**Dreamers and adventurers—
the lifeblood of a young nation**

MEG KINCAID and
SHELDON GERRARD

The promise of great fortune calls them west to San Francisco. But the violence and jealousy of others threaten to shatter their future.

JIM KINCAID

His heart hardened by a devastating loss, he wanders the high wilderness alone— vowing undying vengeance on the man who destroyed his love.

SARA KINCAID DEVERAUX

Confronting jungle savagery and disease, she braves a treacherous voyage—in search of the husband who abandoned her for a dream of gold.

THUNDER EAGLE

A proud, half-breed Crow warrior on the trail of a killer, he is bound to the Kincaids by a remarkable destiny.

Other Avon Books in the
KINCAIDS *Series*
by Taylor Brady

BOOK ONE:
RAGING RIVERS

BOOK TWO:
PRAIRIE THUNDER

BOOK THREE:
MOUNTAIN FURY

THE KINCAIDS

BOOK FOUR

WESTWARD WINDS

TAYLOR BRADY

AVON BOOKS NEW YORK

THE KINCAIDS: WESTWARD WINDS is an original publication of Avon Books. This work has never before appeared in book form. This work is a novel. Any similarity to actual persons or events is purely co-incidental.

AVON BOOKS
A division of
The Hearst Corporation
1350 Avenue of the Americas
New York, New York 10019

Copyright © 1993 by Donna Ball, Inc. and Shannon Harper
Published by arrangement with the authors
Library of Congress Catalog Card Number: 92-97460
ISBN: 0-380-77134-9

First Avon Books Printing: July 1993

AVON TRADEMARK REG. U.S. PAT. OFF. AND IN OTHER COUNTRIES, MARCA REGISTRADA, HECHO EN U.S.A.

Printed in the U.S.A.

RA 10 9 8 7 6 5 4 3 2 1

The Kincaids

Fiona McLeod (Gran) d. 1820 — M — Hugh Cartyle (Dec)

Lillie Reeve (Dec) — M — Nathaniel Kincaid (Dec)

Margaret Dixson (Dec) — M — Edward Cartyle (Dec)

Katherine Cartyle B 1802 — M 1820 — Byrd Kincaid (B 1792 Dec 1837)

Prudence Taylor (Dec)

Matthew Kincaid (Dec)

Nate Kincaid (Dec)

Boothe Cartyle (B 1797 Dec 1843)

Kitty Werner (adopted) B 1820 — M 1837 — Ben Adamson B 1815

Margaret (Meg) B 1822 — M — Fiona B 1843

Caleb O'Hare

James (Jim) B 1826 M 1844 Morning Star Woman

Sarah B 1829 M 1848 Cade Deveraux

Amity B 1832

Luke B 1834

Hilda B 1840

Caroline (Carrie) B 1842

Ben. Jr. B 1849

Chapter One

1851

It was still early in the summer, and snow clung to the high Sierra Nevada peaks. It decorated the crevices between boulders and lay like creamy white frosting on flat, jutting buttes, crunching beneath the wagon wheels on shady parts of the trail. Jim Kincaid had traveled through the mountains half a dozen times in the past eight years, but he never passed this way that he didn't think of the first time. And the snow always made him melancholy.

His first trip west had been through the Rockies. He had entered the mountains in search of his uncle, Boothe, when he was a young man, when the land had been as raw and untried as he was. Only a few hardy pioneers had braved the high passes of the Oregon Trail in search of the Promised Land, and the California Trail hadn't even been heard of.

Now the wagon ruts were deep even at this time of year, the trail worn flat by the tramping of a thousand feet. Jim gave a little shake of his head, a reflection of the wonderment he felt whenever he thought about the number of people going west. His uncle wouldn't have believed it. It was probably best he hadn't lived to see it.

The irony was, it all had happened because of men like Boothe Carlyle, men with wandering feet who set off down the Ohio and across the Mississippi in bark-hewn canoes, who crossed the Great Plains on foot and climbed the soaring mountains and brought back tales filled with glory and awe. They broke the trails for the dreamers to follow.

John Augustus Sutter had been one of those dreamers. He had heard stories of vast unclaimed acres, of fertile valleys and forest cathedrals and endless sunny plains; and he, like many before and since, took the notion to build himself an empire. Past experience had not proved him to be much of a businessman, but he was still smooth enough to talk the governor of California into granting him fifty thousand acres or so just east of the San Francisco Bay. He spent the next ten years carving out an estate that was well on its way to doing justice to the feudal empires of Europe after which it was modeled.

Then in January of 1848, James Marshall was supervising a crew that was building a sawmill on the south fork of the American River, where Sutter intended to set up a timber-cutting business. He left the sluice gates open all night to test the millrace, and when he checked the millrace the next morning, he found tiny specks of what he was convinced was gold clinging to the bottom. The crew laughed at him, but he scooped up the deposits in his handkerchief and showed them to Sutter the next chance he got.

"I believe this is gold," he said, "but the people at the mill called me crazy."

Sutter looked at the material in the handkerchief carefully and agreed. "Looks like gold to me. Let's have it tested."

And that, so the story was told, was how it all started.

By now, of course, Sutter was probably wishing he'd opened that handkerchief to the wind or shot James Marshall on the spot, and Jim wouldn't have been able to say as how he blamed him. The man had spent ten years clearing and building, farming and ranching, and was closer to seeing his dream come true than most men ever got. Now his land was flooded with Argonauts, gold hunters named after the legendary Jason and his men, who once sought the elusive Golden Fleece. The present-day searchers scared off Sutter's cattle, trampled his crops, burned his timber, and dammed up his streams. The way it was looking now, the man least likely to strike it rich off gold was John Sutter himself.

Sutter hadn't been completely stupid, and he'd seen what was coming. He'd tried to keep the discovery a secret, but by May the word had reached San Francisco, and from there it was only a matter of time.

The word spread by ship, first to the Sandwich Islands and then around the Horn to the East Coast, and by foot, mule, and horse across country. By July, San Francisco was a city of women and children, and there was scarcely an adult male to be found in any hamlet or village in California. A stream of eager natives poured off the first ships back from the islands; Mexican laborers, accompanied by their wives and children, livestock and household goods, flooded across the deserts of Arizona and toward the mountains filled with gold.

By December, when newspapers across the country

carried the story of President Polk informing Congress of the "abundance of gold" to be had for the taking in California—accompanied by an impressive display of two hundred and thirty ounces of California gold—the fever was out of control. Men, women, and children had left their plows in the field, their stores unlocked, their stock turned out, and had piled everything they could carry into wagons, sold the rest for ship's passage, and set off for gold country. It was the nature of humans always to be looking for something better, and most often that search turned their eyes west. Jim Kincaid understood that. His folks had always been the wandering kind.

And so the trail west was opened, and it had been worn deep over the next two years. Jim had seen with his own eyes a wagon train that stretched across the prairie to the far horizon: lumbering Conestogas, pack mules, trail horses, women and children on foot, often leading milk cows or carrying crated chickens or being followed by the family dog. Few of the farm animals, not to mention the oxen and pack mules, made it across the deserts. And not everyone who started out for California arrived there.

Disease, Indians, stupidity, the harshness of the land itself—any one of these could decimate a train of starry-eyed gold seekers in a matter of days. But more dangerous than any of the obvious killers was the pure orneriness of human nature. Jim had led one such train across the Sierras, and he could testify to that for a fact.

By the time they reached Fort Bridger, the travelers had endured close quarters, discomfort, and each other's company for two months. They were exhausted, and still had to face forty miles of the cruelest desert man ever crossed, followed by the Sierra Nevada, where anything could happen. Tempers were short and discipline was nonexistent.

Two days out of the fort, an argument developed over a borrowed ax, which resulted in the borrower losing two fingers. A man pushed his wife out of the wagon and drove off without her. An old man was shot for singing too loud. Another man was knifed to death for beating his five-year-old son with a wagon board. By the time they got to Sutter's Fort, Jim had twice come close to shooting a man for pure meanness, and whatever touch of gold fever he'd ever had was completely cured.

But he soon learned, as had dozens before him, that there was money to be made off other people's madness, and one didn't necessarily have to go to the goldfields to do it. Perhaps the first entrepreneurs were the sea captains who, in the summer of 1848, brought word of the strike to the Pacific Islands, then immediately raised their prices for passage—and bought up all the pickaxes and shovels they could find, selling them back for ten times their value.

Sam Brannan, a newspaper man and merchant, was probably the originator of the gold rush in San Francisco, and one of the sharpest traders who ever lived. As soon as he heard the rumors about Sutter's gold, he laid in a supply of staples—flour, coffee, meal, shovels, picks, pans, and buckets—then returned to San Francisco, literally running up and down the streets shouting news of the find and spreading the hysteria. When the would-be prospectors got to the American River, it was to find Sam set up in his camp store, ready to supply the miners with everything they needed—for a price.

That price could be as much as eight hundred dollars for a barrel of flour that in any town east of the Sierras would cost forty, three dollars for a hen's egg, two hundred dollars for a barrel of salt pork, and thirty dollars a bushel for potatoes. It was to the latter that Sheldon Gerrard owed his fortune, and the reason, in a roundabout way, that Jim once again found himself driving a wagon across the mountains.

Seven years ago, Jim and his Cheyenne wife, Morning Star Woman, had set up housekeeping on the South Platte, within the shelter of the trading post Gerrard ran with Jim's sister Meg. At first Jim had started out by building and operating a ferry across the Platte, and it had done right well. Whole trains went past the Kincaid-Gerrard post just to take advantage of the ferry, and while they were there they reprovisioned generously from the store.

Gerrard had always been a shrewd businessman, but he had nothing on Meg, and between the two of them they always seemed to stay one step ahead of the demands of the marketplace. In no time at all, their establishment was almost too fine to be called a trading post anymore, and a nice little community of log cabins and whitewashed houses had grown up around it on the banks of the Platte.

It was along about that time that Jim started driving an occasional freight wagon or leading a mule train up the Oregon Trail, increasing the coffers of Kincaid-Gerrard—not to mention his own—with the profits from goods sold to hungry settlers or sometimes even to pilgrims on the trail. In those early days of Oregon and California settlement, pioneers often arrived at their new homes with little more than the clothes on their backs. The trail was littered with the prized possessions they'd been forced to leave behind—some frivolous, but some, like plow bits and extra wagon wheels, among the very necessities of life. They reached Oregon scraping the bottom of the flour barrel and yearning for the taste of real coffee, but glad to be alive.

So Jim started down the trail with a wagon loaded with staple foodstuffs and hardware—nails for building, wheel frames from the smithy, lantern oil. And as like as not, his supply would be half gone by the time he reached the end of the trail, sometimes taken by Indians, but most of the time sold to travelers he passed who had either underestimated their need or wanted to get a head start on the settlers who would be waiting for goods at the end of the trail.

There was money to be made, all right, and Meg had soon begun to talk about opening up a permanent trading post in Oregon, if Jim and Star would go run it for her. It was something to think about, but Jim knew Star was happy in their snug cabin on the edge of the Platte. Meg and Sheldon accepted her as family, and she was a favored aunt to Meg's daughter, Fiona. Star had even taught Anna, the wife of the Polish blacksmith, to speak English, and now their children were growing up with Fiona and speaking English and gathering around Star in the afternoon to hear Cheyenne legends or to play games with a stick and a rag ball, like the Cheyenne children did. Jim and Star had not been blessed with children of their own, and he knew she would miss her surrogate family if they were to move west. Besides, in another community life might not be so easy for the Indian bride of a white man.

And, though it puzzled Jim to admit it, he wasn't sure how much he'd like being stuck in one place again.

When he'd settled on the Platte to marry Star, he'd thought his wandering days were behind him. He'd come from the shores of the Ohio River all the way to the high plains of the Rocky Mountains, and he'd seen death, illness, disaster, and betrayal along the way. He'd thought he had had enough of adventuring to last a life-time, and was glad to plant his feet by the riverside and spend his days tending store and building a home.

But he must have inherited more of the Kincaids' wandering ways than he realized, because once the houses started springing up around him, he could feel his feet begin to itch. He was glad to have reins in his hand and a clear road ahead—almost as glad as he was to put those reins away and walk through the front door of his own house again.

So he kept putting off making a decision about the trading post in Oregon. And then there was the potato boat, and he didn't have to make a decision at all.

In the early summer of 1848, a passerby brought word of a shipload of potatoes some fool had bought in Panama and was planning to sell in San Francisco. They'd all had a good laugh over that because there were a lot quicker ways to get potatoes to California— even assuming *californios* were too stupid not to grow their own—and if the cargo wasn't eaten up with rot by the time it reached the bay, it sure would be by the time it was sold. They made jokes about the smell and how much they each figured a shipload of rotten potatoes would be going for, or how much a body would have to pay to have it hauled out of the harbor, and about the stupidity of greed in general.

Two days later, word of the gold strike reached the Platte.

Within minutes Sheldon was stripping the shelves of supplies to be sent to the goldfields. A reflection in miniature of the hysteria that had gripped San Francisco was put into motion as word spread throughout the community and people piled into the store, clamoring for provisions and willing to pay whatever price would get them on their way to the gold the fastest. It was Meg who remembered the potato boat.

Jim took off that night, on horseback, with all the ready cash they had stuffed into his pockets, praying he could reach San Francisco before the boat did, praying the potatoes weren't rotten, praying he could make his deal before anyone on board heard about the hungry gold miners less than a hundred miles away.

Jim arrived in San Francisco a mere three days before the *Christo Maria* did and offered two hundred dollars for the cargo, sight unseen, before the stunned captain even had a chance to set foot off the deck. He let the captain talk him up to three-fifty, all the while leading the bewildered man to believe he had discovered a new formula for whiskey and was going to set up a distillery.

Less than one-quarter of the potatoes were rotten. The remainder Jim sold to starving miners whose pockets bulged with ore, to eager hoteliers looking to lure those miners into leaving some of that ore behind in their establishments, to passersby on the street, to enterprising peddlers, and, at last, in the gold camps themselves. Total income from the sales amounted to over two hundred thousand dollars.

Jim had never seen so much money in his life. He had never counted anything that high before, and even trying to comprehend it was more than his brain could take without aching. He assayed the gold out, divided it up between the vaults of the three safest banks in San Francisco—figuring the chances were good that one of them might get robbed or burn down, but not all three—and started back home in something like a daze.

There were some fundamental differences between Jim and his sister. Jim had seen the madness with his own eyes, he had held the gold in his hands and been dragged down by the weight of it in his saddlebags, but he still didn't fully believe in it. He surely never thought about going after more. Two hundred thousand dollars was more money than he had known there was in the *world* six months earlier. It was more than any of them needed in this lifetime, in several lifetimes. Why would anyone want more?

But Meg looked at the insubstantial written receipt, and her eyes lit up like hills on fire. And she said, "This is only the beginning."

Within the month, Sheldon, Meg, and little Fiona were packed up and on their way to San Francisco, where they opened up a mercantile that was making money faster than they could count it. Jim and Star stayed behind to run the trading post and had almost more than they could do, outfitting the Argonauts who streamed by daily, headed for the California Trail.

Then Meg had the idea to open up some kind of "fancy house"—at least that was what Jim called it, earning a slap on the hand in reprimand from his wife every time he did so. Meg called it an "opera house," and claimed she had gotten the idea from a ship's captain who'd just come back from France. She intended to have singing and playacting and dancing women who showed their legs, and that sounded like a fancy house to Jim. Whatever it was called, Meg claimed the newly rich miners would eat it up, and in that Jim had to admit she might be right.

A good majority of the Argonauts were from the East Coast—pale-faced store clerks and bankers and younger sons of the big landholders in the South; many of them were educated, and some of them had even been to places like France, where women pulled up their skirts and kicked their legs when they danced. They'd appreciate the kind of high-class entertainment Meg had in mind. Not that any man, straight from the goldfields, wouldn't appreciate a naked female leg if it was shown to him.

Whether they'd appreciate the bolts upon bolts of red velvet cloth and the crystal chandeliers that filled the two wagons Jim was taking across the mountains into San Francisco was another matter. At least, he thought, and grinned a little as he clucked to the team, they didn't have to worry about Indians. They weren't hauling anything on this trip that any self-respecting Indian would be caught stealing.

Meg had ordered a bar made of solid mahogany, which was coming by ship, and a piano imported all the way from London, England—not to mention mirrors and paintings and barrels full of glassware and china and who knew what else. Those commodities might arrive by autumn if she was lucky, for travel around the Horn was always uncertain. That was why, when she heard she could get the cut-glass chandeliers and the red cloth from a man in St. Louis who had ordered them for a customer who had taken off for the goldfields before they arrived, she'd arranged for Jim to bring them overland.

Though Jim laughed at Meg's fancy house, he was glad of the trip. Star had been feeling downcast since Meg and the little one had left, and he had been thinking for some time that he might take her out for a visit. He found a couple of fellows to help him with the wagons and put Henryk, the blacksmith who'd been with them since the trading post started up, in charge of the store. He figured to have a pleasant trip across country and a fine time showing his wife the sights of San Francisco. According to Meg, the town was something to see by now.

But when they got to the Sublette cutoff, his two

drivers absconded with their hiring-on wages, apparently deciding they could get to the goldfields faster if they weren't driving two wagons loaded down with goods. Since then, the pleasure trip had been nothing but hard work, with Star driving one wagon and Jim the other. Still, there'd been good in it simply because Star was with him.

Jim turned on the wagon seat to look back at her, grinning and doffing his hat. She sat as straight-backed as a missionary, her hair coiled into a jet-black bun beneath her calico bonnet, her coppery skin glowing in the sunlight. When Jim had first married her, she had disdained white women's clothing, but a year or so with Meg had changed all that. Now she wore the muslin petticoats and gentle calicoes with the grace of one born to them. Even now, driving the wagon with the quiet strength and easy competence of a wrangler, she had never looked more beautiful to Jim. He loved her with all his heart.

"There's a cutoff up ahead," he called to her. "We'll stop for the night."

She smiled and raised her hand in acknowledgment.

Jim settled on the wagon seat and urged the team on, aware of a contentment spreading through him that was as clear and pure as a mountain stream, dispersing the melancholia as surely as sun melted snow. In less than two weeks they would be in San Francisco. He had crossed half a continent without a major mishap, the end of the journey was in sight, and the only woman he had ever loved was by his side. He couldn't think of another thing in this world that he wanted.

They called him Lobo. He wasn't certain when it had started or why, though he suspected it had something to do with the chewed-up side of his face, which rumor credited to an attack by wolves in high plains country. Lobo wore the appellation, as he did his scars, proudly, a symbol of the metamorphosis he had undergone on the way back to life from death.

He had survived the lean, hard years by learning to hunt like a wolf, run like a rabbit, and stalk like a cat. He had the patience of a snake on a sunny rock and the quickness of a darting lizard. Some lessons he had learned from the Indians who had rescued him from the snow and for a while given him sanctuary; others he had observed for himself, when understanding those lessons made the difference between life and death.

Part of those eight years of learning he'd spent living in caves like an animal, eating what he could catch with his bare hands, traversing the desert at night, killing or using whatever happened to cross his path. Sometimes what he killed was human. Sometimes what he took was spending money or jewelry or other valuables. More often it was food and blankets, or a new pair of boots. He killed because he enjoyed it, and he stole because that was his right. Soon he became expert at both.

Lobo was an analytical man given to careful thought when it suited him. He therefore could not fail to realize that those early years, when put into the broad perspective of a man who was destined to leave his mark on history, were a necessary period of testing and proving, an ascension into manhood, a trial by fire. All of it was in preparation for this time and this place, when he would at last come into his own.

The long, lonesome trails, the vast deserts, the high mountain passes, which once had been his to command with the quickness of his wits and the cleverness of his skills, were now flooded with the greedy and the desperate. They swarmed across the mountains in hordes, driven by the lust for gold. Many of them never made it to their destination; many more were doomed to disappointment once they arrived. But some of them returned along the same trails by which they'd first come, their pockets bulging, their pack beasts staggering under the weight of their burdens.

Those were the men who interested Lobo.

He was not the first man to realize that it was a great deal easier to steal from the miners than to work a claim himself. He might, however, be credited as the first to realize it was even easier to steal from the thieves.

The first time, he simply watched from a canyon rim as a robber swooped down on a departing miner, relieved him of his gold, and was on his way. Lobo met up with the thief half a mile down the road and put a bullet through his head.

The next time, he stole and allowed the thief to live. And so an idea was born.

Hundreds of thousands of dollars' worth of gold left the fields and camps of the Sierra Nevadas every month. One man acting alone could hope to claim only a small portion of it—and risk getting himself killed in the process. The miners weren't all as dumb as they looked; they were beginning to travel with armed guards, or hiring toughs to take the gold out of the mountains while they stayed back at the camps or traveled with empty pockets. And there was the vigilance committee, whose members would chase a man to the ends of the earth when riled, and string him up where they finally ran him down. There were fortunes for the taking, traveling down those trails, but trying to take it alone was risky business.

There was strength in numbers. And the key to success lay in organization.

There were five battalions under Lobo's command, each composed of from four to six men. Between them they could cover most of the trails leading in and out of gold country. Working together, choosing their targets carefully, they were almost invincible. Already Lobo was a rich man, and those who rode with him had more money than their poor imaginations had ever dreamed. Some might even have liked to quit, to retire and live the kind of life they had only been able to fantasize about before now. Sometimes they even talked about it. But few ever did anything about it. Lobo's method of maintaining discipline was very simple and very effective. No one ever left his employ alive.

Lobo knew that this particular phase of his career was only one step in the master plan. Right now the country was filled with men, but women had a way of following men—and where there were women, churches, schools, and law couldn't be far behind. In a land ruled by greed and lawlessness he was king, but when the preachers and the lawyers and the legislators brought their own brand of civilization to the valley, he would be ready. The ability to adapt was one of the most useful skills he had learned in the desert, and by the time civilization caught up with him, he would know what to do.

Lobo did not ride out as much as he used to, only enough to keep his hand in and make his presence known. It was not superstition, he told himself, but a higher power that convinced him to take the Donner Pass that day. It was a plain and unshakable belief in destiny.

"Cap'n, we spotted him."

Lobo had been amused when the men first started calling him "Captain." When a man was in charge of his own army, he could easily promote himself to general, but Lobo liked the sound of "Captain," so he let it stand.

He answered Charlie, whom he privately thought of as his lieutenant. Charlie—which wasn't his real name, of course—had been one of the first to join him and had since earned a goodly portion of Lobo's respect, if not his unquestioned trust.

"And were you right about him, Charlie?"

Charlie looked smug, which wasn't easy to do with his face distorted by a jawful of chewing tobacco. "Yessir, the fella's got himself a target, all right. Couple of wagons headed down the trail." He chuckled. "Damn fool can't figure out nobody carries gold *into* the fields, I reckon."

"Nonetheless, it doesn't do to dismiss any opportunity."

Lobo's reply was absent, for as he turned his horse in the direction Charlie indicated, he caught a glimpse of the wagons and his curiosity was pricked. They were camped midway down the trail, overlooking Donner Lake, and he saw no indication of a family group. Those could only be supply wagons, so maybe their would-be thief wasn't as stupid as he seemed. These days, as anyone who had ever returned from gold country could testify, there were things a great deal more valuable than ore.

Two of his men were already in position at three o'clock and nine o'clock, so well concealed in the bushes that only Lobo could have spotted them, waiting for the thief to make his move on the wagons. From the looks of it, they wouldn't have to wait long. The man was on foot, creeping through the woods toward the wagons—a miner gone broke, unless Lobo missed his guess, lean and hungry and desperate. If the driver was not a complete fool, the would-be thief was destined to get himself shot before he came within thirty feet of the wagons, and that would spoil it for all of them.

Lobo watched for a moment, then shook his head in disgust. The idiot wasn't even going to wait for dark, and nothing those wagons contained was worth a prolonged shoot-out when the pickings were so much easier up the road. They were wasting their time here.

He started to turn his horse, then stopped, muscles frozen, eyes riveted on the man who came around the side of the wagon.

"Stop him!" he hissed to Charlie without taking his eyes off the wagons. *"Now!"*

Charlie knew better than to question, or even to hesitate for a moment between the delivery of the order and its execution. Almost before the words were out, he was moving down the slope, barking quiet orders to the other two men.

Lobo didn't move. He sat astride his horse, watching the redheaded man until he moved out of sight.

Chapter Two

Sarah Kincaid Deveraux studied her image in the cheval mirror and smiled with satisfaction. The deep bottle green of her new gown complimented her fair coloring and fiery hair to perfection. The low-necked bodice exposed the magnolia creaminess of her shoulders, and the tight waist and full skirt flattered her slender middle. The dress of silk taffeta had been made in New Orleans, several miles down river. It had been copied, the seamstress said, from a French original, and was adorned with bows and flounces and ruches of lace. It was the very height of fashion for the spring of 1851.

Sarah saw a reflection beside hers in the glass. "I love this dress, Tante Emilie. As usual, you're far too generous."

"You look lovely in whatever you wear, *chérie*, but I wanted you to have something special for the party tonight. It's a joy for me to be able to give it to you."

Sarah turned away from the mirror and hugged the short, graying woman with genuine affection. "Shall I take this to California with me? I know there isn't much room for luggage on the ship, but I'd like to have a marvelous dress to show Cade."

Emilie sank down on a little settee, her dark eyes worried. "I wish I were as sure as you that you'll find Cade. It's such a long way to California from here on the Mississippi."

"There's nothing to worry about," Sarah said with more certainty than she felt. "I know where his gold claim is located, and I know the name of the town. My sister Meg will arrange for someone to guide me, and *voilà*—I'll find my errant husband." She had spent years struggling to learn French, with little success, but whenever she could throw in a word or a phrase, she felt a secret stirring of satisfaction.

Emilie, still worried, sighed heavily. "You've heard nothing from your sister . . . nor from Cade . . . in months."

Sarah dismissed Emilie's concerns with an airy wave of her hand. "Which only proves how dreadful the mail service from California is. After I leave, long letters will probably arrive from both of them."

"If the mail can't get through, then how do *you* expect to?"

"We've had this discussion before, Emilie. I'm going. You know that. You worry far too much."

"Of course I worry. You're like a daughter to me, and my nephew, Cade, is like a son."

"Then come with me!" Sarah said with a laugh. "Think of the fun we two could have on the ship."

"Can you imagine me crossing the Isthmus of Panama on a mule?"

Sarah pretended to study the plump form of Emilie Deveraux Gallier through narrowed eyes, as if such an adventure were really possible. "Hmm, actually . . . I can't!"

Both women burst into laughter. Sarah beckoned to the young black woman standing quietly in the doorway. "Come in, Clotilde. I need you to help me get out of this dress. I'm afraid I've rumpled it already."

The slave moved quickly to obey, unfastening the buttons on Sarah's bodice with deft fingers. Clotilde laid the dress on the bed and hurried to fetch Sarah's silk robe from the tall mahogany armoire. She busied herself hanging up the stiffened crinolines and petticoats that her mistress carelessly dropped on the floor.

Emilie was still fixated on the journey that Sarah was undertaking in only two days. "I wish I knew more about this Mrs. Morgan you're traveling with."

Sarah recognized jealousy in Emilie's voice as well as concern, for she knew that if Emilie were younger and didn't feel a duty to remain with her brother at Deveraux House, she would be on the ship to Panama with Sarah.

Sarah formed her words carefully. "Mrs. Morgan's letters are quite nice. She's a minister's wife from Shreveport who's going out to join her husband in San Francisco. She can't travel alone, and neither can I, so that nice ticket agent at the steamship line matched us up. It's the best of all possible plans, since you can't be with me."

Emilie wasn't convinced. "Why don't you wait a month and sail with Father Leseyne and the Sisters of Hope and Charity? I'd feel much better if you were with them."

Sarah moved back to the mirror, pushing her hair back from her face and examining what might be a freckle forming on the tip of her nose. She'd been infinitely relieved when Mrs. Morgan had written her and spared her a journey with the Sisters. Even though she'd converted to Catholicism when she married Cade

Deveraux, she wasn't comfortable with the rituals of the church, or with the priests and nuns she'd met. Her new religion remained mysterious and exotic to her, and in retrospect she wondered at her eagerness to abandon the Protestant faith she'd been raised in and take on her husband's. But then, of course, she would have done anything Cade asked of her.

"When Cade left for the goldfields, I always intended to join him. It's been over a year, and the time is ripe. I can't wait any longer, Emilie. You understand." She went to her friend and knelt by the settee, so that the two women's faces were almost even. "I love him so much."

Emilie took Sarah's face in her hands. "I know you love him, my sweet child. Cade is very special to me, too, but if any harm should come to you—"

"Nothing will happen to me, I promise. I can look after myself, and I think it's time I had another adventure. One I can tell my grandchildren about. Of course, unless I find my husband soon, there won't *be* any children or grandchildren!"

Emilie pretended to be shocked. "Sarah Deveraux, you are shameless!"

"And you love it." Sarah kissed Emilie on the cheek.

"I only pray that all goes well. So many things can happen ... I've talked to Lucien about funds again. He's arranging to have a draft sent overland to a bank in San Francisco—just in case. Now, it may take a few weeks longer—"

Sarah got to her feet. "That's not necessary—"

"One never knows, Sarah," Emilie said firmly. "And, anyhow, arrangements have been made, and once Lucien's mind is made up—"

"He never changes it! I know, and I'm grateful. He's been more than generous, but I have money of my own." She crossed to her dressing table and rummaged in her jewelry box. "I have one of the gold coins that Great-gran Fiona gave to Mama when she left home." It felt cool and solid in her hand.

"*Chérie*, that is a family treasure, an heirloom. You can't think of spending it." Emilie was horrified.

Sarah shrugged. "Mama used one coin to buy passage on a boat down the Ohio thirty years ago, and my sister Kitty used another to start up her horse ranch—so there's no reason I can't use mine to go to California." Sarah knew the coin was hundreds of years old and bore an inscription in a language she couldn't read, but the mystique and sentimentality of the family coin were of little importance to her compared with reaching California and finding her husband. "If I need to spend the gold coin, I will. So don't worry about me."

Emilie stood up, shaking her head. "A gold coin is not enough to stop me from worrying about you, *ma petite*, but I can see my lectures are doing no good. No good at all."

Sarah grinned impishly. "Have they ever?"

"*Mon Dieu!*" Emilie threw up her hands. "You Kincaids must be the stubbornest humans ever born. Once you set upon a course, nothing can dissuade you."

"Be happy for me, *tante*," Sarah said softly. "I'm going to be with the man I love."

Emilie sighed, temporarily defeated. "We'll talk more before you leave; right now I need to see what Cook is doing about dinner. She gets into a state every time we have guests."

"And you can handle her when no one else can. That's why you can't leave Deveraux House. Père

Lucien needs you to keep things running smoothly. I can't believe he agreed to a party for me."

"Lucien loves parties, despite how he grumbles. And he thinks the world of you. He would go with you to California if he could, but his gout is paining him greatly now."

Sarah was enormously relieved that the blustering and overbearing Lucien Deveraux wasn't accompanying her on the trip. She understood why Cade and his father were so often at odds; Lucien wasn't an easy man to live with. His way was usually the only way that something could be done. Only someone as diplomatic as Emilie could get along with him. But her father-in-law did like her, despite his blustering, Sarah knew. He respected her, and had great hopes that she was the woman who could finally domesticate his wayward son. Perhaps that hope was one reason he hadn't opposed her trip to California more vehemently. Someone needed to look out for Cade Deveraux.

Emilie paused at the door. "Let me know if you want to borrow any of my jewelry tonight. I have a necklace that will go perfectly with that dress."

Sarah blew her aunt a kiss. "I'll come by your room before dinner."

Sarah studied her new dress lying on the bed. She called Clotilde to her side. "The trim seems a bit creased. Do you think it needs freshening?" She touched the swath of lace around the neckline.

"The iron's heating on the hearth down in the laundry, Miz Sarah. I kin fix it right up for you."

"Thank you, Clotilde. I want everything to be perfect for tonight." Sarah enjoyed having servants anticipate her every whim, but she was uneasy with the idea that she actually owned a slave, a present from her father-in-law before her marriage. None of the Kincaids had ever had a servant, much less a slave.

Sarah remembered only too well the arguments that had gone on between her sister Kitty Adamson and Kitty's husband, Ben, back in Kansas, about associating with the slave-owning Galliers. Ben hadn't wanted to have anything to do with Emilie or her husband, Charles, who'd come from Louisiana to establish an experimental farm near the Adamson homestead in the Flint Hills of Kansas Territory.

Sarah had been fourteen then, back in 1843, when Katherine, her mother, had sent her to help out Kitty and Ben with their two young daughters. They'd met Emilie and Charles when Kitty had won the argument with Ben, and they'd traveled to the Galliers so the children could be vaccinated against smallpox. The late Charles Gallier had been a man of many interests and talents—and he'd laid in a supply of vaccine to inoculate the Indians and any settlers he could find in the hills.

That day at the Galliers had changed Sarah's life. In Emilie's home, filled with furnishings from their plantation on the Mississippi, she'd gotten a glimpse of another kind of life, a life of graciousness and wealth, of sophistication and ease, so different from the existence she'd known on her family's farm in Illinois and at the Adamsons' horse ranch on the edge of the frontier. Sarah wanted the Galliers' kind of life with an urgent, all-consuming hunger that she couldn't begin to explain to her family. Only Emilie understood and was willing to help.

On that first visit to the Gallier house in the Flint Hills, she'd seen a painting of Emilie's ancestral home in Louisiana, and now she was living at Deveraux House, sleeping in a tall four-poster bed festooned with mosquito netting, eating on Limoges porcelain at a fifteen-foot-long table lit by a French Baccarat chandelier, serving tea to visitors in the morning room, dancing at balls until midnight. It had all been perfect until Cade had decided to go to California.

Sarah pushed open the French windows and stepped onto the gallery outside her bedroom. In the distance, across the formal gardens, she could see the sluggish brown Mississippi winding toward New Orleans. Her eyes drifted to the white lattice of the summer house, tucked amid live oaks draped with Spanish moss. She'd first met Cade Deveraux in the summerhouse.

Of course, she'd known all about him before then, since Emilie talked constantly of her favorite nephew, and Sarah had seen his portrait hanging in the hallway of Deveraux House. She knew he was handsome, but his portrait hadn't prepared her for the reality.

Tragedy had brought Sarah to Deveraux House in the summer of 1847. Sarah had left the Flint Hills and her sister Kitty's family in 1845, when she was sixteen, to return to her mother, Katherine Carlyle Kincaid, in Cairo, Illinois. Grudgingly Sarah had returned home, hating to cut her ties to Emilie and Charles Gallier. Charles and Kitty had become partners in a horse-breeding endeavor, and the families were often thrown together. Sarah made the most of those situations, always thinking of excuses to ride to the Galliers' and stay as long as possible, soaking up like a thirsty sponge what Emilie taught her about art and books and style and manners.

Sarah spent two miserable years in Cairo, despising everything about the place, from its muddy, flooded streets to the low-life types who hung around the wharves and saloons. She was no more interested in her mother's farm than in Kitty's horses. At eighteen, Sarah was lively, pretty, intelligent, spoiled, and manipulative. She had no intention of saying yes to any of the country boys who pursued her. Instead, she spent most of her time plotting ways to get out of Cairo. Katherine, at her wit's end over her daughter's complaining, offered to send her to her sister Meg, who had a trading post on the Platte River.

The idea had horrified Sarah. She wanted to see her favorite brother, Jim, who was living near Meg, but she had no intention of living at a trading post or even visiting one. Sarah had seen enough of frontier life during her two years in Kansas.

What did interest her was seeing Emilie Gallier again, and when the opportunity presented itself, Katherine couldn't object. Emilie wrote from Kansas that Charles had died suddenly, and that she was packing up and moving back to live with her brother at Deveraux House. She felt very alone and longed for companionship. Could Sarah visit, just for a while, to cheer her up?

When Sarah stepped onto the Mississippi sidewheeler that spring of 1847 and said good-bye to her mother, she knew she was leaving Cairo forever. And when the steamer stopped south of Baton Rouge at the Deveraux's own landing and she saw Deveraux House, she knew that this was where she belonged. She made herself indispensable to Emilie, even managing to amuse and entertain the formidable Lucien. But it was Cade who made it possible for her to have a real home at Deveraux House and to become part of the family.

She'd been sitting in the summerhouse, struggling with French verbs and cursing softly under her breath. Emilie had told her it was the mark of an educated lady to speak French, and so, for Emilie's sake, she tried. But who could make heads or tails out of a language in

which half the letters that should be pronounced
weren't?

"Voulez-vous etudier?" she asked herself, and out of nowhere a voice replied.

"No. I hated to study, especially French verbs, and
I'll bet you do, too."

She looked up and there he was, tall and handsome,
with wavy blond hair and eyes the color of fine old
sherry, standing on the steps of the summerhouse. He
was stylishly dressed in a gray frock coat, olive trousers,
and a gray checked vest over a white shirt. He exuded
charm and sophistication from his polished boots to his
well-trimmed hair.

"I'm Cade Deveraux," he said.

She dropped her book in nervousness, her penciled
notes scattering across the floor. "Yes, I know. I mean
I've seen your portrait. I'm Sarah. Sarah Kincaid."

His eyes appraised her thoroughly, and for the first
time in her eighteen years Sarah felt like a grown-up
woman. He smiled as if pleased with what he saw.
"Emilie's young friend."

"I'm not so young," she answered quickly. "I'm almost nineteen." She bent down to pick up the scattered
pages, and he was there beside her, so close that she
could smell the heady scent of his cologne, so close that
she could see the flecks of gold in his brown eyes.

He handed her the papers and helped her to her feet.
Sarah's skin tingled where his fingers touched her
hands, and her heart was beating so loud she wondered
if he could hear.

"Ah, nineteen. So much is still ahead of you." He
shrugged, a world-weary gesture. "I'm twenty-five, you
know."

"And quite the man of the world, I hear." Sarah had
recovered and decided to flirt. She'd been practicing in

front of the mirror in her bedroom and was anxious to try her skills.

"What have you heard about me?" he asked, amused, leaning against the railing.

"That you love to gamble and to travel and—" She lowered her eyes for a moment before raising them to look into his. "And to be seen with beautiful women."

He bowed mockingly to her and extended his hand. "I plead guilty to all the above, Miss Sarah. I am known as the prodigal son of Deveraux House, because I've returned now, and who knows? Maybe with such charming companionship I might stay this time."

Sarah heard both a challenge and a promise in his voice.

"May I escort you in for tea, Miss Sarah?"

As if she'd known him forever, she took his arm.

A year later, they were married. Cade made a valiant effort to become the gentleman planter his father wanted him to be, but the fires of restlessness burned deep in Cade, and when gold was discovered in California, he was among the first to go.

"I won't be away long, *chérie*," he'd told Sarah, who clung to him in tears. "Just long enough to make my fortune and then come home and whisk you away. I'll never have to work again or pretend to enjoy learning about sugarcane to please my papa. We'll have plenty of money; we'll travel. Would you like to go to Paris? You'd love Paris . . . I'll buy you gowns and champagne and anything else you want. We'll take a suite in the best hotel, and we'll go to the theater—"

"But we're happy here, Cade. We have the plantation and Lucien and Emilie—isn't that enough?"

Aren't I enough? she cried inside.

She knew what his answer would be. He needed more. He craved excitement, adventure, danger. He liked to live on the edge and risk everything, and in the goldfields he'd have that opportunity. There was nothing she could say or do to stop him, and so he'd left, feverish with anticipation, his spirits high.

He'd been gone for over a year. At first his letters had been frequent, full of descriptions of the goldfields and the men he'd met. He'd staked a claim and started panning for gold . . . He had such hopes. Then the letters had stopped, and Sarah was doing the only thing she could do. She was going to California to find her husband.

"Miz Sarah, I got your dress ironed."

"Thank you," she said absentmindedly, turning away from the memories of the summerhouse and entering her room. She wasn't as optimistic about her trip to California as she pretended to be in front of Emilie and Lucien, but what else could she do? She loved her husband and she wanted to be with him. She could only pray that everything was all right, and that she and Cade would eventually be together.

"You all right, Miz Sarah? You look kinda sad-like."

"I'm fine," she said brightly. "Just thinking about the trip. We have so much to do to get ready." She sank into a small chair and begin to brush her thick red hair.

Clotilde took the brush from her. "That's my job, Miz Sarah." Slowly, methodically, she ran the brush through Sarah's hair. Sarah closed her eyes and thought of the nights when Cade would brush her hair and then bury his face in the shining mass, and kiss her shoulders and breasts.

She opened her eyes wide and pulled away. "That's enough for now."

"Yes, ma'am."

"Would you like to go with me, Clotilde, to California? Mr. Lucien said I could take you." All at once,

Sarah wanted someone familiar with her, someone she knew. She didn't want to have to travel all the way to California with strangers. The trip seemed daunting and more than a little frightening. "I'm sure I could get a ticket for you."

"California? I don't know, Miz Sarah. It's a mighty long way away." Clotilde looked worried.

Sarah got up and began to pace. "Oh, it's not that far. I hear the trip takes only six weeks. A boat from New Orleans to Panama, then across the Isthmus and on another boat to San Francisco. It's by far the fastest route, and I imagine it's quite safe by now. Why, thousands of people have crossed already."

"Do you need me, Miz Sarah?" Clotilde asked softly.

"It would be nice to have you to wash out my clothes and brush my hair and help me. Of course, you'd have to sleep on the floor of the cabin. It has only two beds, I've been told."

"That wouldn't bother me none, you know that."

"Then do you want to come?"

"You gonna be mad at me if I tell the truth?"

"Oh, of course not, Clotilde. Why should I be angry if you tell me the truth? Just answer me."

"I have a little boy here, Miz Sarah. He's five years old. He lives with the old granny who takes care of the slave babies, but I get to see him once a day. I don't want to leave him, Miz Sarah. His daddy got sold off last year. He needs his momma." Clotilde's large brown eyes shimmered with tears.

Sarah felt a terrible pang of guilt. This was what Ben Adamson hated about slavery. People being owned and families torn apart. Mothers taken from children and husbands from wives. Human beings having no control over their lives. Sarah Deveraux could go to California to look for her husband, but Clotilde might never see the father of her child again.

Sarah knew that the plantations couldn't endure without slave labor, but she was also learning that a terrible price was being paid for the gracious way of life she so enjoyed.

"Then you must stay here with your child, of course. I'll be fine. I'll have my companion, Mrs. Morgan. I'm sure we'll be a great comfort to each other."

"I cain't leave my baby, Miz Sarah. Please don't make me."

Angry at herself and at the system she'd so easily participated in, Sarah snapped at Clotilde. "I'm not going to make you do anything except brush my hair." She hadn't even asked earlier if Clotilde had a child; she'd thought of the young woman only as a convenience to herself and her life, a possession, not as a woman who loved a man or bore a child. Suddenly she was ashamed of her selfishness.

More softly, she said, "I think I'll wear my hair up tonight, with curls hanging down in back. Can you do that, Clotilde?" She seated herself at her dressing table and handed the brush to the slave.

"Yes, ma'am, Miz Sarah. I can do whatever you wants, and thank you for not making me go to California. You mighty brave to be goin' off by yourself, mighty brave."

"Or very, very foolish," Sarah murmured under her breath.

Cade Deveraux felt the steel barrel of a gun against the back of his neck with very little surprise. *Why not?* he thought. The way his luck had been running lately, why the hell not?

He was pressed flat up against a tree, trying to get a

look at the campsite below without making himself a sitting duck to anyone who happened to glance up from below. It hadn't occurred to him to watch his back, but when a man was as cold and hungry as he was, a lot of things didn't occur to him. He raised his hands over his head without turning around.

"That's the time, mister," an approving voice— presumably the one that belonged to the hand holding the gun—murmured behind him. "Now, real nice and easy-like, you slip the strap of that there Winchester off'n your shoulder."

Cade did as he was told. There was a moment—a split second, really—while his hand was near the level of his waist, that it occurred to him to try to reach the pistol that was stuffed inside his waistband. But false heroics had never been one of Cade Deveraux's failings, particularly when such gestures were almost certain to result in a quick and messy death. He was almost relieved, therefore, when a moment later a hand reached forward and divested him of the weapon, removing temptation.

"What do you think?" A second voice addressed the first, sounding a little nervous. "Should we kill him?"

"Boss didn't say." There was a thoughtful silence. "Better not take no chances, though."

Pain exploded in the back of Cade's head, blossomed blood-red, and faded to black.

"What is it?" Star touched her husband's shoulder and followed the direction of his gaze toward the shadowed ridges.

Slowly, she felt the rock-hard muscles beneath her fingers relax. "Nothing, I guess." He smiled at her. "I thought I heard something."

"Probably you did," Star agreed. "We can't be the

only ones on the trail this time of year. Maybe some of the groups we passed have caught up with us."

"Maybe." Jim's voice was a little wary. "But I'll tell you the truth. I'd feel a heap better if we *were* the only folks on the trail right now. This close to gold country, the woods are full of bandits and toughs looking to make away with what other folks sweated for."

She laughed softly, wrapping her fingers around his upper arm. "We have nothing to interest a thief— you've told me *that* much over and over again!"

"Yeah," he muttered, "but they don't know that. Gold makes folks crazy."

And then he relaxed, and smiled down at her. He didn't want to frighten her, or worry her needlessly. It was just that he couldn't help thinking how smoothly the crossing had gone, all things considered, and how close they were. There was a superstitious part of him that couldn't help expecting the worst.

"You're right," he said. "Probably a bunch of pilgrims up there stumbling around in the woods trying to make supper. But now I'm thinking we might be doing better to move on down the pass in the morning, instead of making a longer camp. We're so close, it seems a shame to waste time."

"The animals need rest," she insisted gently, "and so do we. A day or two won't matter, and this is such a pretty place."

She slipped her arm around his waist and they stood looking out over Donner Lake—so named after the leader of the wagon-train expedition that had met its horrible fate in the very place in which Jim and Star were now camped.

"It is that," Jim agreed, but his tone was somber. "It's kinda hard to believe what happened here."

In 1846 the Donner party, as it came to be known,

separated from the main wagon train with which it had crossed the Great Plains and decided to continue the journey by way of Fort Bridger. Though this route decreased the journey by three hundred miles, it also took the pilgrims through the Forty-Mile Desert, which stripped them of energy, oxen, and supplies—not to mention that most important commodity of all, time.

Their numbers were already depleted by the time they reached the Sierra Nevada in late October, as were their food stores, despite a relief expedition from Sutter's Fort. Nonetheless, they forged onward, climbing almost fifty miles into the mountains before the snow became too deep for them to continue.

Eighty-one people took shelter beside the lake below the pass and waited for the storm to end. For over a month they watched the snow pile up until finally it exceeded a height of a dozen feet. Six different groups tried to escape, but only one made it to send back help.

By the time rescue arrived in the spring, the number of people was reduced to forty-seven, and those had survived chiefly by eating the bodies of the dead.

From that time until gold fever drove caution out of men's heads in 1850, the Donner route was studiously avoided, despite the fact that the disaster that had overtaken that party had been chiefly man-made . . . despite the fact that George Donner and his followers were not the only group of pilgrims to be defeated by such misfortune. Boothe Carlyle, Jim's uncle and one of the last great mountain men, had lost half an expedition to a freak blizzard in the Rockies, and that tragedy had haunted him the rest of his life. And in another incident, Jim and Star had been trapped with Boothe in a high mountain blizzard during the final gun battle that had ended the legendary mountain man's life. For Jim, the three incidents—the Donner disaster, Boothe's mountain expedition, and that last crossing—would always be connected in his head.

Jim recalled that the Donner party had elected to linger to rest their oxen, too. The five days they wasted in the Truckee Meadow might have made the difference in their survival.

He repressed a premonitory shiver but couldn't say the lake looked beautiful to him anymore.

Such uneasiness was ridiculous, of course. This route was well traveled now, as the Argonauts had discovered that the savings in time was well worth the risks in the desert and that, in fact, the more northerly routes held far more dangers and for a longer period of time. And snow at this time of year was next to impossible.

Star watched Jim's expression change, and her voice was gentle with perception. "I think you see too many ghosts, my husband."

He smiled down at her. "You're the superstitious one. Are you telling me you don't feel anything, looking down at where all that suffering occurred?"

She was thoughtful for a moment. "I feel sorry," she said. "But it was several years ago, and they were unwise. There are no lost spirits here and . . ." Her dark eyes took on a teasing spark. "I have nothing to fear with you beside me."

After only an instant's hesitation, Jim returned her smile and dropped a kiss on her head. Why should so innocent a remark cause him to be gripped by such fierce protectiveness? But very often, at odd moments like these, he was reminded of just how much he loved her, how desolate his life would be without her.

Patting his arm with satisfaction, Star said, "Good, your dark face has gone away. Kindly keep it that way. I won't have your frown making fear within our child."

Matter-of-factly, she turned to go back toward the campfire. Jim stared after her.

"What did you say?" he demanded hoarsely.

He took half a running step and caught her arm. When he turned her around, her face was glowing, her eyes brilliant with quiet joy. "It is true," she said softly. "I carry your child, Jim Kincaid."

For the longest time he couldn't move, or speak, or even think. He could only stare at her as though he expected her to evaporate before his very eyes.

And then the meaning of her words began to sink in, and waves of emotion washed up from within him. Still he couldn't speak. He could only grab her to him and whirl her around, laughing foolishly and thinking, *A child, a child!* over and over again.

Star laughed back, winding her arms around his neck, holding him tight. If ever there was a moment of pure and undiluted joy, it was then, as they stood together against the setting sun overlooking Donner Lake, holding each other and watching the future unfold before their eyes.

As he opened his eyes to shafts of pain and a groggy consciousness, Cade thought that he was probably dead and this was hell.

He was surrounded by shadowy figures that kept wavering in and out of his vision, swaying trees with skeletal, grasping branches, ground that seemed to undulate beneath him with every breath he took. The only thing missing was the fire of Hades.

After he'd taken several deep breaths, the ground stopped undulating, and after his fourth attempt to focus his eyes, the shadows around him took solid form. But one thing did not change. The central figure, the one that stood over him, did not have a face.

He closed his eyes and opened them again several times. Each time he did he noticed something new about his surroundings. A corral filled with riding horses. A good-sized cabin of hewn timber to his right, with gun ports instead of windows. There were a couple of outbuildings, and a smaller cabin with a lean-to directly in front of him. From the lean-to came woodsmoke and the smells of cooking, which made his stomach cramp with hunger and faintness fill his head. He appeared to be on a ranch of some sort.

"Okay, you, on your feet."

Cade winced as someone grabbed the back of his collar and dragged him to a sitting position. His hands were tied behind his back and his arms were numb; he couldn't use them for balance. Black-and-red blossoms of pain exploded behind his eyes and his stomach heaved, but somehow he was on his feet. The iron hand that gripped his collar jerked him upward again when his knees started to buckle; he staggered and fought for balance, and when his head cleared, he was looking straight at the faceless man.

He didn't really lack a face, Cade realized after several painfully heart-pounding moments. It was simply that his face was swathed in a dark cotton hood that left nothing visible except the eyes and mouth. The rest of his clothing was dark, too, so that he seemed to blend into the twilight—except for those steady, piercing eyes and the straight line of his mouth.

He said, "You're probably wondering what's beneath this hood."

His voice surprised Cade. It was cultured, mellifluous, and he spoke with an educated accent that was distinctly at odds with his appearance—and his surroundings.

"I don't wear it for vanity's sake," he went on, "but

for practicality. My face, once seen, could be easily described, and that's a chance I prefer not to take."

"Who are you?" Cade said hoarsely. "What do you want with me?"

The muffled laughter and snorts of disbelief that went through the small group that surrounded him held a note of genuine surprise. Cade himself was shocked to hear the words come out of his mouth. It wasn't courage that prompted them, but sheer desperation. He had been ambushed, rendered unconscious, and disarmed; he had awakened in the middle of the mountains surrounded by rough-looking men whose leader wore a hood. The only thing he could think of that might save his life was talk. The moment he had spoken he realized how defiant the words sounded.

The faintest trace of a smile seemed to curve what was visible of the other man's mouth. "They call me Lobo. As for what I want from you—that depends. You, sir, are about to be offered a second chance at life. Whether you take it or not is entirely up to you."

Lobo made a sharp gesture with his head and someone took a knife to the rope that bound Cade's hands. The moment they were free, icy hot needles of pain surged upward to his shoulders. His hands hung limply at his sides.

"If you try to run away," Lobo said matter-of-factly, "you will be shot in the back. I suggest it would be more profitable to stay and listen to the proposition I am about to make to you."

Cade said, "I'm listening."

"You were going to rob those wagons down there, weren't you?"

Cade regarded the other man cautiously and did not answer.

"I couldn't let you do that, you see," Lobo continued

mildly. "In the first place, this is my territory. No one brings anything in—or takes anything out—without my permission. And my permission can be costly, I'm afraid. But we'll discuss that later. Because, in the second place, you see, the owner of those wagons happens to be an old friend of mine, and I couldn't just stand by and watch you do him harm, now could I? I wonder if you would have killed him."

Gingerly, Cade tried to rub the fire needles out of his arms. "No," he lied, "I wouldn't have killed him."

Lobo looked at him for a long time. "That sounds like the reply of a lazy man to me."

Cade did not know how to respond to that.

The silence lay heavy and thick around them. Cade watched the twilight deepen with the cold, quiet certainty that he was living out the last few moments of his life.

Then Lobo spoke, with an abruptness that caused Cade to start. His head throbbed powerfully.

"The situation is this, my friend. There are almost as many thieves in these hills as there are miners, and your idea of turning your hand toward robbery is not an original one. There are safer ways to make a living, I'm sure, and I would highly recommend you seek one of them out. If, however, you intend to stay in this line of work, you will be required to make a few changes in your approach."

Once again Cade felt his head begin to spin, and he wondered if it was his injuries that made it so difficult for him to follow the thread of the conversation or whether, in fact, the conversation itself was to blame. First the man had sounded like a preacher, advising him to give up this life of crime, and now he was telling him how to do it better. Cade dared not do anything except play along.

"Like what?"

"First of all, you will be required to turn over to me half of everything you steal. Secondly . . ." And he smiled a little from within the hood. "You really must learn to be a better thief."

And then he made a gesture with his hand that seemed to dismiss the subject—and Cade. "But my men can explain the details as well as I can, and I have a rather important campaign to plan. No doubt you're hungry. Take him over to the shed, boys, and have Cook fill up his plate. You think about my proposal and give me your decision in the morning."

He started to walk away.

"Do you mean—do you mean I'm free to go if I want to? You knocked me out, tied me up, and dragged me back here, and now—I can just go?"

The other man turned back. "But of course," he said mildly. "It's entirely up to you. But have something to eat before you go. I can't turn you loose so hungry that you'll go back down there and make the same mistakes again, now can I?"

With a last faint, polite smile, he turned and entered the larger cabin, closing the door firmly behind him.

It wasn't until he was gone that Cade felt free to breathe normally.

A big, mostly bald man said, "You're lucky, son. He was in a good mood. Gen'ly we'd string a skinny thing like you up and shoot at him for target practice."

There was a burst of laughter from the group, and the big man flung an arm around Cade's shoulders, making him stagger. When Cade saw his broad, gap-toothed grin, he realized it was meant as a companionable gesture.

"You're lucky in more than one way," the man said. "If you'da stumbled around out there much longer, you'da starved to death—if you didn't get your head blowed off first. Come on, we got orders to feed you."

It had been the code of Cade Deveraux's life to follow the course of least resistance, and this was no exception. He let the big man lead him over to the lean-to, where the aroma of camp stew made his head spin. The cook filled a tin plate to dripping over with stew and skillet biscuits, and Cade ate most of it standing up while the rest of them were filling their plates. He got in line a second time, and when his plate was full once again, he followed the others inside the small cabin.

It was lit by a couple of stubby tallow candles—no windows here, either—and a moment or two passed before Cade's eyes adjusted to the dimness. There was a long table lined with benches in the center of the room, a fireplace at one end, and bunks lined up along the sides. The place was not luxurious by any means, but far superior to the accommodations Cade had been used to during the past few weeks.

He gave his surroundings no more than a cursory appraisal as he sat down at the table and dug into his second plate. But when his stomach was full enough to let him think again, he started paying attention to what was going on around him. What had seemed until this moment a bizarre, injury-induced dream began to take on the sharp edges of reality. He wasn't sure that was a good thing.

There were six men, not counting the one in the lean-to. They had names like Sarge and Noose and Partridge and Stump—the kind of names a man picked up once he crossed the Mississippi and thought it best that his past now follow him west. They were unbarbered, uneducated, and unwashed, and they had a hard, mean look to them that—to a man—warned Cade not to underestimate them.

He leaned back in his chair, toasting them slightly with his coffee cup. "Gentlemen," he said, "I have dined in some of the finest restaurants in New Orleans, but that, without a doubt, is the most exquisite meal I have ever tasted. My compliments to the chef."

No one seemed to think his remark was amusing. Their stares ranged from blank to suspicious; then they turned back to their meals without a further display of interest. One man—Skunk, Cade thought it was—grunted.

"You talk funny. No wonder the boss likes you."

Cade refilled his cup from the coffeepot in the center of the table. The brew was black and bitter and tasted as if it had been boiled with shoe leather. He tried to keep his demeanor casual.

"What is this place anyway?"

It was a moment before anyone answered. Then Charlie, the big man who'd first taken him prisoner, replied around a mouthful of biscuit. "We call it the Fort."

Cade nodded consideringly. "I don't remember passing anything on the trail that looked like this."

Somebody guffawed. "And you wouldn't either. That's the point."

"We call it the Fort," Charlie said, pointing with his fork for emphasis, "because it ain't so easy to get into. Even harder to find."

"I see. A perfect arrangement for a gang of thieves—no offense intended, of course."

Charlie stared at Cade intently. "You go bust in the mines, did you?"

"In a manner of speaking."

The truth was that Cade Deveraux had never held a

pick or a shovel, nor did he have any intention of doing so. He had managed to go broke at mining in spite of that. He was a man who lived on luck and charm, and he'd arrived in California only to find that the one had run out and the other wasn't enough. He had made and lost several fortunes at the gambling tables in his lifetime, but these miners were a hard and unforgiving lot, and it hadn't taken him long to realize he was not cut out for the rough life of the mining camps. He had abandoned all notions of making his fortune in the West. All he was trying to do now was stay alive long enough to make his way back to San Francisco.

He was not so naive as to believe his chances for doing so had improved since stumbling onto these men.

He said, "Do you mind if I ask you something?"

They continued to eat.

"You rob the miners coming out of the fields. A smart way to make a living, and I don't guess you're the first to think of it. But why do you give that man half of everything you steal? Why not just keep it for yourselves?"

Only a couple of them thought his question was worth even glancing up from their plates for. It was Charlie, once again, who answered.

"Well, there's a lot of reasons, if you think on it," he said. "First off, there's this place. A hideout in case of trouble. It increases your chances of staying alive considerably, son. Also, not a bad place to come home to after a hard day at work."

A few chuckles went around the table.

"Then there's the man himself. Smart man. Plans every job, and damn good at it, too. I been with him more'n a year and, you know, in all that time we ain't had one man kilt or hurt." He shrugged. " 'Cept, of course, the ones we kilt ourselves."

"Then there's the dust," put in the man called Sarge.

"He assays it out for us, turns it into hard cash once a month. We don't go risking our hides down in the hollers."

Cade sipped his coffee. "You don't worry about him cheating you?"

Six pairs of eyes pinned him. He knew immediately he had made a mistake.

Charlie said quietly, "No."

The subject was closed.

After a long, uncomfortable moment Cade put down his coffee cup. "Is one of those bunks mine?"

No one answered, so he got up and helped himself.

It wasn't too much longer before they all started drifting off to bed. The candles sputtered and burned out, and within an hour the room was filled with sporadic snores.

Cade lay stiff and wakeful, his head throbbing from the injury and spinning with desperation. He wondered if he was physically capable of making an escape even if he could work up the courage.

Charlie was the last to come to bed. He came in from outside, and Cade had the feeling he had been over at the big cabin, consulting with the boss. Maybe about him.

Charlie sat down on the bunk across from Cade and began pulling off his boots. Cade spoke quietly into the dark.

"Let me ask you something. Just supposing I decide not to take Mr. Lobo up on his generous offer. What do you think my chances are of getting out of here alive?"

One boot squeaked and thumped to the floor.

"Not very good, son. Not very good a'tall." The other boot fell. "Even if you did manage to find your way out of the canyon, why, we'd just have to track you down and shoot you. Might take a couple, three hours, that's all."

Cade was thoughtful for a moment. "That's what I thought," he said.

Charlie stretched out on the bunk. "Better get some sleep," he advised. "The boss is laying out a big job, and we got a lot of getting ready to do. One way or another, you got an early day ahead."

"Yeah. You're right about that."

Cade closed his eyes and slept.

Chapter Three

On their second morning at Donner Lake, Jim was up before sunrise, stirring up the fire, watching his wife sleep. She lay wrapped in a blanket on the ground near the fire, one hand pillowing her cheek, her face serene with peaceful dreams. He had tried to get her to sleep inside the wagon, even before he'd learned of her condition, but in fair weather she insisted upon sleeping beneath the stars. In a place as beautiful as this, Jim couldn't blame her.

He was torn between the desire to linger in this lovely spot, where his new life as a father had begun, to pamper Star with the rest she deserved and to savor the plans they were making; and the need to push on to San Francisco, where all their dreams would begin to come true. The baby would be born there. And by the time it arrived, Jim would have finished building their house—a fine house up on a hill somewhere, with glass windows all around and a room for every member of the family and big porches to sit on in the evenings and catch the breeze. They were never going back to the

Platte. Why should they? Jim had seen California, and it was beautiful country. There was plenty of room there for a man who had already made his fortune to carve out a place for himself. A pretty little ranch, with whitewashed fences and glossy-coated horses . . .

"You look thoughtful, husband," Star murmured, watching him drowsily across the low flames of the fire.

He smiled at her. "That's because I was thinking. I was thinking about money, and how much we have and how it never meant anything to me until now. Until I could do something with it, build something with it, for my family."

Star sat up, smiling tenderly at him as she began to unbraid her hair. "Our child is fortunate indeed to have such a good provider for a father."

And then Jim's expression sobered, became slightly troubled. "Is he?" he inquired. "Do you think he's lucky to be born to me, Star?"

Her fingers fell still against the dark rope of her hair. "I do not understand."

Jim got up and filled the coffeepot from the barrel on the wagon. When he returned he said, "When I first started to fall in love with you, my uncle Boothe tried to talk me out of it. He said it was unfair to you, to try to make you fit into the white man's world. He made it sound as if I'd be stealing something from you—your heritage. And the same for our children, if we ever had any. He tried to make me see what it was like for the Indian wives of white men and their half-breed children, but I was so young and so crazy about you. I didn't half listen. I was just wondering . . ." He looked up at her. "Are you ever sorry? Do you ever regret marrying me?"

Star came around the fire to him, kneeling beside him. She laid her hand lightly atop his. "Jim Kincaid," she said softly, "I regret nothing. There was nothing in the world of the Cheyenne for me. How could there be when my heart was in your world, and would be forever?"

Her hand tightened on his, and her eyes, deep and luminous, searched his. "You have given me seven perfect years in our little cabin on the Platte, Jim Kincaid," she said. "You have given me glass windows with white curtains and a wood floor. You've given me meat for my table in the dead of winter and friends to share it with. Now . . ." Her hand moved to her abdomen. "You have given me a child. No woman could ask for more. No woman has ever been happier."

Jim cupped her face with his hand. "And no man has ever been luckier."

She entwined her fingers around his and pressed her cheek against them briefly. "And now," she said, "you promised fresh game for breakfast, and neither your son nor I will have any unless you go and hunt."

Jim grinned and got to his feet. "What makes you so sure it's a boy?"

"A mother knows."

Jim picked up his rifle, then hesitated. "Star . . . if it is a boy, I was thinking maybe we could call him Boothe."

She smiled. "Of course we will. And," she assured him, "it *is* a boy."

Jim slung his rifle over his shoulder, the pleasure in his eyes sparking with the gentle light of the morning sun. "Warm up that skillet," he said. "I'll be back before the sun hits the treetops."

Star watched him move down the trail and into the woods, her heart swelling with affection and contentment. Then she turned to her morning chores.

She knew what worried Jim. The times were not

what they once had been. White men were flooding into the West, more white men than Star had ever thought existed, and they brought with them their own set of rules, their own sense of right and wrong, their own preferences and hatreds.

The child of mixed parents was not a rare thing; such births had been taking place since the first white man crossed into Indian territory. The lives of these children had never been easy. Often they were rejected by their own tribes, but even if they were not, the societies of many tribes had no place for half-Indian children. Yet even so, life had been easier for half-breed children in the past than it would be in the future, and Star knew that as well as Jim did.

For while mixed-race children were not uncommon, a white man's marriage to an Indian woman was. Star had been fortunate to find acceptance and friendship among the settlers in the small community that had been established by Jim's sister. But as more and more white men crossed the mountain, she came to recognize the uneasy, suspicious look in their eyes.

That look—that hating without knowing, which seemed to be an exclusive product of the white man's world—was what Jim dreaded for the sake of their child. The fact that it was the infant he worried about and not himself only made Star love him more. Because of it, she was not afraid. Her husband would protect her—and her child—from whatever unpleasantness the world might hold.

She took a bucket down to the lake to replenish the water barrels. When she turned, four Indian men on horseback surrounded her.

They had come upon her so suddenly, so silently, so completely without warning, that for the longest moment she simply could not believe what her eyes told her. Two of them dismounted. The other two held their rifles on her. That was when she knew something was wrong. A multitude of observations came together in her head, but she did not stop to analyze them. She dropped the bucket and ran.

She got perhaps half a dozen yards in the slippery mud before a strong hand caught her hair and flung her down. She screamed.

Just before the blade came down, she saw the shadowy figure watching from the woods, and she screamed again.

When he saw the tracks in the woods, Jim decided that he and Star would be moving on today. The droppings that accompanied the tracks were no more than an hour old and sufficient to scare off game for half a mile in any direction. As far as he was concerned, this country was becoming too crowded for comfort.

He circled back through the woods toward a creek where the hunting was usually good, and didn't find so much as a rabbit track. There were, however, signs of several horses having stopped to drink in the predawn hours.

The smell of woodsmoke led him back down the trail the way he'd come. Not once did he see anything worth shooting at. For all the disturbance the party with the horses had created, he expected to see a whole wagon train camped beside the trail; he was somewhat disconcerted to see nothing but a couple of miners and half a string of mules.

He announced himself long before he was within shooting distance. These days, a man approached a stranger's camp at his own risk.

"Come on up to the fire," called one of the men, giving him a gap-toothed grin as he waved him over. "We ain't got nothing to steal even if you was a mind to. Not yet, that is."

He was a squat, gray-haired man who looked too old to be chasing rainbows all the way to California, but that wasn't an unusual sight. His companion was thin and bearded and a little more cautious about putting his rifle aside. Both of them carried enough trail dust to map their route by.

"Name's Shorty Bramlett," said the first man, pouring Jim a cup of coffee. "This here's my partner, Sid Hayden, from Tennessee."

"Jim Kincaid." He accepted the metal cup. "Me and my wife are camped down by the lake. We're hauling a load of goods into San Francisco." He glanced around. "Where're your horses?"

"We've got nothing but mules, mister," Hayden answered, filling his own cup. "Damn stubbornest creatures God ever made, too. If I get out of these mountains without shooting one of them, it'll be a miracle."

"There must be another party behind you," Jim said. "There are horse tracks all over the woods."

The two men exchanged a glance and a shrug. "Not that we noticed."

Then Bramlett said, "You made this trip before, have you?"

"A couple of times," Jim admitted.

Excitement gave new life to their trail-weary eyes. "Then you must know—"

Sound carried clearly in the mountains, and the noise, though far away, was sharp enough to make Bramlett cut off his sentence and cock his head, listening intently. Jim felt everything inside him freeze. They all must have recognized the sound and known what it signified, even though part of their minds simply refused to accept it.

Then it came again, high, sharp, terrified, cut brutally off at the end. The coffee cup tumbled to the ground as Jim grabbed his rifle and ran.

Tree branches slapped at his face and leaves blinded his eyes. Undergrowth snatched and tore at his feet and clothing as he plunged through the woods, sometimes sliding, sometimes running. He kept thinking about the horses, something about the tracks he should have noticed. He should have headed for camp immediately; he should never have left Star alone. He thought about how foolish they had been to stay here in the shadow of death, how he had wanted to leave that first night and she had persuaded him to stay. Yet he had known, somehow he must have known, that nothing good could come of it. And he thought about Uncle Boothe, about high mountain passes and death in the snow, and he thought, quite clearly, *We never should have come here. I never should have brought her* . . .

The smell of smoke reached him long before he saw the lick of flames sparking in the clearing at the lake. And the silence . . . the most horrifying aspect was the silence. The absence of screams.

He broke out of the woods, firing his rifle at a barely clear target on horseback. The wagons were on fire. There were three of them—no, four—breechclout-clad Indians painted for war, their long dark hair decorated with feathers and beads, their rifles held aloft. Their horses were similarly painted and decorated. Through the haze of oily black smoke and the agony of terror and disbelief, Jim took aim and fired again. One of the Indians staggered sideways on his horse but kept his seat. They were on the run and their distance from Jim was increasing. One of them wore something over his face, like a hood.

Jim would remember later that in all that time they never made a sound. The explosion of gunfire, the retreating thunder of hooves, the crackle of fire . . . but not a human voice.

The riders disappeared into the horizon and the last echo of gunfire died away. Nothing remained but the whoosh and crackle of flames as the canvas wagon tops were devoured and the wooden crates inside began to catch. Dimly Jim was aware of the two miners, who had bravely followed him down the trail with their rifles in hand. But they had arrived too late. They had all arrived too late.

He called hoarsely, "Star?"

Nothing.

He staggered a few steps forward. "Star!"

His mind flashed back to another smoking, burned-out campsite when panic had risen in his chest as he called for Star . . . And she had appeared from the shelter of the woods, her clothes scarred with cinder burns and her skin sooty but otherwise unharmed. He had known he would marry her that day. That day their life together had begun.

Today it would begin again. Any moment now she would step out of the woods and come running to him . . .

A gust of wind cleared the smoke briefly, and he saw the form at the edge of the lake. He took a step toward it, and another. He started running.

Within a dozen feet he knew what he was going to find. Still he kept moving. A hand grabbed his shoulder and a harsh voice cried, "For God's sake, man, don't look."

He shook off the hold and plunged forward. He fell to his knees in a puddle of blood beside her.

Jim Kincaid gathered up the mutilated body of his wife and held her close. Then he threw back his head and began to scream.

It was almost sundown by the time they laid the last stone on the grave. Sid wanted to say a few words, but it didn't seem right, with her husband the way he was. So they just stood over the grave with their heads bowed for a few moments and hoped the good Lord wouldn't hold it against them.

They had put out the fire with water from the lake, and managed to save quite a few of the crates. Not that anyone cared in light of what they had not been able to save. They had rounded up the horses and the oxen that had scattered. And all the while Jim Kincaid had simply knelt in that pool of blood, rocking back and forth, holding the corpse.

It had taken them the better part of the morning to pry the mangled body of the woman out of her husband's arms. When they saw what he was holding, what was left of her, they wished they'd left well enough alone. Sid was sick in the bushes for almost half an hour, and Shorty knew the sight would haunt his nightmares for years to come.

While they dug the grave, while they wrapped the body in blankets and lowered it into the ground, Jim knelt where they had left him, soaked in so much blood it looked as though he had been gut-shot himself.

And then, when the last stone was laid, Jim Kincaid did the strangest thing. He got up and walked into the lake, fully clothed.

Sid tried to run after him, but Shorty held him back.

"Don't be a fool, man—he'll drown you, too! Can't you see he's lost his mind?"

They watched in growing horror and helplessness as Jim waded deeper and deeper, and the water turned red around him. And then, when the water was up to his neck, he turned and walked back. Moving heavily, streaming water behind him, he climbed out of the lake.

Sid and Shorty stood back as, still soaking wet, Jim started saddling a horse. In a low voice, Shorty said, "Sid . . . them Indians. They look like Crow to you?"

Sid nodded. They had come upon a hunting party on their way out and the look of them was unmistakable, with their extraordinarily long hair and brightly painted ponies. They had heard the Crow weren't hostile unless provoked; and, sure enough, Sid and Shorty had passed unmolested.

Sid could only assume that somebody had done a powerful lot of provoking to this group to make them do what they'd done to the wife of Jim Kincaid.

"You figure he's going after them?" Sid said, also in a low voice.

His partner looked at him soberly. "God help him if he does."

"God help us all."

They watched as Jim finished saddling his horse, a big black-and-white spotted creature, and mounted. Water still dripped from his clothes, but it was clear water, untainted by blood. Shorty pulled his courage together and stepped forward.

"Mr. Kincaid," he called. "About your wagons. Is there somebody we should notify . . ."

Jim Kincaid turned the horse and looked down at them. Both Shorty and Sid would swear to their dying day that just the memory of that look could turn their blood cold. It was the look of a man who had left his soul in hell and brought back the will of Satan. It was the look of a man who had nothing left to lose.

Jim Kincaid wheeled his horse around and rode away without ever saying a word. The two men he left behind were glad to see him go.

Chapter Four

Kitty Kincaid Adamson leaned against the split-rail fence and looked at her house through narrowed, appraising eyes. Its pale limestone walls gleamed softly gold in the spring sunshine, and she decided, as she had each day since the house was built, that it was the most beautiful house in the Flint Hills of Kansas Territory.

"Are you going to stand there all day, wife, staring at that house, or are you going to get me my dinner?"

Kitty jumped at the sound of her husband's voice behind her and then relaxed against him, drawing his arms around her waist. "Stand here all day and look at my house."

"It's been over seven years, Kitty. I'd think you'd be used to it by now."

"I may be used to it, Ben, but not tired of it. I'll never grow tired of it." She turned so that she could look up at him. "Remember how I wanted a stone house when we first moved here back in '37, and we had to settle for logs?"

"I remember."

"But the fire took care of that."

"You act as if that fire was a good thing."

Kitty was contrite. "I didn't mean that; it was awful. It's just that ... well, sometimes things have a strange way of working out that puny little humans like us can't control."

Kitty would never forget the prairie fire that had swept up from the plains into the hills in the autumn of 1843. It had been sudden, devastating, and, in the end, almost miraculous. Ben and the Adamsons' hired man, Billy Threefingers, had cut a firebreak between the fire and the horse ranch. The barrier had held, except at one place—the Adamson house. The flames had jumped the cleared patch of land and engulfed the log cabin so quickly that nothing could be salvaged.

There had been a human cost also—an eighty-foot cottonwood tree had crashed to the ground and pinned Ben under its flaming branches. Kitty had screamed and run wildly, blindly, toward her husband. If she closed her eyes, even now she could feel the heat of the flames and smell the acrid scent of smoke and hear Ben's terrible cries of pain.

Somehow she and Billy had managed to pull Ben free and drag him away from the fiery tree. As Kitty crouched by her husband, his head in her lap, the pain she felt from the burns on her hands and arms was nothing compared with the hurt inside as she watched her house and all her belongings burn to the ground. There was nothing to do, she decided, but load Ben and the girls into the wagon, free all the livestock, and try to outrun the flames ...

Then the miracle happened. As Ben had predicted when he and Billy cut the firebreak, the wind shifted and drove the fire back on itself, away from the barns and horses and the springhouse, where Sarah, Kitty's sister, huddled with the young Adamson children.

Ben, his face blackened with soot and ashes, his leg broken, and his clothes singed and charred, gathered his family around him and thanked God for mercifully sparing the rest of the ranch. Before the prayer ended, Billy set off for the nearest neighbor and brought back Charles Gallier, who knew more about medicine than anyone in the hills. He'd set Ben's leg and offered the hospitality of his home until the Adamsons could rebuild. He'd even offered his slaves, who'd built his stone house, to help with the new construction.

That had been a hard favor for Ben, an abolitionist, to accept, but he bent his ironclad principles and said yes. The alternative was for the Adamson family to live in the barn until Ben and Billy could start on another log cabin, and while Ben could have endured that for himself, he didn't want it for his children, especially not with autumn and cold weather fast approaching. So together, the slaveholder and the abolitionist had shared in the building of the Adamson home.

Even though both Ben and Kitty disapproved of slavery, they'd grown close to the Galliers and were grateful for the older couple's help over the years. Charles had been a founding force in the Adamsons' successful horse-breeding business, and his influence at Fort Leavenworth, where the First Dragoons were quartered, had allowed Kitty and Ben to carry on a solid business with the Army. Each spring and autumn, Ben and Billy Threefingers drove the Adamson horses, bred for endurance and swiftness, to the fort, where the Army quartermaster paid top dollar for them.

After the fire, with the help of the Galliers, the Adamsons had not only endured but also prospered. Kitty had her stone house, their two daughters were strong and healthy, and in 1849, Kitty and Ben had been blessed with a son, Benjamin, Jr. After years of struggle, their dreams seemed to be coming true. And miracle of miracles, she and Ben cared for each other more than ever. Adversity had bonded them closer, and their commitment to each other and their family was absolute.

Kitty hugged Ben tightly. "Whatever the reason—fire or not—we're doing pretty well, Ben Adamson. Better than we ever thought." She stood on tiptoe to kiss him. Just then a small, blond-haired figure appeared on the front porch of the Adamson house. "Mo-thur!" The second call was louder. "Mo-thur!"

"She has perfect timing, doesn't she?" Ben murmured.

Kitty sighed. "Now, why does Carrie call me 'Mother' and Hilda call me 'Ma'?"

"Because Carrie's a prissy miss like her aunt Sarah, and Hilda is more like you."

Carrie Adamson, aged nine, marched across the yard toward her parents. Her blond curls bobbed on the shoulders of her pinafore and her forehead was creased in a frown.

"What is it, Carrie?" Kitty called out.

"Hilda won't set the table. I told her to, but she won't. It's her turn. I did it last night."

"I'll tell her," Kitty said. "Older sisters don't like young ones to give them orders."

"I wasn't giving orders," Carrie said precisely. "I was just reminding her. She's so . . . so pigheaded."

"I can't imagine where she gets that from," Ben murmured.

Kitty poked him with her elbow. "I'll be there in just a minute. It's so nice out here, I hate to come inside."

"You just don't want to start dinner, do you, Mother?" Carrie said accusingly.

A sharp answer was on the tip of Kitty's tongue, but she bit it back. She was learning that her daughters knew her very well, and lying to them was impossible. "No, I don't, but I will. Right now I want to stand here with your papa and look at my beautiful house and think about how happy I am."

Carrie raised her eyebrows in resignation. "All right, Mother, I'll start dinner. Billy will probably help me."

"Thank you, sweetheart. I think there's stew left over from last night, and there're potatoes in the cellar. Is your little brother awake?"

"He's still having his nap, but I think I'll wake him up. He's slept long enough," Carrie called over her shoulder as she marched back toward the house.

"Sometimes I wonder who's the mother and who's the child," Kitty said with a laugh.

Ben removed her hat and ran his fingers through her curly fair hair. "You don't look old enough to have three children," he said. "You still look like a little girl."

"I'm thirty-one, Ben. That's old." She sighed again. "It seems like a lifetime, though, since I came to these hills."

"I know you get lonely, Kitty."

She shook her head. "I'm too busy to get lonely, with you and the children and the horses—"

"And the dogs and the cats," Ben teased. Kitty had a rapport with animals that was remarkable, and the ranch was overflowing with assorted four-legged beasts.

She ignored his interruption. "But I miss Emilie and Charles. I wish she hadn't moved back to Louisiana."

"She didn't have much choice after Charles died. She wasn't like you; she didn't know anything about running the farm."

Emilie, who was twenty years older than Kitty, had served as a surrogate mother to her and as a grandmother to the Adamson children. They'd celebrated holidays together and nursed each other through illnesses and hard times. When Charles had died, the first person Emilie had sent for was Kitty. Although Ben and Charles had continued their dialogue about the institution of slavery, Kitty and Emilie never discussed it. Neither was going to change her views, and so they just accepted each other, warts and all, as Emilie had said.

When Emilie packed up her belongings to move back to her ancestral plantation, Deveraux House, she'd given generously to the Adamsons. She left them the big four-poster bed she'd shared with Charles, saying that now, since he was gone, she couldn't sleep in it alone. She insisted that Kitty take her drop-leaf walnut dining room table and the eight chairs that went with it; she had no room for them at Deveraux House, and it would give her pleasure to think of her friends celebrating holidays around the big table. She also left Kitty her cabinet of medicinal supplies. Kitty tried to soak up all that Emilie told her—blackberry root as a poultice for swollen eyes, pumpkin seeds to cure tapeworms, peppermint tea for stomach upsets, rose hip tea for a cold—but she knew she'd never have the skill that Emilie had.

"It's too bad the Conrads aren't our kind of folks," Ben commented.

The Conrads, who'd taken over the Gallier house, were from Missouri, slave owners, too, but they lacked the humanity and kindness of Charles and Emilie. After their first meeting, Kitty and Ben knew they would never be close friends with the new family. There'd be no sharing of holidays or frequent visiting back and forth. Still, in times of trouble they'd rally with their neighbors as people on the frontier had learned to do. There were less than eight hundred squatters in Kansas, and nothing like a real town. The territory was still mostly unsettled, with Fort Leavenworth serving as its center.

"I don't even like to see the Gallier house anymore," Kitty said. "I rode over last week to take Mrs. Conrad some dried apples, and it just made me so sad. They've torn out Charles's grape arbors and gotten rid of his sheep, and Mrs. Conrad has no idea how to take care of Emilie's flowers. It wasn't the same. I hate to lose people, Ben."

"I know. Like Emilie and Charles and the Cheyenne and High Backed Wolf."

Kitty nodded. For years Ben and Kitty had traded with the Southern Cheyenne for horses, and tight bonds of friendship had been forged between the Adamsons and the tribe. Kitty's brother Jim had married a Cheyenne woman, making the ties even stronger.

Then in 1849, an outbreak of cholera had decimated the Cheyenne, and High Backed Wolf had moved his people into the mountains. And so they were lost to the Adamsons, too. Since Kitty and Ben bred their own horses now, the Indian's departure had been a loss of friendship rather than a business setback. From the fine Spanish horses that they'd bought from the Cheyenne in the late 1830s, Ben and Kitty had developed their own strain of Western horses.

"It doesn't seem fair, Ben, that so many folks have passed out of our lives!"

"Like our families back home in Cairo."

"It's funny," Kitty said thoughtfully. "Now that I'm a mother myself, I miss Ma more than ever. Letters help, but I'd just like to talk to her—" She shrugged. "Oh, well, no sense whining about it. Let's go see if we can find something to cook for dinner." She started for the house.

Ben grabbed her hand. "Let's talk a minute, Kitty."

She looked up at him. She couldn't read the expression on her husband's handsome face, and for a moment she was worried. "Is something wrong?"

"For once, no. We've got the best herd of horses we've ever had. The Army's going to buy every one of 'em, I guarantee, and I'm going to raise our prices—"

"Are you sure?"

"Yes, Kitty, we're raising our prices, and they'll pay. Believe me, the Army'll pay for these horses. Didn't Colonel Stephen Kearney and his whole contingent go riding off to fight the Mexicans in '46 on our horses? Seems like he forgot pretty quick he had a grudge against your brother Jim when he saw that roan stallion he wanted."

Kitty nodded. Colonel Kearney had briefly carried out a vendetta against the Adamsons and refused to buy their horses because of a murder that Kitty's brother Jim was accused of committing. Finally Kearney, a practical man, had been persuaded by Charles Gallier that he'd be foolish not to trade with the Adamsons, who had the finest horses west of the Mississippi. Kearney's successor at the fort had continued to buy, and, in fact, each year he increased the number of horses purchased for his growing garrison on the Missouri River.

"So we'll be rich, have money to burn—is that what you're telling me?" Kitty joked.

Ben laughed. "We'll never be rich, but after this spring sale, we'll have a little extra." He cleared his throat and proudly announced, "Enough to buy four tickets on the steamship that stops at the fort."

Kitty's heart skipped a beat. "Four tickets?"

"You and the girls and little Ben. I thought you

might want to travel down the Missouri River to St. Louis and get a Mississippi steamer and then—well, maybe you might want to show the kids off to your ma."

Her breath caught in her throat and a hot rush of tears filled her eyes. "Go home? To Cairo, and take the children—" She flung her arms around him. "Oh, Ben, yes, yes!" The tears were flowing now, wetting the front of his shirt. "It's been fourteen years since I left home, since I've seen Ma—"

"Don't cry, honey." He wiped her cheek with his thumb. "I wanted to make you happy."

"You know I'm happy, Ben Adamson, but I just can't help crying." She stood on tiptoe and kissed him long and deeply. "Let's go tell the girls that they're going to see their grandma and their aunts and uncles—"

"And cousins," Ben added. "Don't forget, my sisters will be there, too, with their broods."

"Ben Adamson, you're the best man I've ever met. Why don't you come with me?"

"One of us has to be here, you know that. Foaling time is coming up, and Billy can't handle things alone."

"Then maybe I shouldn't go . . ." Kitty said tentatively.

Ben put his arm around his wife and led her toward the house. "There's nothing in the world that's going to keep you off that boat. You and I both know that, so don't play noble with me, Kitty."

She grinned at him. "I never could fool you, could I? I'm writing Ma tonight; you can mail it from the fort when you take the horses, and you can buy the tickets then, too. No, maybe I'd better come along. I want to be sure we get a good cabin. I've never been on a riverboat, Ben!" She stopped and gazed up at him, her eyes shining. "What an adventure for my children!"

"And for their mama, too," he said softly.

Kitty paused at the foot of the porch steps and sighed deeply. "It's a beautiful house, isn't it?"

"The best in the world, Kitty. The best in the world."

Remarkable changes had taken place in the sleepy little village of Yerba Buena, which for years had huddled almost unnoticed on the edge of San Francisco Bay. The change began in 1846, when President James Knox Polk went to war with Mexico and declared California part of the United States of America. Soon afterward, Yerba Buena became San Francisco. Then, when gold was discovered at Sutter's Mill and forty-niners poured by the tens of thousands into San Francisco, it swelled to a town of over twenty thousand. In 1850, California became a state, and more changes were set in motion.

The gold mines kept on paying off, and San Francisco continued to grow. By 1851, it was no longer a town of tents and wooden shacks. Brick and frame houses, some as high as three stories, clustered near the bay and straggled up the chaparral-covered hills. The city boasted saloons and stores, hotels and restaurants, laundries and barbershops, and the population seemed to be made up of every nationality under the sun. The Irish congregated south of Market Street, the Germans at the end of Montgomery. The Sydney Ducks, undesirable Australian ex-convicts, lived in Sydney Town near Telegraph Hill, and the Chinese had taken over an area near Sacramento Street. There were also French, Peruvians, Mexicans, Hawaiians, British, and Chileans. In the streets a polyglot of languages was spoken, and the city had a vitality that was impossible to repress.

San Francisco was bold, bawdy, and booming, and it seemed to re-create itself into something new and exciting every year. That's what Meg Kincaid liked best about the place—the constant possibility of rebirth. She was somewhat of a phoenix herself, and San Francisco seemed the city for beginnings.

When she and Sheldon Gerrard, her business partner of eight years, and her daughter, Fiona, first arrived in San Francisco, they'd ignored the mud and rats and shantytown atmosphere and concentrated on the opportunity the city represented. They bought a lot on Portsmouth Square for fifty thousand dollars, a bargain, they agreed, for one of the best locations in town. This was where they'd build their new store.

The problem, they quickly learned, was that although land was available, building supplies were not. There were no bricks to be had, and very little lumber. Meg was undaunted. She looked around and saw a veritable forest of masts in San Francisco Bay. There were six hundred ships at anchor, many of which had been abandoned when captain and crew took off for the gold camps.

"We'll simply buy a ship," she announced to Sheldon. "Tear it apart and use the wood for our store."

"Why not just drag the ship on shore and use it intact, like others have done?" Sheldon asked. He knew the answer, but he liked to challenge Miss Meg and listen to her reasoning. At one time he'd thought he had the better business mind of the two. Now he wasn't sure.

"Because that would look cheap and easy and as if we don't care. There are enough tacky-looking boats pulled up on shore and turned into stores and hotels and restaurants. That's not for us. Kincaid and Gerrard Emporium isn't going to be some thrown-together shack that caters to failures. There're lots of miners with lots of money—and we're going to get it."

Sheldon had nodded in agreement. She was exactly right. They needed to establish themselves as quickly as possible among the high rollers, the entrepreneurs, the people who counted, and running a two-bit store out of an abandoned ship wasn't going to do that for them. Or for Fiona.

Fiona, who was eight years old, wasn't Sheldon's child. When he'd met Meg in a woebegone little town on the Missouri, ironically named Bellevue, she was already pregnant and on the run from her abusive husband, Caleb O'Hare, whom she despised. But having been with Fiona since the day she was born, taking care of her and loving her and worrying about her, Sheldon felt as if she were his own. Meg wanted Fiona to call him Mr. Gerrard, which she did, but Fiona, like all the Kincaid women, had a mind of her own. She called him Papa, and loved him even more than she loved her mother.

Meg and Sheldon built an elegant, solidly constructed store, and it was immensely successful. They brought to it their experience of running a trading post on the Platte and combined that with their ambition, their willingness to work eighteen hours a day, and an uncanny ability to anticipate what their customers needed. Rains were frequent and the streets were often flooded. Sometimes the mud was deep enough to swallow up a wagon. Meg went down to the harbor and made an outrageously high bid for a shipment of hip boots and made a tidy profit by selling the boots at an inflated price.

Most people were making money in San Francisco, in all kinds of ways. The stories were legion. Four laundresses decided it was ridiculous for the miners to ship their dirty clothes all the way to Canton, China, to be cleaned, so they opened their own establishment. In two years the women retired with profits of twenty thousand dollars each. A sea captain, knowing about the huge rat population plaguing the city, brought in a shipload of stray cats and sold each one for ten dollars. An enterprising meat-shop owner began to raise his own cattle and sell the fresh beef in his store. Meg heard of a man named Levi Strauss, who was selling his canvas pants down on the docks, and she contracted with him to sell them exclusively through her store. The pants leapt off the shelves, and Strauss made enough money to start up a factory.

Meg also sold a more upscale line of goods, when she could get them—cigars and sherry, silk cravats for men, and crinolines and petticoats for the ladies. When the miners came down from the hills, their pockets loaded with gold dust, they were determined to spend every penny before going back to the camps—and many times they didn't care what they bought. It was bad luck not to spend all the money they had, so if a miner who lived in a shack in Grizzly Flats or Mad Mule Gulch wanted to wear a satin vest decorated with ivory buttons over his dirty overalls, Meg would sell it to him. If she had it in stock . . .

. She soon learned that shipments were a problem. Nothing ever seemed to arrive on time, and there were periods of glut with more items on the Emporium shelves than she ever thought they could sell, followed by lean times when the shelves were bare.

Fires frequently swept through the city, most of them blamed on the Sydney Ducks, who, it was rumored, set them and then looted the burning businesses. Meg's store didn't escape the hazard. The first time the fire surged near Portsmouth Square, she lost only the roof.

The second time, two months later, the whole store burned down, along with many of the hotels, saloons, and businesses on the square. Fortunately by then, she, Sheldon, and Fiona had moved from living above the Emporium to a two-story frame house in Happy Valley.

The name amused Meg, who'd seen the area before its metamorphosis. It had once been a tent city, filled with refuse and reeking with human waste, a place where rats and dogs fought in the mud over scraps of food. But as with all things in the city by the bay, things changed; a fire swept through the tent city, burning it to the ground, and when Happy Valley was rebuilt, it became one of the most desirable neighborhoods in San Francisco.

They shared their home with Monserrat and Tonio Ramirez, whom they'd met soon after they arrived in San Francisco. Monserrat took care of Fiona and cooked, and Tonio did whatever needed to be done, from helping to put a new roof on the store to driving Sheldon in the carriage he'd bought. But Sheldon wasn't happy in the frame house; he worried about fire, and he didn't think the neighborhood was prestigious enough for him and his family. He'd begun buying property—even Meg didn't know how much or where it was all located—and had decided to build a brick house at the base of Fern Hill. People were already calling it Nob Hill—some, Snob Hill—and Sheldon's intuition told him that one day it would be a fine place to live. He wanted a brick house like the one he'd owned in St. Louis before he'd lost his first fortune; he wanted a little garden in back and a big barn for the horses and carriage. He wanted it to be a house of style and substance, a house for Fiona and for her children to call their own.

Meg was more interested in her new enterprise than

in their future home, and couldn't understand why
Sheldon wasn't as enthusiastic as she. She ignored the
fact that he was in his fifties, or that he'd been complaining more often of not feeling well. Meg accused
Monserrat of using too many chilies in her cooking and
ordered Sheldon to watch what he ate.

He and Meg made a point of having breakfast together each day with Fiona before she left for school;
sometimes it was the only time they saw each other all
day. After Fiona left, they took the opportunity to talk.
Morning sun streamed through the lace curtains in the
dining room. It was a pleasant room, furnished with an
ornately carved table and six high-backed chairs in
what Sheldon called "the Spanish style." He'd bought
them from a departing family, rancheros, old Californi-
ans of Spanish descent, who decided too many Americans were ruining California, where their families had
lived for a hundred and fifty years. They moved to
Mexico City, and Sheldon bought most of their furniture. He liked the heaviness of it, the substance, and the
fact that it was old, possibly a hundred years or so.
"Family heirlooms," he told Fiona proudly, as if the
items had been passed down to him through his own
relatives.

Sheldon put down his newspaper, took a sip of coffee,
and listened to the lecture Meg was giving him.

"You see, Mr. Gerrard, if you'll eat a boiled egg in
the morning with plain toast, potatoes and beef for
lunch, and—"

"My health is fine, Miss Meg, as is my stomach, as is
my ability to choose what food I eat. Despite what you
think, you don't know what's best for everyone." He
picked up his paper again.

Unperturbed, Meg buttered a piece of toast. "You
must not have slept well last night."

"I slept fine," Sheldon answered, not looking up from his paper. "For once there were no fire bells going off. I'll be glad when the new house is done."

"It is worrisome, isn't it? No one seems to be able to control the fires. You'd think the vigilantes could catch whoever is setting them."

San Francisco had no organized system of law and order, and frequently when the citizenry became upset about crime, a vigilante group would spring up to take action. Sometimes, it turned out, the vigilantes committed criminal acts themselves and had to be hunted down by still more bands of outraged citizens.

Sheldon put aside the paper for good and warmed to his topic. "There's no law in this town, Miss Meg, and until there is, I don't like the idea of you building this gambling house, consorting with low-life—"

Meg had known the discussion would come around to this. It always did. She had decided it was foolish to rebuild the Emporium; there was more money to be made other ways. "It's not going to be a gambling house or a saloon. I'm going to call it an opera house—"

Sheldon snorted.

"No one will sing opera," she said firmly. "I've told you that fifteen times, although there will be a stage for the orchestra. Maybe a string orchestra. They seem popular these days. Downstairs we'll serve food and drink and upstairs we'll have gambling rooms, and they won't be open to just anyone. I want people of a certain class—"

"Anyone with money, you mean."

"Mr. Gerrard, you have a very narrow way of looking at things."

"Miss Meg, I see reality." He took another sip of coffee. "Did Captain Tyler get that bar unloaded and into the warehouse for you?"

"Yes, he did." Meg hid a smile. Even though Sheldon pretended a lack of interest in her latest endeavor, she knew he was aware of every move she made. "It's wonderful. Fifty feet long, shipped in two sections, carved of mahogany. It will be the talk of the city."

"That and your chandeliers."

"Jim will get here—with the chandeliers and everything else we ordered. Don't you trust my brother?"

"I've trusted him for years. I just don't trust the Rocky Mountains, my dear. We should have had them brought by ship."

"It takes far too long, and too many ships go down around the Horn. This is the best way by far."

"Whatever you say, Miss Meg."

"So you're agreeing with me."

"Maybe about the chandeliers, not about the sal—I mean the opera house. There's a lot of competition out there. This town has hundreds of saloons."

"There were stores in San Francisco when we opened the Emporium, but we made it a success. My opera house is going to be different. I'm not trying to compete with those places with sawdust on the floor and women of no particular virtue in the back room."

"May I remind you that right on Portsmouth Square, in our neighborhood, are some fine establishments. The Verandah, the Parker House, the El Dorado—"

"I know their names, Mr. Gerrard," Meg said sweetly. "I pass them every day. Those are the places I'm going to compete with. My opera house is going to have style and class . . . and dignity. I'm going to hire a chef—"

"A chef?" Sheldon laughed. "Miss Meg, may I remind you this is not Paris, France?"

"I am hiring a chef, not a cook," Meg insisted, "and I'm going to offer free lunches—just at first, to draw in a crowd—"

Sheldon sighed. "You know how men in this town feel about women going into business and showing them up. They might not be pleased with you giving away free food to steal their customers."

"You're the person who taught me about being successful. I can't help it if I learned my lessons well," she said with an emphatic shake of her red hair.

"You may have learned too well, Miss Meg. There're some dangerous men in this city who run gambling halls, and they won't appreciate your taking their customers. I hear Yancey Connor's moving his saloon over to Dupont. Now, that's right around the corner from your opera house, and he's a rough one. That's why I don't like the idea of you working at night, consorting with that element of society. I don't want anything to happen to you. I couldn't bear that." His voice shook with emotion.

Meg, surprised, for once was quiet.

"We have plenty of money, Miss Meg. I can build you and Fiona a grand house. We can entertain and meet the right people and ensure Fiona's future. Don't you want that?" His eyes were bright with a kind of desperate passion as he leaned toward her.

Meg clasped her fingers firmly together in her lap, stifling the desire to reach out and touch his hand. She and Sheldon Gerrard had been business partners, antagonists, spurs to the other's ambition, and devoted parents of Fiona, but never intimate or loving with each other.

"Of course I want that. That child is my life, but I want more. I want to do something on my own—to succeed. To be someone. You can understand that, can't you?"

Sadly he nodded. "Oh, yes, I can understand that,

Miss Meg, but I can't condone it. Look at me. I lost a leg because of my ambition and greed. Lost my money and my fortune back in St. Louis, and except for you and that darling red-haired child, I would have lost my life. I'm thinking of you. I want to protect you from what happened to me."

Meg was a little frightened by the depth of emotion in Sheldon's voice, and she didn't know how to respond. Except for her love for her child, her own feelings had long ago been transformed into a driving ambition, goaded by a fear of failure. Finally she responded. "I thank you for your concern, and for your help over the years." The words seemed inadequate and sounded much too formal. She saw Sheldon's lips tighten and his expression change.

"My God, Miss Meg, you don't need to thank me."

"Yes, I do, and I don't do it often enough. I still need you to help me, Mr. Gerrard. I value your opinion more than that of any man I know. I mean that with all my heart."

He sighed deeply, as if defeated. "I'll be here to help you as long as I can. Would you like me to drive down to the square today and take a look around at the opera house?"

"Yes, I'd like that. It's hard to keep the carpenters working. As soon as I hire one crew, they decide to take off for the goldfields and I'm without laborers again."

"I'll see what I can do."

Meg pushed her chair back from the table and stood up. "I'll get dressed so I can ride with you."

"Only on one condition. I want you to drive over and see the lot I've picked out for the new house."

"This morning? I have so much to do."

"It's important to me."

"Then I will," she agreed. She turned to leave the room but stopped. "Is everything all right?"

Sheldon was staring at his paper. "Everything is fine; go change your clothes."

Meg went upstairs, the conversation with Sheldon playing over in her mind. *I'll be here to help you as long as I can* . . . As long as he could? She knew Sheldon would never leave her or Fiona, not willingly. It wasn't like him to talk that way. She pushed the alternative from her mind. No, she wouldn't think of it. Sheldon was as healthy as he'd ever been; his diet gave him those stomach pains, nothing else. He wasn't ill; he was just . . . bored. She could solve that part of the problem by involving him more in the opera house, and she'd talk to Monserrat herself and be sure that his food was properly prepared.

Things were going wonderfully for all of them now, and she wouldn't allow that to change.

Chapter Five

Less than half of the settlers who started out for California ever made it to the Promised Land. Travel on the Overland Trail was harsh and the suffering real, and abandoned wagons, the carcasses of dead pack animals, and the graves of emigrants littered the way.

Having experienced the dangers of the Rockies, the desolation of the Great Basin, the relentless sun of Nevada Territory's Forty-Mile Desert; having survived broiling heat and freezing nights, stampedes and storms and raiding Indians, poisoned water, starvation, accident, and illness—having endured all this, the pilgrims seemed to be overtaken by a certain madness on their last two-mile descent toward the Carson River at the foot of the Sierra Nevadas. California and the goldfields lay ahead, across the treacherous spires of the mountains, but now there was only one goal for the travelers—the river.

They came barreling down the slope, on foot, on horseback, or driving their rickety wagons at breakneck speeds, flinging their hats and their empty canteens into the air, letting forth savage cries of triumph. Before them were the cool, shady shores of the river, the first trees they had seen in weeks, and water, endless water. Many of them kept on running, right into the river, or flung themselves spread-eagled onto the grassy shore, or sank to their knees and pressed their parched faces against the cool bark of a cottonwood tree. It was a sight to see.

A little encampment had sprung up on the trail west, straggling along the Carson River. Across the Sierra Nevada, a formidable boundary, lay the goldfields of California. The settlement, which was well on its way to becoming a town of sorts, was called Ragtown because of the wind-strewn litter discarded by the emigrants. Along with the iron skeletons of wagons that had been discarded because the beasts, having brought them this far, were unable to go another step, there was the acre or so of goose feathers that had gotten loose from a split mattress during a high wind. The population of Ragtown was a mostly transient one, but already a few enterprising gamblers had set up shop to welcome the travelers, along with a general store whose only commodity was whiskey.

Here anxious friends and relatives waited for news of those who had been lost on the trail. Here those who had been depleted by the desert recovered from their ills. Here, too, the occasional miner—most likely played out on his own and looking for a grubstake—might wander down from the mountains, bringing news of the riches, or lack of same, that waited across the range.

Just such a miner had passed through a week previously, on his way back to Fort Hall, where he had left his family. He brought news of an encounter with two pilgrims headed for the goldfields, and the massacre they had witnessed at Donner Lake. Those who ventured onward had better beware: the Indians were on the warpath.

After all they had endured to get this far, the thought of Indian trouble in the mountains was too much for the emigrants. Grumblings of defiance spread from camp to camp and, fueled by whiskey, reached riotous proportions inside the big tent that served as the general store. They had been through hell and beyond; a mere two weeks' travel stood between them and the Promised Land, and they were prepared, if not altogether able, to kill on sight anything that stood in their way.

The man called Thunder Eagle had no way of knowing this, however. He came from the Snake River, across the Great Desert on the Humboldt, and into the Carson River like any other pilgrim. But a pilgrim he was not. He was headed West, though it wasn't gold he sought. He traveled alone by choice, a tall man dressed in cotton pants and a calico shirt, a wide-brimmed hat atop his head. His features were broad and full, his skin nut brown. His blue-black hair was plaited into a single braid that hung below his waist.

He came down the trail at sunset, long after the usual influx of emigrants had arrived. In the quiet of the cool evening the click of a rifle bolt was clearly audible above the sound of his horse's hooves—then another one, and another. A voice came from his left.

"Hold it right there, you thieving, murdering, son-of-a-bitchin' bastard."

Thunder Eagle considered his choices briefly, and brought his horse to a stop, holding the reins lightly in one hand while he lifted both arms to the height of his shoulders. Even from that position he could have had his rifle out of its scabbard before anyone saw him move, but he judged it to be an exercise in futility. By his estimation, not one of the three barrels that were aimed at him was more than five feet away, and the chance of even one of them missing at that range was remote.

They stepped out from behind the rocks one at a time, cautiously. They were thin and grizzled, trail-hardened and tough as rawhide. Thunder Eagle was glad he had followed his instinct and kept his hands high.

"Who are you, Injun?" one of them demanded. "And what d'you want here?"

"You speak English?" demanded another.

"Where's the rest of 'em? Where's your war party?" Another man was darting his eyes about a little wildly. "They come out of them rocks and you're dead first, you hear that?"

Thunder Eagle gazed down at them coolly. "My name," he said, "is Thunder Eagle, and I haven't murdered anyone." He looked them over measuringly before adding, "Lately."

He had the satisfaction, brief though it was, of seeing an Adam's apple bob in one skinny throat. The other two men just jerked their rifles at him.

"Git down off that pony, Injun."

"Real easy-like," added the other man. "And keep them hands high."

Thunder Eagle did as he was told. Not a flicker of expression crossed his face, not even a glance toward the weapon and the mount he was leaving behind.

They gestured him to walk in front. One of them led his horse, and the other two covered him with their rifles at two paces. It was so quiet on the trail, he could hear them breathing and judged their distance, as well as their concentration, by the sound of it. When they reached the bottom of the trail, where tents and lean-tos were scattered over the ground like so much added rubble, the atmosphere changed.

"We got us one, boys!" one of the men behind him shouted. "We by God damn got us a killer Injun!"

"Look here! Look what we caught!"

"We found him trying to sneak down the trail and murder us in our sleep! God knows how many others of them are hiding up there in the rocks!"

Knots of men began to form. Tired, long-faced women pushed open the flaps of their tents and glanced out with frightened eyes. An occasional child broke loose and started to run toward him, only to be jerked back and severely reprimanded by a parent. The men who were sober looked angry and disturbed; the drunken ones just looked angry. The truth was, if it had been only an hour later and those men had been a little more drunk, Thunder Eagle might not have survived his sojourn into Ragtown.

"I'll get a goddamn rope!" somebody shouted from the crowd.

"Save your rope! Shoot him down where he stands!"

A rangy, pale-haired man emerged from the big tent and leaned one shoulder against a support post, chewing on a straw and watching the proceedings with little interest. Thunder Eagle gazed back at him.

"Well, we ought to do something! We can't stand here staring at him all night."

"I'll tell you what we ought to do! We ought to form a posse and hunt the hills for the rest of the war party, that's what we ought to do!"

At that point one of the men in the group outside the big tent pulled a pistol from his waistband and, reeling a little, took aim.

As quick as a snake, the blond man's hand went out and grabbed the other man's wrist. The shot went wild.

Women screamed and men jumped back as the bullet split the dust. No one seemed quite as anxious to raise objections as he had been before, and into the stunned silence the blond man spoke.

"Now, boys, don't you think you might be acting a bit previous, there? Why, you don't even know what kind of Injun you got here, or what he might be worth."

He moved forward, his thumbs hooked under his galluses, and with a studious look on his face, made a slow circle around Thunder Eagle. The men who were holding weapons relaxed them a little as the tension on their faces became mitigated with curiosity.

The blond man's name was Evan Thompson. He had made the Overland Trail six times now, first as a scout for some of the best wagon masters in the country, then for the Army. More than half of those presently gathered in Ragtown knew someone who owed his life to Evan Thompson; and those who didn't, knew his reputation. There wasn't a man in the country, they would all readily agree, who knew his business better than Evan Thompson. When he spoke, people listened.

"Well, now, boys," he drawled at last, coming to stand in front of Thunder Eagle again, "you know who you got here, don't you? His name is Thunder Eagle, and he's wanted by no less than the United States government. You go stringing up this here Indian and you got to do a lot of explaining to some mighty powerful folks."

The three who had brought in the Indian started to look nervous. "Thunder Eagle, yeah, that's right," muttered one uneasily. "That's what he said his name was."

"What's he wanted for?" asked another.

Evan glanced at him. "Questioning," he answered. "Seems some Army folks think this Indian can give 'em some answers that might save a lot more folks from being murdered and robbed on the trail."

Gun barrels started to lower uncertainly. "Well, what the hell are we supposed to do with him?"

Evan shrugged. "Turn him over to the Army, I reckon."

"There ain't no army around here."

"You could take him back to Fort Hall."

"Damn it, Evan, you know we can't— Hey! You work with the Army. Seems to me like you're the one we ought to be turning him in to."

Evan frowned. "I'm not a soldier. And I sure as hell ain't taking him all the way back to Fort Hall." He looked thoughtful for a moment. "But I tell you what. I could take him on to the Army post at Sacramento for you, see what they want to do with him there."

There was little more discussion after that. No one wanted the responsibility of an Indian who was both dangerous *and* valuable, and they were glad to get him off their hands. It was agreed that Evan would take him downriver, away from the family encampments, and guard him that night, to start out early in the morning for Sacramento. Thunder Eagle offered no resistance as his hands were bound and he was forced to remount his horse. Evan took his reins, and his rifle, and led the way.

They had gone about two miles downriver when Thunder Eagle spoke. "You want to untie me now? This pony's blind in the dark."

"Hell, I figured you'd've taken care of that yourself by now," Evan replied without looking back. "You still got that knife in your boot?"

"I've got it, I just can't reach it. Not without falling off, anyhow."

Evan chuckled. "You could ride a buffalo bareback in

a high wind without falling off, Thunder Eagle. You're getting lazy, that's all."

"Or maybe smarter."

Evan led the horses to the riverbank and dismounted. He cut Thunder Eagle's ropes with his own knife and resheathed it without a word. Thunder Eagle dismounted, rubbing his wrists briefly. He jerked his head back toward the camp. "What was that all about?"

His English was as American as Evan's, as were his mannerisms. Some said that came from having a white father. The truth was that, though he had grown up in the Crow village among his mother's people, between his mother and himself, English was the only language they ever spoke. She insisted on it.

In certain Indian tribes he was becoming known as the Prophet, hearkening back to the renowned visionary and leader of the Shawnee, brother of the famed Tecumseh. As far as Thunder Eagle was concerned, it was his mother who was the prophet. She had known that the time of the white man was coming, and she had done everything within her power to prepare him for it.

Evan looked at Thunder Eagle steadily in the gathering gloom. The two of them had been friends for many years and had never lied to each other. Evan had never been tempted to do so until now.

"A fellow came through a few days back," he finally said. "Told about a woman killed at Donner Lake. Not just killed. Mutilated. There were witnesses, came up as the killers were riding away." Here he hesitated. "Said they was Crow."

Thunder Eagle's expression sharpened briefly, then relaxed. "And those fools believed them."

"It's more than just the fools back in Ragtown," Evan replied soberly. "From the descriptions we've been getting, they're damn sure shaping up to be Crow in any-body's book."

Thunder Eagle said quietly, "You know that's impossible."

"Yep. I know it. You know it. Up until a few years ago, any trail-smart man in these parts would've known it. But things is such a goddamn mess nowadays, it's hard to be sure what to think anymore. The Pawnee are raiding the Comanche. The Crow are chasing off the Pawnee, and the Sioux are after all of them. Time was when a man knew what territory belonged to what tribe, and that was damn well what he'd find there, but not anymore. Crow have been seen this far west. Nobody'll argue that."

"You said the woman was mutilated."

There was another brief pause, as though Evan were wishing he did not have to answer. "They took her scalp."

"No Crow did that, Evan."

He didn't answer.

After a moment Thunder Eagle walked past him to the riverbank. He squatted down and scooped up a handful of stones. One by one, he tossed them into the water.

Evan came over to him. "So you can see why it's not exactly smart for you to be seen right now, where there's white men with guns. They're mighty worked up about this, and it's only going to get worse. From now on, every stolen horse, every accidental fire, every drunk that hauls off and shoots another, is going to be blamed on the raiding savages. It'll just be a matter of time before a white man actually does harm to an Indian, thinking he's protecting himself, and then . . ."

"It never ends." Thunder Eagle's voice was quiet, almost obscured by the *plop* of another stone hitting the water. After a moment he inquired flatly, "Colonel Foster?"

"Well, that's what I was sent up here to tell you." Evan sounded uncomfortable. "The colonel doesn't think it's—what was the word he used?—appropriate to go ahead with your meeting. He said he hopes the climate will be more . . . Hell, what he meant was, maybe we'll try again when things calm down." He paused again. "I know it's not much, but at least he didn't cut you off completely. At least he left it open."

Thunder Eagle gazed into the water. It was black and oily. "It took three years for me to get a member of your government to agree to meet with me. And then only a colonel. This might be our last chance to unite the tribes to make a lasting peace with the white man."

"I'm sorry." Evan didn't know what else to say, though his sentiment was genuine. "I know how much this meant to you."

"To us." Thunder Eagle's fist closed around the last remaining stone, and his voice, though low and steady, took on a hoarse edge. "To all of us."

"Yeah." The single word sounded empty in the dark, and then there was nothing else Evan could say.

The night grew deeper. Somewhere a tree frog started up a chorus, and through a gap in the foliage along the riverbank, there was the flicker of a distant campfire.

Thunder Eagle stood and looked at his friend. "Is there anything else you can tell me about the killers?"

Evan thought for a moment, frowning. "There is one thing. I don't know what kind of sense to make of it, though. Could be just panic talking, you know. But the story is that when the white men came up on the scene and the Indians were riding away, one of them, the one they took to be the leader, was wearing something over his head and face. Like a mask or a hood. I never knew any kind of Indian to do that, have you?"

Thunder Eagle was very still. "Lobo," he said softly.

Evan stared at him. "What?" When Thunder Eagle made no reply, Evan translated mentally from the Spanish. "*Lobo*—wolf? You mean it was Pawnee?"

Wolf was an appellation commonly given the Pawnee because of their expertise at thievery. If the raiders were Pawnee, things might make a bit more sense, though why they would attack without stealing anything was still baffling—as was why Thunder Eagle would refer to them by a Spanish name.

But Thunder Eagle said, "No, not Pawnee." His expression was thoughtful in the dark. "Just a man . . . I heard of, who lived with a band of Crow for a while."

"You don't think this man's been stirring up the tribes just to bring ruination to this big powwow of yours, do you?"

Thunder Eagle shook his head. "I don't know. It's possible. Not much is known of him these days, but it's said he lives in the mountains with an army of thieves under his command. It's said he's responsible for more than half the ambushes on the gold trails."

He shrugged. "Or it could be just stories. Superstition. It doesn't matter. Whether it was Lobo, or Pawnee, or even renegade Crow, the damage is the same."

He turned for his horse.

Evan followed. "I'll ride with you a spell."

Thunder Eagle paused with his hand on his horse's mane and smiled. "You're a good friend, Evan Thompson, but I don't think we're going in the same direction."

Evan's eyes narrowed. "You wouldn't be thinking about tracking down them killers, would you?"

Thunder Eagle swung astride his horse.

"All by yourself with half the countryside out to nail *your* hide just because you look like an Indian?" With a sharp, impatient shake of his head, Evan strode to his horse. "Like I said, I'll ride with you."

With a gentle nudge, Thunder Eagle moved his horse in front of Evan's. "I ride faster alone," he said. "Besides, if I don't come back, I want someone to remember why. And maybe even remember what I tried to do."

Evan looked at him gravely. "If you don't come back, one way or another we've got a war on our hands. You know that, don't you? The Indians will blame the whites, the whites will blame the Indians, and as fast as the word spreads, there'll be killings. Everything you've been working so hard to keep from happening will happen that much quicker if you go out and get yourself killed."

"Then I guess I'd better try not to get killed."

Thunder Eagle wheeled his horse and rode away.

Evan muttered, "Yeah. You do that."

He listened until the hoofbeats faded into the night, then mounted his own horse and turned its head toward Sacramento.

Chapter Six

Brave and foolish, and more than a little crazy, Sarah decided. The small, chunky coastal steamer, *Panama Queen*, was barely out of the port of New Orleans, and she was already wishing she'd never set foot on the ship. Her doubts were intensifying with each mile that passed; she missed home and Emilie already, and she had the awful feeling that her great adventure might turn out to be a failure.

Her anxiety hadn't lessened when she'd met her traveling companion the day before at the St. Charles Hotel, where they'd engaged a room for the night. Molly Morgan wasn't at all what Sarah had expected. She was young—even younger than Sarah—and very slight, no more than five feet tall. She looked as though a strong sea breeze might blow her overboard. Her brown hair was pulled back from a pale face dominated by huge blue eyes; her voice was soft, her speech hesitant.

Molly knew less than Sarah did about the journey to Panama and beyond, and Sarah felt as if she were chaperoning a younger sister instead of enjoying the company of a traveling companion who might be of some support to her. Sarah tried to hide her resentment at Molly's dependency, which was evident from the first moment they met. Molly seemed unable to make a decision about anything, from what to order for dinner to what to wear the next day, without asking Sarah.

Sarah looked at the young woman standing beside her at the rail; her face was streaked with tears, and again Sarah's irritation rose.

"I can't imagine why you're crying, Molly. After all, you're traveling toward your husband, not away from him. I, for one, am delighted that I'm going to meet Cade." It was only half a lie, Sarah decided. She did want to see her husband, even though she felt a growing dread of the long trip that lay ahead.

"I guess . . . I mean, I think I'm just worried and afraid. I've never been away from my family, and California is so far, and—"

Brusquely Sarah broke into her recital. "Let's go find our cabin. We can hang up our clothes and get settled in. We'll feel better when we're comfortable." She looked at the cabin number on their tickets, took Molly's arm, and started off. As they left the deck and entered the narrow companionway that led to the cabins, Sarah began to notice the other passengers on board. Mostly men, rough-looking men who stared boldly at the two women. Sarah looked straight ahead and marched Molly along with her to their cabin.

She unlocked the door and took half a step into the room. "Oh, dear Lord . . ."

Molly crowded in behind her but, like Sarah, was stopped at the door. The little cabin, no more than six feet by eight, was overflowing with luggage. Sarah's two small trunks took up most of the floor space, while suitcases and hat boxes were piled on the beds. The room contained two berths, one upper and one lower, a shelf with a washbowl and pitcher, and a slop pot in the corner. And piles of luggage.

"Oh, no," Molly wailed. "We'll never have room. What shall we do? Ask for another cabin?"

Sarah gritted her teeth and picked her way gingerly among the trunks and cases. "We'll have to decide what we need for the voyage and have someone take the rest away. Surely there's storage space on this ship. As for another cabin, the steamship line's been sold out for weeks."

Molly stood in the doorway wringing her hands. How in the world, Sarah thought, was this child going to deal with the hardships of California when a crowded stateroom overwhelmed her? "Come on, Molly. You can stand on my trunk to get to yours. You don't weigh enough to make a dent. We'll go through your luggage first, then mine."

Two hours later, after Sarah had found and bribed a cabin boy to take their excess luggage to the hold, she and Molly made their way to the dining room. They'd have to make do with two dresses, she'd decided, one for day and one for evening, though it hurt her to send her nicest dresses into storage. Of course, Molly had been delighted to go along with Sarah's decision about how to dispose of their belongings.

Sarah's humor was somewhat revived when she realized that she and Molly would be seated at the captain's table. With a pleased smile and her head held high, she swept into the dining hall, Molly following meekly in her wake.

"Ah, Mrs. Deveraux and Mrs. Morgan. We're delighted you could join us." Captain Tom Simpson got to his feet and held out chairs for them.

"And we're delighted to be with you." Sarah looked at the two empty places across from her. "Will others be joining us?"

"My purser and my first mate, but today they're taking care of last-minute details. Alas, you'll have to put up with me alone."

Sarah sized Tom Simpson up immediately. He was middle-aged and handsome in a coarse kind of way, with curly graying hair and a rakish mustache. He was the kind of man some women might find attractive, but she didn't. He lacked Cade's refinement and innate breeding, but on the other hand, he might prove useful if she and Molly needed help. Sarah decided the best course of action would be that of impersonal friendliness. She'd find out about the ship and the passengers, but would never discuss his personal life or hers. Emilie would approve of that—ladylike, charming, and aloof.

After the first course of soup had been served and cleared, Sarah looked around the dining room. "So many men on board. I had no idea that Mrs. Morgan and I would be so much in the minority."

"Indeed you are. Most of these men are going to California to look for gold, but a few will be going on to Colón and working for the railroad."

"Railroad?" That caught Molly's interest. "Can we take a train across Panama?"

Captain Simpson laughed patronizingly. "In three to five years, I'd wager. The railroad was only begun this year, and they've probably not laid more than a few miles of track. No, you ladies will be disembarking in Chagres with the others and crossing by boat and mule."

"How far is it?" Sarah realized she was as ignorant as Molly about the details of their trip across the Isthmus.

"About seventy-five miles."

"Seventy-five miles? Why, that's hardly anything." Sarah thought of the miles she'd traveled with Ben and Kitty across the Kansas plains. Seventy-five miles wasn't daunting.

Again the captain smiled with a superior air. "In Panama, it's a journey of at least a week. Or longer, depending on the rain and mud. It's not a pleasant journey, ladies, but I expect you know that."

"A week isn't really that long," Sarah said dismissively. "And however long it takes, it's shorter than sailing around the Horn or going overland."

"You're right about that. It's fifteen thousand miles or so around the Horn. I calculate you two ladies will cover less than half of that before you reach California."

Sarah felt a wave of despair wash over her—it sounded so terribly far—but she refused to give in to it. "What an adventure that will be," she said brightly. "I can hardly wait to begin."

"Then I toast two brave and fearless ladies." Captain Simpson raised his water glass and smiled. Sarah made it a point not to meet his eyes. With only a small amount of encouragement, she decided the captain might become a nuisance.

A burst of female laughter saved her from making a response. She turned to look, as did most of the other passengers, at three women who were entering the room.

"The other members of our female contingent," Captain Simpson said, a mocking undertone to his voice.

Sarah understood why. One of the women was in her late thirties, the other two some ten years younger. All three wore far too much rouge on their lips and cheeks, and their dresses, even given the excesses of the time, boasted too many bows, ruches, and frills to be judged stylish.

Molly's eyes grew wide, and she whispered so that only Sarah could hear, "Sarah, do you think—are they—"

"Yes," she answered. "They most certainly are."

Captain Simpson had observed the interplay between them, and the look on his face was one of bemusement. Sarah deliberately glanced down at her plate of food and tried to remember everything that Emilie had told her about the conduct of a lady in private and in public. A lady would definitely not discuss a covey of New Orleans fancy women with anyone. Such people were to be ignored and not dignified with acknowledgment. Out of the corner of her eye she noted that Molly was staring straight ahead, her face beet-red from embarrassment. Sarah was determined to handle the matter with more sophistication, and she allowed herself no pity for Molly's display of . . . of *gaucherie*. She felt an inward sense of accomplishment. Sometimes the French did have the right word.

After an appropriate amount of time, Sarah addressed the captain. "Please tell us a little more about this Chagres place. Mrs. Morgan and I want to learn all we can before we arrive in Panama."

After dinner, Sarah and Molly took a turn around the deck, and while Sarah listened absentmindedly, the younger woman talked about her husband, the Reverend Peter Morgan.

"I've known him since grammar school," Molly explained. "His family and mine were very close, and everyone knew we'd get married when we were old enough. Just as everyone knew that Peter would be a preacher like his father."

"Umm," Sarah answered, thinking how boring it must be to have known your husband all your life.

"I thought we'd stay in Louisiana. I never dreamed Peter would want to go to California." Molly's voice quavered slightly.

"Well, men are like that. Taking off and thinking that their women will follow."

Molly gave a little sniff, and Sarah hoped she wasn't going to cry. "It scares me, Sarah, thinking of how far away I'll be from home and my mama and papa. I've never really been away from them. What if I never see them again?"

"You can visit your parents, and no one really stays in California. People go there to make their fortunes and then they leave." As she spoke, Sarah wondered what kind of fortune a minister would make in California. Not much of one, she figured, and Molly probably had some hard times ahead.

"I miss home so much."

In a gesture of camaraderie, Sarah took Molly's arm. "I miss my family, too, but I guess it's different with us Kincaids. All of our family are travelers. My great-grandma Fiona came all the way from Ireland and ended up in the mountains of Kentucky. Then my ma set out down the Ohio River all by herself, and my sister Kitty went to Kansas, and Meg's in California, and Jim—who knows where Jim is these days?" The mention of Jim made her sad. He was her favorite in all the family, and she hadn't seen him in a long, long time. But she was hoping to catch up with him in California.

"Oh, my," Molly said in awe. "Your family sounds very daring. But maybe they wanted to travel. I don't think I like traveling at all."

Sarah was at a loss for words. No wonder Molly couldn't make a decision; all her life someone had told her what to do, and now she was being ordered to follow her husband to a place she didn't want to go to. There was nothing Sarah could do about it, but maybe she could think of some way to give Molly a little bit more gumption. She had plenty to spare, and they'd have the rest of the trip to build up Molly's spunk.

As they rounded the corner of the wheelhouse, they came face-to-face with the three women they'd seen at dinner. The scent of their perfume was heavy on the night air. Two of the women kept on walking, but the third stopped. She was pretty in a dark, gypsy kind of way, with wavy black hair and heavily made-up eyes. Boldly she looked Sarah in the face, her bright lips curving in an enigmatic smile.

"Why, good evening, Miz Deveraux. Enjoyin' the sea air?"

Molly gave a strangled cry of dismay. Sarah grasped her arm more tightly and swept past the woman, keeping her head turned away. "Don't say a word, Molly," she hissed. "Not until we're in the cabin."

Sarah breathed a sigh when she closed the cabin door behind them. She sank down on the lower berth, still confused over the encounter on the deck. "She knew my name, Molly. She stopped to . . . well, to accost me. Isn't that extraordinary? How in the world—"

"Oh, Sarah, I was shocked. A woman like that. A . . . a . . ." Molly could not bring herself to pronounce the dreadful word. "Do you know her?"

"Molly Morgan! What a ridiculous thing to say! Of course I don't know her," Sarah snapped.

"I mean . . . I thought . . ." Molly's lips quivered. "But how did she know your name?"

"I have no idea," Sarah said coolly, "but I can say

absolutely that I've never met any of those ... those women." She thought for a moment. "Maybe she saw my name on the passenger list. It's posted, I think, in the main cabin. Yes, that's it."

"But why would she single you out?"

Sarah didn't try to hide her irritation. "I have no idea, nor do I care to speculate on it. Would you like to wash up first?" she asked. "I'm tired and I want to go to sleep."

"No, you go first," Molly said meekly.

Three hours later, Sarah was still struggling to sleep. The little ship bounced and wallowed and swayed with each wave that struck it. Her mattress was thin and lumpy and smelled slightly of mildew. The room was airless and stuffy, but when they opened the porthole, noise from the lounge on the deck above kept them awake. They could hear the low rumble of men's laughter and the tinkle of coins, as if they were playing cards or gambling. There were women's voices, too, and the strumming of a banjo and the sound of someone singing. "Old Black Joe" and "Oh, Susanna" floated on the sea breeze.

Sarah pulled a pillow over her head and closed her eyes tightly. She wouldn't think about Panama or the ship or the tawdry woman who'd spoken to her. She'd think about more pleasant things—Emilie and Deveraux House; the smell of roses on the soft summer air and Cade's arms around her; her mother sitting by the fire, her red hair gleaming in the soft glow. She'd think of home and all the people she loved.

She woke to the sounds of her own screaming. Molly's face was a pale blur above her.

"Sarah, what is it? Please, tell me. Are you all right?"

Sarah's heart was racing wildly and her breath came

in short, gasping spurts. It had been so real . . . so real
. . . She struggled for words and finally they came. "A
nightmare, just a dream . . . nothing . . ."

Molly reached for the oil lamp, and in a moment its
soft light enveloped the cabin. "Would you like some
water?"

Sarah sat up on the edge of the bed, feeling dazed.
She hadn't had a nightmare like that in years. "Yes, water. Please." Eagerly she drank the glass that Molly
brought her. Her throat felt parched, her skin hot.

Molly's scared eyes examined her. "Are you sure
you're all right?"

"Yes, I'm sure," she lied. "I'll probably fall right back
to sleep. You can turn off the light now."

"Well, if you're sure . . ."

"Yes," Sarah said softly. "I am."

She lay in the darkness, still trembling and shaking
inside. It was the same dream she'd had in Kansas. The
dream about her brother Jim being stalked by a great
black wolf, the wolf circling the campfire where Jim lay
sleeping, the wolf lunging at her brother's throat—

Eight years ago, her dreams had proved dangerously
prophetic. Jim had been pursued by a man who wanted
him dead, a man who wore a signet ring emblazoned
with the head of a black wolf. But Captain Marcus
Hunt Lyndsay was dead, and there was no reason for
him or his wolfish image to invade her dreams anymore. Her family's enemy had died in an avalanche in
the high ranges of the Rockies. He'd killed her uncle,
Boothe Carlyle, and then been killed himself by one of
nature's accidental rampages.

The Black Wolf was dead. Jim had assured her of
that, and she hadn't thought of Lyndsay in years, so
why was she dreaming of him now? She didn't want to

face the answer, but it was there, hovering above her in the darkness. It was her brother Jim. He was in danger, and, as before, she was powerless to warn him that an enemy lurked nearby.

Chapter Seven

Sheldon Gerrard balanced against his crutch and looked at his pocket watch. "Fiona, we have to pick your mother up in fifteen minutes. Are you ready, girl?"

He stood at the bottom of the stairs looking up. His bedroom was on the first floor, Fiona's and Meg's upstairs. He'd been up the stairs only once, when he'd decided to buy the house. Over the years he'd become adept with his crutch, negotiating other stairs slowly but safely. His one leg didn't keep him from venturing up these stairs; it was the knowledge that he'd be treading into territory where he wasn't welcome. He and Meg Kincaid had always maintained separate bedrooms, respecting the other's privacy. There'd never been a hint of intimacy between them; something that Meg had no interest in, she said, and something that Sheldon had long ago stopped hoping for. Instead, he'd given all his love and affection to Meg's daughter.

Monserrat appeared at the top of the stairs. "Señor Gerrard, she cannot decide between the blue dress and the green. We are having a terrible time."

Sheldon snapped his watch shut. "Tell her the white, Monserrat. It's new, and it will show up best in the photograph."

He'd bought Fiona the new white, lace-trimmed dress at Easter for her to wear to church. He'd decided that it was befitting for all of them, as stalwarts of the up-and-coming San Francisco gentry, to become churchgoers, and so he'd chosen a new Presbyterian congregation where services were conducted in a tent. He liked the idea that he could be involved in the fledgling church from its beginning, and almost at once he'd gotten himself appointed to the building fund-raising committee, much to Meg's amusement.

"I guess you're going to make us respectable or die trying," she'd commented wryly.

Sheldon hadn't answered. Both he and Meg had dark secrets in their pasts that they never discussed with anyone—not even with each other. Sheldon, protecting Meg, had once killed a man, and they'd burned his body and then stolen his wagon of trade goods, on which they'd built their fortune. Sheldon knew men who'd done worse, but he was at a point in his life when he wanted—no, craved—forgiveness from a higher power. And he thought, from a practical standpoint, it didn't hurt a man's reputation to be a pillar of an up-and-coming church.

He moved to the sideboard in the sunny hall and poured water from a cut-glass decanter into a glass. He added a drop of liquid from a vial he carried in the pocket of his brocade vest, swirled the liquid, and drank.

"What are you drinking, Papa? Is it wine?" Fiona was coming down the stairs.

"You know your papa never drinks wine. Just a little something to settle my stomach."

"Too many chilies," Fiona said sagely.

Sheldon laughed and beckoned her down the stairs. He found her mothering tendencies charming; in fact, he thought everything about the child was extraordinary. "Come down here and let your old papa look at you. My, my, you are something to see."

Fiona pirouetted in the hall, her white skirt billowing out around her, showing her white stockings and shoes. Her red hair, perfectly straight and the color of wild strawberries, hung in a shining fall down her back.

"You look wonderful, princess. Now get your bonnet. Tonio's waiting with the carriage."

"Isn't Mama going to have her picture taken, too?"

"I told you, angel, she's waiting for us at the post office, hoping to hear something from Uncle Jim. You know your mama; she's worried about her chandeliers."

"I miss Uncle Jim and Aunt Star. I thought they were coming to visit."

"They are. Bad weather probably held them up. Nothing for you to worry about. Now give me your hand. Let's go find your mama."

On the days when the mail boat arrived in San Francisco, lines began to form at the post office on the corner of Clay and Pike streets before dawn. It was common for San Franciscans to hire someone to stand in line for them, and that morning Meg had taken advantage of the custom. Tonio had waited in line for two hours before she appeared at nine A.M. to take his place. After two more hours, she'd finally been able to collect the mail.

She left the post office and hurried across the planked street toward the corner where Sheldon was to meet her. Due to a lack of rain, streets that had been muddy rivers were now dry dust bowls, and Meg held the hem of her blue-and-white taffeta dress high off the ground.

She was so intent on keeping her dress clean that she didn't notice the man who blocked her path until she ran square into him.

"Mr. Connor," she said coolly.

"Miz Kincaid. Or is it Gerrard? I can't seem to figure out if you're married or not."

Meg's mouth tightened. She didn't care whether people thought she and Sheldon were married or not; in fact, she cared very little what anyone thought about her. "Miss Kincaid will do. What is it that you want, Mr. Connor?"

"What's this I hear about you building a saloon across the street from my new place?"

Yancey Connor wasn't much taller than Meg. He had a thin face that reminded her of a weasel and a scraggly ginger-colored mustache and beard. His breath smelled of garlic and stale beer, and instinctively she drew back from him.

"I own the property, Mr. Connor, and I can build whatever I want. And for your information, it's not a saloon. I'm building an opera house."

"Fancy, eh?"

"Very much so. Now, if you'll excuse me, I have an important appointment."

Connor still blocked her path. "My casino's opening within the next month. I plan for it to be the most successful business establishment on the square, and I don't want nothing to stand in my way."

"Then I wish you well. San Francisco is big enough for all of us to do well. There are more than sixty casinos in this town already."

"But most of 'em are dives or low-class hangouts, not like what I'm putting up. Why don't you forget this opera house and go back to selling dry goods and rub-

ber boots and ladies' bonnets? Now, that's fit work for
a woman."

Meg was furious. More than anything, she wanted to
lash out and slap the sneer off Connor's face. She
clenched her fists and said in as calm a voice as she
could muster, "Just like other business people in this
city, I'm always looking for an opportunity to better
myself. Surely there's nothing wrong in that."

"That man of yours involved in this? I hear he's
kinda retired."

"That is really none of your business," Meg snapped.

"A woman needs a man in this city—for protection,
if nothing else." There was a nasty tone to Connor's
words.

Meg lifted her skirt and swept past him, head high,
not looking at him or responding to his remark. As she
crossed the street, dodging carriages and pushcarts, she
heard his last remark, muttered low: "Bitch."

She kept walking. Sheldon was right. The male entrepreneurs who were making money hand over fist in
San Francisco didn't want a woman involved in business, unless, of course, she was a laundress or ran a
bawdy house or clerked behind a counter. There were
few women in San Francisco, in fact in all of California,
and men—at least the men in power—seemed to want
them relegated to specific and submissive roles. Well,
Meg had never conformed to anyone's pattern, and she
wasn't about to start now.

She knew she wouldn't mention her run-in with
Connor to Sheldon, or the implied threat in the man's
comment about her needing protection. Sheldon would
only be upset and intensify his efforts to stop her from
building the opera house, and no one was going to stop
her.

She saw Tonio proceeding down Clay Street. The

new carriage was polished to a high sheen and pulled by a fine team of matched bays. Meg's anger and distress over Connor and his kind dissolved as she saw Sheldon and Fiona. She smiled proudly. He had dressed in a stylish gray jacket and fawn trousers and was even wearing his top hat today. Anything that involved Fiona was a cause for him to look—and act—his best. And Fiona, she looked like a little angel in her white dress.

Sheldon held out his hand for Meg. "Sorry to make you wait, Miss Meg, but Fiona couldn't decide what she wanted to wear." He helped Meg into the carriage, and she seated herself across from her daughter and Sheldon.

"Papa said I should wear my new dress. Does it look all right?"

"Perfect. Papa was right." She handed Sheldon a packet of mail. "Nothing from Jim. I'm getting very concerned."

He nodded obliquely toward Fiona, whose eyes were bright with interest. "Fiona and I have been talking about Uncle Jim, and I've told her he's fine."

"I'm sure he is. Just late." Meg looked at the one letter she'd kept for herself. "It's from Sarah. What—" She removed her glove and slit the letter open with her fingernail. She read for a moment before looking up. "My Lord, she's coming to California!"

"You don't want to see her, Miss Meg?"

"Of course I want to see her. It's been years. Maybe ten." Quickly she read through the rest of the letter. "She's traveling by way of Panama, and she's coming to look for Cade. She hasn't heard from him in over six months." She raised her eyebrows meaningfully at Sheldon. They'd seen Cade when he'd first traveled to California, and neither had been impressed with Sarah's husband, especially Sheldon, who said he was enough of an old trickster to recognize the quality in someone else.

"She's supposed to catch a boat called the *Laura Lee* out of Panama City. It should dock in a week or so." Meg looked back up at Sheldon. "Of course, she may miss her connections in Panama City. She probably has no idea what's going on there." Meg and Sheldon had heard stories of people who'd waited for months on the west coast of Panama for a boat to California.

"She's planning to go to the goldfields to look for her husband, I assume."

"That's what she says she wants to do. Of course, it's quite impossible. She can't travel alone, and I don't have time to go with her, and I know you won't go with her."

"You're right about that," Sheldon agreed. "My traveling days are over."

"Well, maybe I can talk her out of it."

Sheldon let out a bark of laughter. "Not likely, Miss Meg. I've never known a Kincaid woman to be talked out of anything she's set her mind to do."

Meg regarded him fondly and then motioned to her daughter to lean closer. "Come here, Fiona, and let me fix that bow on your collar. Neither your papa nor Monserrat has any idea how to tie a little girl's bow. I want you to look special for this picture. After all, it's for Grandma Katherine, back in Cairo."

Photography was a booming business in San Francisco. Louis Daguerre had invented the process for portrait photography in France in 1837, and now, almost fifteen years later, it seemed as if every miner in California wanted his picture taken, a memento of his days in the goldfields, whether he'd been successful or not.

Monsieur Claude Bertrand billed himself as a student

of Louis Daguerre, and therefore the prices at his studio in San Francisco were twice as high as those elsewhere. Still, he had an excellent reputation, and Sheldon, who wanted only the best for Fiona, had booked the appointment with him.

Meg's sharp ears caught the inconsistencies in Bertrand's accent almost as soon as they arrived. The closest he'd ever been to France, she decided, was the Gay Paree Saloon near Portsmouth Square. But like everyone else in San Francisco, she mused philosophically, the man was out to make his fortune. Fussily, he posed Fiona alone and then with Meg on a small red velvet settee and commenced to take his photographs, admonishing his subjects to smile, hold their breath, and not move a muscle.

"And Monsieur—" he said, gesturing to Sheldon, who was hovering behind the camera in the background. "Do we not want Monsieur Kincaid in one of these beautiful photographs?"

Meg found the idea amusing. "Monsieur Kincaid, come and pose with us."

Sheldon shook his head. "No, I don't think so. This is for you and Fiona."

"Papa, we want you in the picture. Mama said so!"

"Oh, come on," Meg said. "Why not a family portrait?"

Sheldon hesitated and then swung forward on his crutch and his one good leg.

"*Très bien,*" Bertrand said. "Monsieur will sit here on the settee . . . so, and little Mademoiselle will sit beside him, and the lovely wife—"

Meg rolled her eyes and allowed herself to be pulled into place.

"You will stand behind your husband with your hand

on his shoulder. Ah, *magnifique*. A perfect family, *n'est-ce pas?*"

That night the rains began, and Meg felt more restless than usual. Rain would delay construction on the opera house, which would put her further behind schedule. She paced up and down the parlor, feeling gloomier by the moment. She could hear Sheldon and Fiona in the dining room going over her lessons, and from the kitchen came the chatter of Monserrat as she prepared dinner with Tonio's help. But even the familiar sounds of her household couldn't mitigate Meg's unease.

She looked out the rain-streaked windows at the street, which was quickly becoming a quagmire of mud. The air was chilly, and she thought about asking Tonio to light a fire, something to brighten her mood. She picked up Sarah's letter from the little marble-topped table where she'd laid it and read it once more. She was glad her sister was coming; despite all her avowed independence, Meg realized, she'd never outgrown a need for her family around her.

She watched the figure of a man splash across the road, stepping off the planks into mudholes. His hat was worn low over his eyes and a serape was draped across his shoulders. For a moment her heart leapt. He was heading for her house. Maybe it was Jim! In the foggy darkness she couldn't be sure.

At the first knock on the door, she pulled it open.

"Miz Kincaid, ma'am?"

The man wasn't her brother. "Yes, I'm Meg Kincaid." She pushed the door almost closed, leaving only a crack to talk through. "What do you want?"

"I had some kind of a hard time trackin' you down, ma'am. I got news about a supply train of yours . . ."

Meg opened the door again and ushered the stranger in as Sheldon appeared from the dining room. "What's going on, Miss Meg?"

"This man—he has news of the supplies. And Jim?"

The man stopped just inside the door. "Name's Shorty Bramlett, and I'm awfully wet, ma'am. I wouldn't want to dirty up your nice rugs."

"Oh, bother the rugs," Meg said. "Hang your coat and hat over there." She pointed to a coat rack. "Monserrat," she called out, "bring some coffee. You would like something hot to drink, wouldn't you?"

He nodded. "Mighty obliged, ma'am, and sir." He nodded to Sheldon.

Ignoring the muddy tracks across her carpet, Meg settled the man in the parlor. He was rough-looking, short, and squat, dressed in muddy boots, trousers, and a stained cotton work shirt, the uniform of the gold miner. Long gray hair hung limply around his grizzled face.

"Now, tell me about the supplies and my brother Jim Kincaid. Did you see him, Mr. Bramlett?"

Shorty looked down at his work-worn hands, folded on his knees, as if it were difficult to meet her eyes. "Yes, ma'am, I seen him. Oh, Lord, I seen him." He shook his head sadly and was quiet for a moment, as if entering his own private hell.

"Mr. Bramlett—" Sheldon urged.

He looked up at them. "I got your pack animals camped outside town with my partner, Sid. We brought down one of your wagons and a big crate with a chandelier in it. Other wagon done got burned up pretty bad, along with the carpets and the drapes and a whole mess of other goods. Took us a while to get down to Frisco and then to track you from Portsmouth Square out here to your house."

"I don't care about the wagons or the chandelier. Tell me about Jim—and Star. Mr. Bramlett, for God's sake, tell me now!" Meg was filled with a terrible foreboding, and she swayed for a moment, feeling sick and faint.

Sheldon moved to her side and steadied her with his arm. He nodded at the man.

Drawing a deep, long breath, Shorty Bramlett began his story.

Chapter Eight

Panama was much worse than Sarah had imagined. Chagres, where the *Panama Queen* docked, wasn't really a town at all, only a collection of bamboo huts on stilts surrounded by mud and garbage. The stench of decaying vegetation and putrefying bodily wastes hit the two women before their small boat put them ashore. A group of Indians, sick-looking and surly, came down to meet them and to barter with the first mate, who had volunteered to make the final arrangements for Molly's and Sarah's passage.

Sarah held a perfumed handkerchief under her nose to mitigate the stench, and Molly, her cheeks flushed from the heat, clung to Sarah's arm.

"It's not all that bad," the first mate, Mr. Denver, said cheerfully. "You'll be traveling in a group of about fifty people, going upriver in a bongo with the other ladies—"

"What did you say?" Sarah interrupted.

"In a bongo, ma'am. It's one of them canoes over there, hollowed out of a giant tree trunk. Why, some of 'em's up to ten, twelve feet across. Now, it's perfectly safe—"

"No," Sarah interrupted again. "That's not the part I object to. What is this about other ladies?"

Denver still wasn't sure what she meant. "The only other women on board, ma'am. Miz Camille and Miz Marie and Miz Lisanne. Those ladies." He gave a nod of his head.

Sarah cut her eyes to the side. "They are not ladies," she said icily, "and you cannot expect respectable married women like Mrs. Morgan and me to share a . . . a bongo or anything else with them."

Denver looked down at the ground and shuffled his feet. "Well, then, Miz Deveraux, I guess you're just gonna have to get back on the *Panama Queen* and go home, 'cause Sanchez"—he pointed to a villainous-looking man with a bushy black mustache and a two-day growth of beard—"says he can only account for you ladies' safety if you stick together. He'll put two of his best Indians with you, and he'll be in the boat in front of you, but that means all five of you. In one bongo and in one hut at night, separate from the men in the party. Señor Sanchez is the man hired to take you folks across the Isthmus."

"Oh, Sarah, what shall we do?" Molly pressed even closer.

Sarah shook her off as one would dismiss a tiresome dog. "Molly, it's too hot for you to cling to me like that!" She had never felt such heat, even in the midst of a Louisiana summer. At least a breeze blew off the Mississippi now and then. Here the air was still and heavy, and the heat was all-enveloping.

Perspiration trickled down Sarah's forehead into her eyes; her underwear was soaking wet and clung to her until she felt imprisoned by it. She wiped her face with her now stained and clammy handkerchief and tried to remain calm. "We have only two choices, it seems—to travel with those other women or to go home. Which is it for you?"

Molly raised her tearstained face to Sarah. "Oh, Sarah, I don't know. I want to go home, but I can't travel by myself."

Sarah wasn't sure what she wanted to do either, but she wasn't about to admit it. She, too, thought longingly about returning home. But what would happen then? She'd be no closer to finding out about Cade than before. Surely seven days of torment with a gaggle of prostitutes couldn't be as bad as more months of worry and anxiety about her husband.

"We're going, of course," she announced. "Other women have made the journey safely, and we shall, too. Thank you for your help, Mr. Denver, and thank the captain also. And will you see to it that my luggage is safely loaded in the baggage canoe?"

Sarah raised her parasol and started toward the bongo where the three other women sat, fanning themselves languidly in the stifling heat. Molly trailed dolefully behind Sarah, eyes downcast, looking utterly miserable and afraid.

The oldest of the three women spoke first. She was heavyset, with a mass of blonde hair piled on her head. "Well, now, looks like we've got company, girls. Step on in and make yourself comfortable. It'll be hours before these savages get our baggage loaded." There were low benches along the sides of the canoe, and a piece of canvas had been stretched over the top. It gave partial shade, but didn't reach the edges of the boat.

Molly and Sarah found a place and sat down. The river smelled, too, with a disgusting odor of rot emanating from the shallows, and along its surface lay green scum. Mosquitoes hovered in great hordes around the bongos, and voracious gnats seemed determined to fly into Sarah's nose and ears and mouth.

"We might as well introduce ourselves," the woman went on. "I'm Madame Camille, and these are my traveling companions, Mademoiselle Marie LaFleur and Mademoiselle Lisanne deVille. We're all on our way to San Francisco."

Sarah gave a cool nod and said nothing. Molly moved closer. Sarah could tell it was going to be a long, long trip.

Travel up the Chagres River was so slow that it was almost unmeasurable. The Indians who poled the bongos did so at their own speed and rhythm. They ignored the passengers and paid little attention to Sanchez, who ranted and raved each time they took a rest stop. But the Indians, a mix of native Americans, Spanish settlers, and Negro slaves, didn't care. They knew they were in control. Until the railroad was built across the Isthmus, their bongos were the only means by which travelers could cross.

Their schedule seemed to depend wholly upon their whims. Sometimes they roused their sleepy passengers before sunrise and hurried them into the boats; on other days they lay around the camp until the heat of noon before starting out, and then a few hours later, when the afternoon rains began, called a halt for the day. It was frustrating and nerve-racking, and everyone's temper was on edge.

Nights were spent in flea-infested huts along the way, and the meals prepared by the Indian guides were inedible, at least to Sarah's way of thinking. She was sure they'd been served roasted monkey one night, and after that she stopped eating with the others. Emilie had provided a farewell tin of tea, coffee, and sweet cakes, and Sarah lived almost entirely on that and the hardtack and beef jerky that Sanchez sold at inflated rates. Bananas grew in abundance in patches behind the huts, and she picked and ate them gratefully. Molly scarcely ate anything at all and complained of fierce headaches each evening when they stopped. Sarah, lost in her own discomfort, had little sympathy for her.

It was interesting, Sarah mused, what people worried about. She'd been alarmed at the rough band of men making the crossing with them and then she'd been upset about traveling in a bongo with three prostitutes. All the while she should have been worried about obtaining food and a decent bowl of water to wash in and trying to find a private place to change her underdrawers. The men showed little interest in her and Molly, and when they had energy to flirt, which wasn't often, they turned their attention to Madame Camille and her girls. Sanchez had been paid only part of his money, and he knew full well it was in his best interest to deliver the women safely to Panama City. His future as a guide depended on it, and so he always seemed on guard, his mustache bristling, a machete clasped in his right hand.

The heat, humidity, insects, poor food, and bad-tasting water had deleterious effects on the ladies of the evening as well as on Sarah and Molly. They were looking ill, bedraggled, and pale, especially Madame. Sarah felt sorry for them, but no sorrier than she felt for herself. Like Sarah and Molly, the other women were too tired to initiate conversation, and therefore much of the day passed with them sitting in a heat-induced stupor, fanning away the gnats and mosquitoes as best they could.

Heavy green vines hung low over the river and made the heat more intense. Sarah was the first to see the green-and-brown snake that dropped from the vines onto the canvas top and then writhed off the edge into the bottom of the bongo. Her terrified screams roused the others from their naps. Instinctively, she stood on the bench, and the sudden shift of weight caused the bongo to rock dangerously in the water.

The snake twisted frantically on the floor of the boat; the other women screamed and started to scramble for safety, drawing up their feet and crouching on the benches until they were stopped by a stentorian shout.

"You fool children, you'll turn this damned boat over for sure if you stand up. We'll be thrown in the water and eaten whole by them god-awful gators. Sit down, right now. I mean it! That snake is more scared of you than you of it."

In a half crouch, Sarah hunkered down and held onto Molly, who was too scared to utter a sound. Lisanne and Marie stopped their screaming and sat down, their legs extended in front of them.

Madame turned her attention to the boat polers, who were laughing and pointing at the hysterical women and the terrified snake. "You grinning fools, get that damned serpent out of this boat. Vamoose! Did you hear what I said? Vamoose!" She raised her parasol threateningly.

Either her fractured Spanish or her body language motivated the Indians. One of them languidly raised his pole out of the water, thrust it under the snake, and lifted the reptile easily back into the river.

The women breathed a collective sigh of relief. Marie laughed nervously and shuddered. "Thank God that's over."

Sarah let go of Molly's arm and settled back on the bench. She knew she'd acted foolishly and she had to say something. She took a deep breath. "I'm sorry for causing such a fuss; I was just so startled."

Madame shrugged. "Nobody likes a snake dropped in her lap, I guess, but I grew up on the bayou and I'm used to the critters. Well, as accustomed as anyone can get."

"Thank you," Sarah said quietly. "Thank you for taking charge."

Madame simply nodded, but all the women knew that something had subtly changed among them.

As the boat moved up the river, Sarah was more aware of the dangers all around her. Giant alligators slid silently off the muddy banks, and she had recurring visions of the bongo overturning and the women providing a feast for the reptiles while the men continued upriver and didn't bother to look back. She wished she'd turned back at Chagres, but it was too late now. Occasionally there was something pleasant to see—a flight of blue butterflies flickering in the dappled sunlight, or the flicker of a bright-colored parrot in the lush green jungle, or a glimpse of a rainbow through the heavy green foliage of the jungle.

But pleasures were few and far between.

On the third night of their trip upriver, a sound woke Sarah in the middle of the night. She looked around in the faint glow of moonlight that filtered wanly into the straw hut and saw that Molly was missing. Sarah, who'd grown used to sleeping in her clothes, crawled out of her hammock and shook out her shoes. She'd learned not to be surprised by a spider or a scorpion nesting in the toe.

She crept outside and called, "Molly! Molly, where are you?"

A low moan was her answer. She found Molly sitting

on a fallen log, hunched over, her arms wrapped around her stomach. "I feel so bad, Sarah. So sick."

Sarah felt her forehead. "You're burning with fever. Come back in the hut."

"No." Molly wrenched away, her body shaking in a violent spasm. "My bowels—please, I have to go into the bushes. Please."

"I'm going to get help. Just stay here." It was a foolish command, she knew. Molly was too sick to move.

Sarah burst into the hut and shook the first form she found. "Madame! Wake up, I need help. My friend, Mrs. Morgan—"

Madame struggled to an elbow and regarded Sarah with bleary eyes. "Lord, girl, what's the screaming about?"

"My friend is so sick . . . I don't know what to do."

Madame put a hand to her head. "I don't feel so good myself, honey. Got a terrible headache." She fell back onto her hammock. "I don't think I'll be much help."

"Madame—" Sarah was about to shake her again when she felt a hand on her shoulder and looked up. The dark-haired Marie was standing beside her.

"Leave her alone, Miz Deveraux. I think she's coming down with something, too. She didn't feel good at supper and neither did Lisanne. They've been complaining for the past three days about headaches. I thought it was just the heat."

"It's Mrs. Morgan. She's terribly ill. I don't know what to do." Sarah could hear the panic in her voice.

Marie LaFleur was calm. "The first thing we do is find Sanchez. He should have medicine of some kind and know what to do. It's probably just a stomach upset. He can handle it."

"Do you think so? Really?"

"Well, honey, I ain't no nurse, but I can hope. Come on, I'll go with you."

Sanchez wasn't about to tell them much. He carried Molly back into the tent and stared worriedly at her in the glow of his lantern. "I don't know, señora, what it is. Could be the yellow jack from the mosquito, or maybe cholera—"

"No, not cholera," Sarah said. "Please, no."

"I am not sure. There hasn't been an outbreak this year, but who knows? In '49 it was very bad." He shrugged. "Maybe some kind of fever from the heat and bad water. Maybe something from the food."

"She's hardly eaten anything the past few days," Sarah said. "She lost her appetite."

"Before that?" Marie asked.

"I can't remember."

"Could be from the ship, you know. Happens all the time. People get sick on the boat and then bring the fever here to us." Sanchez bent down and touched Molly's forehead. "I think it's the fever."

"Then do something," Sarah demanded. "Help her."

"Nothing I can do, señora. *Nada.* Either she's strong and fights it or—" Again he shrugged.

"Well, she's not strong. She's not strong at all and she can't fight it." Sarah knew she was shouting, but she didn't care. "You must do something." She grabbed Sanchez's arm and shook it. "Help her."

"Now, Miz Deveraux, yelling at him isn't going to help your friend." Marie pulled Sarah away. "Señor Sanchez, I know you must have something that can help the lady."

"I got laudanum. Just a little."

"Well?" Marie demanded.

"I'll bring her some. At least it can make her sleep."

Molly was moaning and talking erratically, calling her husband's name and then crying out in pain. Terrified, Sarah bent over her. She felt powerless, and she had a terrible foreboding that the worst was yet to come.

More of the travelers, including Madame and Lisanne, contracted the fever. A dozen of the fifty travelers in the party were stricken, but the fever didn't affect the Indian guides or Sanchez. Sarah began to believe it was something they'd caught on the boat, something that Molly and Madame and the others had eaten or drunk and she and Marie had not. She knew that Molly Morgan was very, very sick and would likely die in the steamy jungle along the banks of the Chagres River. And there was nothing she could do to stop it.

She and Marie took turns sleeping and looking after the sick in their hut. They kept a pot of water boiling constantly and ate or drank nothing that wasn't cooked or washed in the water. It made sense to Sarah that the illness had come from eating dirty or ill-prepared food, and this was the only way she knew to guard against that. Each day she waited for a sign that she was becoming ill, and each night she breathed a sigh of relief that she was still alive. The men who were well tried to care for the others, but there was little anyone could do except to fan the flies away and hope.

Early one morning Marie awakened her. "Come, look." She took her to Molly's bed. Sarah hated to even glance at her; she looked like a skeleton with skin stretched over the bones. She was dying; there was no doubt about it. Marie loosened Molly's bodice and pointed to the oval, rose-colored spots on her abdomen.

"Smallpox? Is that what it is?" Sarah asked.

Marie shook her head. "No. I've seen it before. It's typhoid fever."

"Is it . . . do people die?"

Marie's answer was to the point. "Yes, sometimes."

Sarah turned away from Molly, her shoulders shaking. "She's too young to die, and too sweet. And I've been so cross with her and so mean, and I wasn't patient—"

Marie held her by the shoulders and shook her. "Stop it! You can't do this. You can't fall apart. Yes, she may die, and so may Claudie and Myrt—"

"Claudie and Myrt?" Sarah sniffed and wiped her eyes with her hands.

"Camille and Lisanne. You don't think whores are born with names like Camille and Lisanne, do you? I love them, too, and I owe them. We were going to go to California to live the good life, and here they are, burning up with fever in this hellhole of a place. God sure knows how to play jokes on people, don't He?"

Sarah sighed and studied the other woman. Marie's face was thin and haggard, her dark hair hung in limp strands around her face, and her skirt was stained with mud. She didn't look hard or coarse anymore; she looked like Sarah felt, desperate and scared.

"Yes, He does," Sarah said softly, and then for some inexplicable reason, she held out her arms. Maybe it was because Marie looked so pathetic, or maybe it was because Sarah needed the comfort of another human being. Marie walked into her arms and they stood for a moment, hugging each other tightly, as if to verify that they were still alive and able to fight.

"I'm not going to die," Sarah whispered. "I'm going to get to California. I'm going to find my husband." She held Marie at arm's length. "And you aren't going to die either, do you hear me? I need you to help me. Swear to me, Marie, that you won't die."

Marie forced a wan smile. "Honey, I ain't about to die. I'm too mean and too greedy. I'm gonna get me some of that California gold. I swear it."

Chapter Nine

In a two-hundred-mile stretch of the Sierra Nevada, between the Mariposa and the north fork of the Feather rivers, there were so many gold camps that a mapmaker couldn't fit them all in on a carrying-sized map without blurring the dots together. It started with a bar—a spit of land on which a few pieces of metal ore were found scattered around—or a nugget dug out of a stream, or sometimes no more than a rumor. It started with a single man standing hip-deep in icy water or digging out the hillside in one-hundred-degree heat until his muscles gave out, collecting just enough dust or ore each day to keep him wanting more. Then he'd usually take on a partner to help him build a dam and divert the stream to make the bed more accessible, and pretty soon others were coming in, staking their claims upstream or down. A rich bed could support as many as forty men within a two-hundred-yard radius, and before anyone knew what was happening, a mining town was born.

To call these tent and shanty camps "towns" was

something of a glorification. Their population was almost exclusively male, and these were the kind of men who required very little in the way of luxury. Though a surprising number of the Argonauts were young adventurers from well-to-do families back east, a few months in the goldfields sapped the strength of even the heartiest among them, so that they were indistinguishable from their less privileged counterparts. The typical miner was whipcord-thin, his skin burned by the sun and scarred with flea and mosquito bites, his joints arthritic from long periods of submersion in icy streams. He commonly suffered dysentery or scurvy from poor nutrition, and was often in one of the progressive stages of pneumonia. Sanitation was rudimentary and personal hygiene was generally ignored.

In such a place the only necessities were a saloon, a gambling table, and—in the most fortunate of camps—a fancy lady or two. Once these requirements were met, a heretofore-undistinguished band of loosely connected claims might reasonably call itself a "town." They took on names such as Red Dog, Poker Flat, Downieville, Liar's Flat, and, the most famous of all because it lay right at the end of the long Overland Trail, Hangtown.

As its name implied, Hangtown was arguably the roughest of all the gold-camp towns, and the reason was simple. It was here that men who had traveled three thousand miles or more, sustained by the promise of fortunes beyond their imagining, met their first defeat.

They arrived at the end of the trail drained by the desert and beaten by the mountains, half starved, weakened by cholera or typhoid fever or any one of a dozen diseases that winnowed out all but the most determined of them. They had known desperation and they had survived despite it, yet the cost of that survival had often been greater than they had planned. They had lost children, wives, and loved ones along the trail. They had fought Indians and killing storms. They had done murder, some of them, to protect what was theirs and had found, afterward, that murder was not nearly so terrible a thing as they had been taught to believe.

They arrived at the end of the trail that led to the pot of gold lean, hungry, and toughened by endurance, only to find they couldn't afford a bag of flour to fill their empty barrels. They found the best diggings were up-river and their pack animals were too spent to go another step. And, perhaps most discouraging of all, they discovered that they themselves were too physically depleted by the effort of simply getting this far to work a claim. There were those who tried, of course, and who, after a day or two of swinging a pick or squatting in icy water, broke their health completely and spent months recovering from their foolishness, if they recovered at all.

The one thing these men could afford in a place like Hangtown was rotgut whiskey. The one thing they were still capable of doing was lifting the glass to their lips. And the only thing that dulled the pain of the defeat they had journeyed so far to find was the haze of alcohol. These were bitter, angry men with little to lose and even less reason to care.

When Jim Kincaid rode down out of the Sierras and into Hangtown that gray afternoon, he was taken for just another pilgrim at the end of the trail. His weary horse moved with its head down and its steps slow, but it was in better shape than most that came off the trail. It was a fine-looking spotted creature, the kind of animal you'd notice right off, and it stirred up some attention, even among the most jaded of onlookers.

Jim rode with his shoulders square and his head high,

his hat pulled low over his bright hair. His lower face was obscured by a ginger-colored beard and his eyes were dark and deep. No one who looked into those eyes that day ever forgot them. Some said it was a deadly fever that made them burn so. Others said it was simply madness.

He dismounted and looped his reins around the hitching post outside the false-fronted mercantile. A man with bloodshot eyes and a half-pint bottle of whiskey leaned against the building and watched Jim warily while he drank. A younger man, his eyes wide with wonder and admiration, circled the Appaloosa. Jim went inside, taking his rifle with him.

The Hangtown mercantile was somewhat better than the one in Ragtown, but not by much. The wooden false front concealed a low canvas roof that sagged and leaked in wet weather and walls that weren't much better. Though supported by wooden studs, they, too, were made of canvas that could and frequently did blow down in high winds. Whiskey was still the most popular item for sale, and those who came to purchase it stayed to make themselves at home on rough-hewn stools at hastily constructed tables, telling one another tall tales of the fortunes they were going to make and drinking just enough to pretend the stories were true.

But the mercantile did possess a counter and several shelves of genuine dry goods behind it, along with precious few lanterns, shovels, and picks displayed in front. There was a big barrel in front of the counter from which a faintly rank and rotting odor emanated. The sign atop it read "Potatoes $20.00 a lb.," and the barrel was almost empty. Jim did not even smile.

A man in a clerk's apron got up from one of the tables and took his place behind the counter when Jim came in. He didn't say anything; idle chat was not in his nature, and something told him this was a customer who knew what he wanted.

"Side of smoked bacon, ten pounds flour, ten pounds coffee," Jim said, his tone flat.

"No bacon," the clerk said, turning to fill the rest of the order. "Only five pounds of coffee left. Come back tomorrow and I'll have more. That'll be thirty-two dollars."

Jim peeled off the bills without blinking. "And four hundred rounds of ammunition for this here Sharps."

The clerk hesitated, visibly startled by the request. His movements were noticeably slower as he bagged the last of the coffee and tied it firmly with a strip of hemp. He made no attempt to disguise the curiosity in his eyes.

"You expecting trouble, are you, son?"

Jim did not answer.

The clerk reached under the table and started bringing up boxes of cartridges, taking his time. The atmosphere inside the building had grown considerably quieter as several men tried to overhear the conversation.

"Guess you ain't been to the mines yet."

Jim started filling the pockets of his coat with cartridges.

"Or maybe," suggested the clerk, "you ain't a miner. If I had to, that'd be my guess."

There was no answer, nor any discernible change of expression on the bearded face.

The clerk gave up. "Fifteen dollars," he said.

Jim paid him and picked up the flour and the coffee.

"Hey, mister."

A lean, stubble-faced man was standing at the open door, looking out. He glanced over his shoulder at Jim.

"That your spotted horse out there?"

Jim came to the door, looked out, and pushed his way through. Other men followed curiously, but they got no farther than the threshold.

A small-to-medium-sized crowd had gathered in the street, grinning and elbowing one another and watching the antics of the two drunks who'd made the spotted horse the object of their afternoon's entertainment. Somebody had placed a straw hat between its ears. Somebody else had crawled astride it, backward, and was holding its tail like a rein. Yet another had dug into the saddlebags and found, of all things, a blue calico dress. He was holding it up before him and mincing and giggling like a girl, to the vast amusement of all who watched.

Jim came out of the store and let the sacks of flour and coffee drop. The men up front noticed it first—a whitening of the flesh across his cheekbones, a darkening of his eyes. Their laughter stopped. They nudged their companions, and the amusement faded throughout the crowd as gazes turned toward the ginger-bearded man. But it was slow in happening, and the two pranksters didn't notice.

"Get off my goddamn horse."

Jim's voice was low, but it carried. In the uneasy silence that had descended on most of the crowd, it practically echoed. The man with the blue dress did a little dance step and brought himself up short as he came face-to-face with Jim. The man on the horse turned around, still grinning. The grin died when he saw the face of the man who had spoken.

"Hey, mister, we didn't mean no harm—"

Jim cocked his rifle.

The man on the horse slid off with such haste that he fell to the ground. He caught himself on all fours, righted himself, and backed away.

Jim lifted the rifle and shot him.

The impact of the Sharps at that range cut his chest in two. Blood splattered on men standing twenty feet away. The body itself flew back two yards or more before falling, face-up, the eyes wide open and fixed in an expression of eternal disbelief.

Horror rippled through the crowd in slow waves. The man holding the blue dress dropped it and began to run. Another rifle shot exploded and he fell facedown in the dirt, his spine shattered and his back torn open.

Jim Kincaid walked forward and picked up the blue dress. He folded it carefully and replaced it in his saddlebag. He went back for his provisions and packed them away. No one spoke a word. No one moved.

He mounted his horse, the rifle still ready in his hand. He looked down at them and said, "Where I come from, they hang thieves."

He nudged his horse and rode down the street at a walking pace. Among the twenty or so men who had gathered by that time, not one raised a gun, or suggested going after him, or thought about stopping him. It was true enough, they convinced themselves later on. You can't blame a man for shooting a thief who was caught in the act.

So they just stood and watched and were glad to see him ride out of town.

Sarah found Marie sitting by the river, staring out over the yellow-green water. She handed her a cup of tea. Marie sipped gratefully, then asked, "How are they?"

Sarah dropped down onto the fallen tree trunk beside her. "Lisanne seems better. She drank some tea and ate some hardtack that Sanchez sold us. But Madame and Molly—" Her voice shook. "Molly's tongue is . . . it's all brown and awful, and she can't eat or drink. Oh, God, this is so horrible."

"Go on and cry, honey. I don't blame you."

"No." Sarah shook her head. "No, I won't cry, not now. I'll cry when I get to California. I'll cry when I see my husband." She imagined for a moment how wonderful it would be to feel Cade's strong, comforting arms around her. Then she could cry and let out all the pain; then she'd feel safe.

"So your husband's working in the goldfields?"

Sarah was grateful to Marie for asking the question. For a moment it took her mind off Molly and Madame and the miasma of death and despair that hovered over the camp.

"I think so. I haven't heard in a while. I've tried to tell myself that he's all right, that I'll find him. Now I'm beginning to wonder."

"It's just because you're tired and worn down that you're having doubts. Things'll be different when you get to California."

"Maybe," Sarah replied without much conviction. They were quiet for a while, and then she asked, "How come you knew my name on the boat?"

"Saw it on the passenger list."

"But why me? Why not Molly? Her name was there, too."

"Because she wasn't married to Cade Deveraux and you were. I wanted to make you feel uncomfortable and—hell, I just wanted to be a bitch. I'm sorry."

"You know him, don't you?"

Marie turned her face away, not answering.

"You might as well tell me, Marie," Sarah persisted. "It doesn't matter. Not now, not here with all this going on around us."

"I knew Cade Deveraux," Marie said carefully.

"Down in New Orleans. He used to come to the Verandah Hotel to do his gambling and card playing. Honey, who wouldn't know Cade Deveraux? Why, he was the handsomest man in the city."

"Oh," Sarah said. She shouldn't be surprised. Cade was older than she and had had a romantic, adventuresome life before she met him; but it seemed somewhat ironic that she should learn details about it from a prostitute in the middle of Panama.

"Of course, I haven't seen him at all since he got married, but I was curious about what kind of woman could catch Cade Deveraux. So when I saw your name . . . It was just curiosity, honey. I wondered if he'd married some stuck-up bitch."

Sarah smiled. It had been so long, she was surprised that she still knew how. "Sometimes I am just that!" She got to her feet. "I don't care if you knew Cade. There's nothing I can do about the past. After all, I'm his wife, and he loves me."

"That's right, honey, and don't you forget that. Just hold onto that when things get rough."

"Señoras, señoras." Sanchez came along the bank toward them. "I have bad news for you. We can't afford to stay here any longer. The connecting ship leaves Panama City in four days. We'll just make it if we leave today."

Marie was on her feet in an instant. "There are a dozen sick people here. There's no way they can travel today."

Sanchez shrugged. "Five of the men can travel, and the others . . . Well, they are very sick indeed and need to stay here. I'm not sure if they will last the day. I will leave an Indian and one of the bongos behind."

Marie confronted him. "You're not trying to run out

on us, Sanchez, are you? We paid our money to get to California, too."

"Please," Sarah begged, "please don't leave us."

"I must take those who are well to Panama City," he said stubbornly, "or they will miss the ship. They have paid for their tickets."

"So have I," Sarah countered.

"Then you can come with me."

"But Mrs. Morgan and Madame—they can't travel," she argued.

"We'll come back for them and the others," he said.

"You go on, honey," Marie volunteered. "I ain't leavin' Madame and Lisanne. We'll get another boat to Frisco sooner or later. You go on and make your connection."

Sarah was torn. There was nothing she'd like more than to walk away from the sickness and smell of death, the heat and bugs, the suffering and sadness all around her. She wasn't really responsible for Molly Morgan, was she? Why did she have to stay and take care of her?

And then she thought about her mother, the indomitable Katherine Carlyle Kincaid, who'd led a whole troop of women and children down the Ohio River to safety through Indian-infested terrain. Her mother hadn't given up or run away, and Sarah knew that she couldn't either. If she left, she'd be haunted by Molly's face for the rest of her life, and that was a kind of guilt she couldn't live with.

"I'll stay, too. When will you be back for us?" she asked Sanchez.

"It's one day, maybe two, to Cruces. There I will put the others on mules for the trip across the mountains, and I'll come back for the rest." His eyes narrowed. "It may cost extra, these two trips."

"We don't care," Marie said. "We'll pay, but you be

sure you show up or I swear, Sanchez, I'll track you down, and when I find you, I'll cut your heart out. I know how to use a knife."

Sanchez smiled, showing broken and rotted teeth. "I bet you do, señorita. I will be back. *Es verdad.*"

The two women watched him swagger away. "Is he lying?" Sarah asked. "Will he be back or will he leave us here to die?"

"I don't know, but we ain't dyin', honey, no matter what, even if we have to pole our own bongo out of this hellhole."

Sarah felt her spirits lift. "If that's what we have to do, then we'll do it!"

"Good for you, girl. Now, I guess I better git back to Madame—Lord God, I guess we'll have to nurse those other sick fools, too."

"I'll go. I want to see how Molly is. I'll call you if I need you."

Marie nodded and sank back on the tree trunk. What a joke, she thought, she and Cade Deveraux's wife becoming best of friends in the middle of a stinking jungle, acting as nursemaids to a preacher's wife and two sick whores.

Marie knew lying was a sin, but she was glad she was good at it. Sarah Deveraux had accepted her story that she hadn't seen Cade Deveraux in three years, not since he'd married. The truth was that Cade had been a regular at Madame's for years and hadn't let a wife stand in his way. He hadn't been able to visit New Orleans as often as before, but he'd found reasons to come to the city and always spent time playing cards, drinking, and visiting with the girls.

It was too bad, Marie thought, that he was cheating on his wife. Under that snobbiness, she was a right nice woman. But men—what else could a woman expect, especially from a handsome devil like Cade?

Marie had no expectations of men at all, not since she was eleven and her pa and brother began to have sex with her out in the barn on their farm in Mississippi. If her ma knew about it, she didn't try to stop it, and Pa had warned her that if she told anyone, he'd kill her. She believed him. Pa had a hell of a temper. They'd gone to Natchez the summer she was fifteen for Pa to sell his cotton crop, and when her pa and brother went into a saloon, she managed to slip away and hide on a riverboat. The captain had wanted to throw her off until she offered to pay her passage—in his bed.

In New Orleans it took her a while to find Madame; Marie had been beaten up and abused and used in all kinds of ways by the men she'd met up with, but all that changed when she met Madame. The woman ran a high-class establishment catering to gentlemen who knew how to treat a lady—at least for an evening. Madame told her to forget the past; everything would be different from now on.

She changed her name from Mary Scroggins to Marie LaFleur and learned how to curl her hair and apply powder and rouge. She pierced her ears and used perfume and even had a pair of silk stockings. She slept in a clean bed every night and ate three good meals a day and bought lots of pretty dresses and lacy lingerie. It wasn't, of course, the life she'd dreamed of. Like most young girls, she'd wanted a home, a family, and a man of her own, but it was a hell of a lot better than living on a dirt-poor farm in Mississippi and having her pa's or her brother's baby.

She'd thought California would be like New Orleans—high living, good times, lots of money—but now she wasn't so sure. If Madame died and Lisanne didn't make it, she'd be on her own again, and to someone who'd grown to depend on her friends, it was a very frightening thought.

Molly's hand was hot and dry. It was like holding bones in her hand, Sarah thought, little bird bones with skin stretched tight over them. She knew Molly couldn't live much longer. Her frail body was burning with fever, and she had begun to jerk and twitch in convulsive spasms. Her breathing was labored and shallow, and Sarah wondered if each gasp would be the last. She sat beside Molly and wiped her brow with a cool cloth. There was nothing else she could do.

Molly began to talk randomly and wildly, as she had all day. "Tell Mama not to worry . . . I'll get my lessons done . . . I always do . . . It's all right, Mama, I promise . . ."

Sarah felt the sting of tears against her eyes. "I'll tell her, Molly."

"Peter!" She called out her husband's name. "I don't want to go to California. It's so far away. I don't want to leave my mama and my papa. Please, Peter. Please."

"You don't have to go," Sarah soothed. "You don't have to go to California."

But Molly didn't hear her. "Midge just had puppies, Mama. Can I keep one? Can I keep the black one? I'll take care of it all by myself. Can I, Mama?"

Sarah couldn't bear it anymore. She stumbled outside and leaned against the side of the hut, her shoulders shaking with sobs. Marie patted her awkwardly on the shoulder. "It's all right now, honey."

Sarah shook her head and said in a strangled voice, "I swore I wouldn't cry—"

"It ain't the first vow that any of us broke. I'll go in and see to her. You get yourself some coffee."

"No." Sarah's eyes were swollen with tears, her skin mottled and splotchy. "No, I'm going to be with her until the end. I won't let her die without me."

Molly lay quietly, breathing so shallowly that her chest barely moved. The racking tremors had stopped, and she lay silent. Sarah sank beside her and held her hand. Marie stood beside her. "The Lord is my Shepherd . . ."

Marie's voice joined hers. "I shall not want . . ."

Sanchez returned in time to dig the graves for the two women and the three men who'd died from the fever. They buried Molly Morgan and Madame Camille in two deep graves beside each other. Sarah took Molly's wedding ring and the gold cross she wore around her neck. She'd do her best to find Peter Morgan in California and give him the last remembrances of his wife. Those and Molly's Bible were all she'd be able to take with her.

"So little," she said to Marie, "for a whole life."

"She didn't have a chance from the beginning," Marie replied. "She wasn't tough like you and me and Lisanne."

"What about Madame? Wasn't she tough? And look what happened to her." Sarah's despair had turned to a dark, brooding anger. She was angry at Peter Morgan for compelling his frail wife to follow him to California, angry at Madame for being greedy for gold, and angry at her own husband for his wanderlust and irresponsibility.

"Maybe in her case it was the luck of the draw. Oh, God, am I going to miss her." Marie sighed. "But I've got Lisanne to take care of. She's weak as a kitten and twice as mewly. She always was a skinny little thing;

now she looks like a hant. Honey, you've got to help me get her to Panama City. Will you do that?"

Sarah slipped her arm around Marie's waist. "I'm not going to give out on you. If I have to walk across the mountains to the Pacific, I'm going to do it—I'll even carry Lisanne if I have to. I'm getting out of this hellish place today."

"Sanchez says those that ain't dead are well enough to travel. Come on, honey, let's rejoin the land of the living."

Chapter Ten

Among the Crow people, the story of their origins was clear and explicit. As tradition went, they were the oldest of the American people, the Father of All Nations. The Toltecs and Aztecs, the Apache, the Snake, the Sioux and Cheyenne—even the Blackfoot, mortal enemy to the Crow—all owed their existence to a common Belantsea, or Crow, father. The legend told how the Crow once occupied the entire range of the Rocky Mountains and the vast valleys on either side, from the far stretches of Canada to the end of the mountains in the Bay of Panama.

And so, the legend continued, the Crow was once the greatest nation that ever lived, until the coming of the Flood. The Deluge swept away the tribes of the valleys, and only a few who climbed the highest peaks of the mountains survived. From these few the world was repopulated, but the numbers of the Great Ones, the Father of All Nations, were never again as great as they once were.

The Belantsea still lived in the Rockies when Thunder Eagle was a boy. He grew up in a village of forty tents, learning the legends and skills, the traditions and games, of his mother's people. He remembered wondering why, if they were all one people of a single father, there was so much war among the tribes.

And he wondered: who was the father of the white man?

He grew up in the certain knowledge that the Belant-sea were the most perfect of men—tall, pleasing to the eye, graceful in form, and strong in battle. Theirs was a civilization older than time; they had mastered the art of living. Though their numbers were depleted and many of the Old Ways had been lost to memory, still there was room within their society for the things of luxury—the art of fine quillwork and brilliant dyes, of storytelling and picture making and the dressing of hides.

The beautifully ornamented white hides from which Crow women fashioned their tents and clothing were things of beauty unparalleled throughout the Indian culture. It had been said by early frontiersmen that a Crow Indian could be identified at some distance by the elegance of his costume and the whiteness of the skins of which his clothing was made.

As a child, Thunder Eagle had watched the women of the tribe go through the ritual of dressing the buffalo hides, a task which commonly took weeks. First the skins were immersed for a few days in lye made of ashes and water, or until the hair was soft enough to remove. After that they were stretched on the ground, with the edges pinned down with stakes, and covered with the brains of the buffalo for several days. Once the skins were conditioned, the women took a specially prepared bone, usually the shoulder bone of the buffalo, which had been shaped at the edge like an adz, and used it to scrape away the fleshy side of the hide. At this point the skins were serviceable, and most tribes would have been satisfied with that, but the Crow women were proud of their skills and took the process another step.

First a small hole was dug in the ground and filled with rotten or green wood, which would smoke but not flame. Over that a tent was erected, and the skins that were to be cured were placed inside. The wood was set to smoke and the tent sewn together at the edges to keep the smoke from escaping. The skins were smoked for several days or a week and, when done, were able to retain their resiliency, soil resistance, and pale color even when wet.

The women of the tribe would then spend the better part of the winter cutting, sewing, and decorating the skins for use as garments or lodges. The lodges of the Crow were without dispute the most striking on the plains. Constructed of linen-white skins and highly ornamented with the brilliantly hued dyes that were used in pictographs that described the accomplishments of those who lived within, often decorated with colored porcupine quills and scalp locks much like their clothing, these tents were of no mean design. They were often large enough to house extended families of forty people or more, with as many as thirty poles used in construction, all cut of sturdy Rocky Mountain pine and often passed down from generation to generation. Such a lodge might stand twenty-five feet high and fifty feet in diameter at the base. An entire village of such tents spread out across the plains was an impressive sight indeed.

As elaborate as these lodges were, they could be disassembled and packed for long-distance transport in a matter of mere minutes. And so they were, at least twice a year, when the Crow village moved to its summer and winter camps.

There was never much notice given of these moves. When the chief decided, he would send runners through the village to announce they would be moving at a certain hour, often no more than half a day distant. The women would begin packing furniture, tools, skins, and supplies so that, when the signal was given at the appointed hour, all was in readiness.

After the lodge poles of the chief were removed, the rest of the village went into action. The maneuver was a thing of beauty to watch, as thrilling as a perfectly executed strategy of war, for within two minutes from the first signal, all forty lodges lay flat on the ground, ready to be transported.

The poles of the lodge were divided into two parts and strapped to either side of a horse at the withers. A bracing pole was tied across them in the center, forming a travois for the lodge, which was rolled up and attached on top. Blankets, household furnishings, cookware, and personal belongings were then secured to the travois, and as many women and children as the horse poles could support rode on top. One woman led the horse, while another, commonly with a nursing child or a toddler, rode astride the beast. All the women carried packs, as did many of the dogs that trotted alongside or brought up the rear of the procession.

The band of travelers stretched out for miles along the prairie, the braves riding the best and strongest horses up front, the women and beasts of burden following at a more sedate pace, while the dogs— hundreds of them—raced and played at the rear.

Upon arriving at their destination, the people would reconstruct the lodges and unpack their belongings as quickly as the whole had been disassembled, and a feast would be held to celebrate their safe arrival.

The culture of Thunder Eagle's youth was one of pride of heritage and ease of living, of contemplation and matters of the spirit. His grandfather, whose lodge he and his mother shared, had taught him the value of honesty and fair dealing; thievery was considered an act beneath contempt among the Crow, and killing appropriate only in battle. He remembered that his grandfather was known to have the longest hair in the tribe—for the length of a male's hair was a matter of considerable pride among the Crow—and during feasts and ceremonies unbound it from the leather scabbard in which it was usually tucked at the nape of his neck and combed it out. Dressed with bear's grease to the high gloss of a raven's wing in the sun, decorated with rows upon rows of brightly colored feathers, his grandfather's hair trailed the ground behind him for almost a foot and garnered the admiration and envy of all he passed. Such a growth of hair was the goal of every young man in the tribe, and though few had matched that length, none had exceeded it, even now.

Thunder Eagle's grandfather had died when Thunder Eagle was seven, and as a gesture of respect to him, and to the people who would always be his family, Thunder Eagle had never cut his hair. He knew, however, that he would never approach the length of locks about which the Crow boasted. The blood that ran through his veins was, after all, half white.

Of the man who was his father, he knew little, nor did he want to know. He had discovered as he grew older that legends often fared best if they weren't investigated too closely. According to those legends, his father was, much above the ordinary, as he would have to be to merit the daughter of a chief. He was a renowned hunter, a climber of mountains, a rider of rivers, and a teller of tales extraordinary. His medicine, it was said, was very great. It was for that reason that Thunder Eagle, though sired by a white man, had no reason to feel shame for his heritage. For three winters his father had lived in their village before taking Burning Bright as his wife. In the spring he would leave, then return to winter with his Crow family. Then one winter he did not return, and so it was that he never knew of the birth of his son.

This was not an uncommon story among the trappers, explorers, and mountain men who were the first whites to venture into Indian territory. The same ambition and determination that had brought them as far as the Rocky Mountains would inevitably take them farther, and the wisest of them knew it would be much more cruel to take their Indian families with them than to leave them behind. Burning Bright had understood this, and though she mourned the absence of the father of her child, she never resented it. Thunder Eagle was raised in a shadow of greatness that no white man, before or after, could match.

After the death of his grandfather, in Thunder Eagle's eighth year, his mother woke him on a cool fall morning before the mist had yet dried. She commanded him to dress and handed him a pack. "Your youth," she said, "has been spent among your mother's people, as it should be. But soon you will be a man. It is my wish that you come to manhood among your father's people, as it should be." She had placed her hand upon his head and added softly, "You will need all you can take from both worlds to face what the future holds for you, my son."

He had ridden away that cold dawn in the company

of his mother's brother, knowing he would never see her again.

He was delivered to the care of a man named Crater and his wife, who operated a small trading post on the Colorado River. Crater was a trader well known to the Crow, and indebted to Thunder Eagle's grandfather from a time long ago. He welcomed the grandson of so noble a friend, as did his wife. Thunder Eagle lived with them there on the banks of the great Colorado until he was sixteen. He spoke their language and read their books and learned the things that were important in their world. But he never forgot his first people. And he never cut his hair.

He returned from fishing one summer evening to an eerie quiet. The cabin was still, its windows unlit. The corral was empty. He found his foster father sprawled across the doorstep, pierced through with sixteen arrows. His foster mother was inside the cabin. Bloody handprints marred the wall and painted the picture of her attempted escape. She had not succeeded.

The arrows were Blackfoot.

Thunder Eagle returned to the village of his mother's people. His mother was dead, as were both of his uncles and a surprising number of the friends of his youth, lost to the ever-increasing ferocity of ongoing war between the Crow and the Blackfoot. Thunder Eagle would wonder for the rest of his life whether it was his presence that had brought on the attack by the Blackfoot on the trading post, or whether it was simply a random display of malice against white incursions into their territory. In the end it didn't matter, for his rage was on behalf of both his birth family and his foster parents, and his village was happy to welcome another warrior.

Thunder Eagle killed many Blackfoot over the next two years, and he saw many more of his own people die. Women outnumbered men three to one in his village because of the ravages of the Blackfoot. The situation in the Blackfoot village was even worse, and yet they kept coming. While their children starved, Crow braves rode out again and again to meet the enemy.

The last Blackfoot brave Thunder Eagle killed was thirteen years old. It was not his youth Thunder Eagle remembered, however; it was the look in his eyes.

He came upon him in the aftermath of battle. Thunder Eagle knelt to drink from a stream, and a reflection appeared beside his own in the still water. Mere seconds comprised his observation, but those seconds were indelibly imprinted on his mind. The reflection beside his belonged to a boy. Though he might be a man in his tribe, he was a child of half the size and a quarter the experience of Thunder Eagle. He had been wounded, for one arm sagged limp and bloody at his side. In the other hand, however, he held a knife aloft. And in his eyes was a hatred so pure, a determination so fierce, that it was clear and chilling even through the murky reflection in the stream.

Their tribes were decimated, and still they warred. The white man swarmed across the plains, stealing their lands and bringing disease, and still they warred. Their children learned to hate before they could walk. And it occurred to Thunder Eagle then that he could stop it all by simply moving away from the stream and the child with the knife.

But the flash of insight was too brief and came too late. He turned to defend himself, killing swiftly before he himself could be killed. And that was the day Thunder Eagle walked away from the war. His people were the father of all tribes. He could no longer kill his children.

It was a long road from that place to this, as he sat

across the campfire from the Paiute brave Talks With His Hands. Talks With His Hands had been sent from his village with a party of four and their pack animals, to trade hides and horses and stones set in silver with the white man for corn and flour and rifles. He was returning to his village, his beasts laden and travois full with soft blankets, foodstuffs, and sturdy rifles. The braves who accompanied him would boast for months of the shrewd bargains they had made. After such an excursion, he always frowned and claimed he had been badly cheated by the white thieves, but it was well known that Talks With His Hands was the sharpest trader of any tribe west of the Rockies.

He scowled at Thunder Eagle across the low flames of the fire. "You ask foolish questions. Let them kill each other, white throat to white throat. We will all be happy of it."

Thunder Eagle drew deeply on the pipe and passed it to his friend. Mixed in with the tobacco was a mild narcotic that caused dizziness to dance before his eyes when he held the smoke in his lungs. He exhaled slowly and answered, "You always will speak first and think later, Talks With His Hands. Maybe someday they will kill each other. But first they will kill us. You know I say the truth."

Though the two men spoke enough of the other's language to make themselves understood, the subtleties were often lost. Each of them therefore elaborated the spoken word with sign language, painting pictures in the air with their hands.

"I think it is your white blood speaking," challenged Talks With His Hands shrewdly. "I wonder whose battle it is you fight."

This was an old argument between them, almost comforting in its familiarity. "I come to stop the battles," Thunder Eagle replied, "for there is no honor in the murder of a brother. The white man will come. We cannot stop him. We make ourselves weak fighting each other, while the white man takes our hunting grounds and spoils our water and drives his horses through our lodges. Far better we join together, a People under one father as it once was, to reason with the white man, to preserve what is ours. Together we are a mighty nation. Apart we are easy to defeat. The mighty oak has many branches, and will not fall easily to the ax. But the branches, when hewn from the oak . . ." He let the sentence finish itself by picking up a stick and thrusting it into the fire. They both watched as it was consumed.

Talks With His Hands nodded once. He had heard this speech before and had passed the wisdom of it on to his people. He nonetheless enjoyed testing his friend's sincerity by challenging him, now and then, to see whether his convictions had changed.

He passed the pipe to Thunder Eagle. "Your words are noble. The white man's words are false. Your Colonel Foster has said words and now he makes them unsaid. Yet you think there is reason in such men."

It took a moment for Thunder Eagle to understand what the Paiute brave meant, and when he did he heaved a mental sigh. How could he explain the politics of the white man to someone whose very language barely accommodated the concepts around which white civilization seemed to revolve? How could he explain what he barely understood himself?

He handed back the pipe and said, "Colonel Foster can only speak for his people what they will have said. They will have nothing said when they think my people are killers of women."

The other man's lips turned down in a sneer. "Such

is the work of the white man. They paint their horses and their faces and fool each other, but no one else."

Thunder Eagle nodded soberly. "But what the white man believes will anger him. He will seek out the Crow and the Paiute and the Pawnee and the Sioux, and instead of coming together to reason, we will stand alone to fight. Our children will starve. Our old men will freeze. Our young hunters will be killed in battle. This is not the way I would have it, old friend. Help me if you can."

Talks With His Hands was quiet for a moment, regarding him steadily across the flames. Then he inclined his head slightly.

"Tell me what you know of the man called Lobo," said Thunder Eagle.

Talks With His Hands drew on the pipe for a while, thinking. "This is a hard thing. He steals like a wolf out of the mountains and carries off his prey. They say he makes his home in a cave, but I have heard it is a much finer lodge, hidden in the rocks where only the weasels and the rabbits can find it. He knows the way of the Indian, it is said, but he is white. And he uses his wiles against his own kind. He does not concern me."

"Do you know where he can be found?"

The other man shook his head slowly. "That I do not know. The white men in the villages below, they have many troubles, and they do not talk of Lobo so much these days. Perhaps they should."

Thunder Eagle watched him alertly. "What do they talk of?"

"Now they talk of another man, who rode out of the mountains and killed two of their own with a rifle. They say this is not a usual thing." He made an elaborate gesture with his shoulders to demonstrate the unfathomable ways of the white man. "He rode a spotted pony into the mountains again."

Thunder Eagle accepted the pipe that was passed to him. They smoked together in silence until the tobacco was spent, and Thunder Eagle thought about what he had learned.

Talks With His Hands rolled himself into his blanket and lay down beside the fire to sleep. After a time he said, "You will go into the mountains?"

"I think I must."

There was no reply for a while. Then Talks With His Hands said, very quietly, "I think you are a fool."

Thunder Eagle tossed the last of the kindling into the fire and watched it flame. "You are probably right. But wish me good fortune anyway."

His friend said nothing. After a long time, Thunder Eagle slept.

Jim Kincaid was seventeen when he left home and hearth to make his way in the world. He came from a long tradition of trailblazers, adventurers, and explorers, and the footsteps of the men who had gone before him were hard to follow. Jim's father, Byrd Kincaid, a trapper and a keelboat pilot, one of the first men to set his eyes upon the great Northwest Territory and the high mountain peaks. And Boothe Carlyle, his mother's brother, who had become a legend in his own lifetime. Some Indian tribes still spoke of the Firebird, as they called him, though Boothe had been dead for eight years now. He had left his mark upon history along with that of Kit Carson and Jim Bridger. Jim Kincaid's great grandpa Hugh Carlyle had crossed an ocean and cleared a forest to make his home in America, and his father before him had fought kings for his freedom. The shadows of such men were long, and to a seventeen-year-old boy in search of a chance to prove himself, they seemed particularly so.

His mother had seen him off with a few quiet words, and placed around his neck the talisman pendant that had accompanied every adventurer or adventuress in her family since time immemorial—a Celtic cross surrounded by a circle of iron that some said was older than the first king. That cross had once saved his mother's life when a band of Shawnee had recognized the symbol and let her pass in safety. Uncle Boothe, the legendary Firebird, had worn it as he crossed a continent on foot, navigated the mighty Mississippi, fought with Sam Houston, and climbed the Rockies with John C. Frémont. Jim's sister Kitty had worn it when she led a band of Shawnee renegades to rescue a group of stranded travelers under attack.

On his quest for manhood, Jim had run afoul of a renegade military man named Captain Marcus Hunt Lyndsay who had sworn to kill him. Fleeing into the mountains to find his uncle Boothe, Jim had found the only woman he would ever love, Morning Star Woman, a Cheyenne held captive by a well-meaning but half-mad white trader.

Trapped by a freak blizzard in one of the high passes of the Rockies, Lyndsay had caught up with them. It was there that Boothe Carlyle had died. Sometimes Jim replayed that scene in his head, and every detail was as clear as it had been the day it happened. Boothe Carlyle, the legendary Firebird, had at the crucial moment lowered his rifle and walked straight into the line of fire. It was almost as though something about Lyndsay had distracted him, as though he had seen something at the last minute that confused him. But as often as Jim reviewed the scene in his head, he still could not understand what had happened.

Star, who had been held hostage by Lyndsay, believed Boothe's sacrifice had been his way of giving her and Jim a chance to escape. And perhaps it had been, because as Lyndsay fired, Star broke free and hurled a flaming log from the campfire into his face. Lyndsay's wild shots had caused an avalanche that had buried him alive.

In his first season as a man, Jim had lost his uncle and his archenemy, but he had found the woman who would be his wife. Now he had lost her, too.

His uncle Boothe had ridden a big spotted horse that had been given to him by the Indians of the Northwest. Jim had taken it out of the mountains and eventually to Kansas and his sister Kitty, who was already gaining renown as a breeder of fine Western horses. The animal he rode now was the first offspring of his uncle's big Appaloosa. Often when he was astride the stallion, it seemed as though the Firebird rode beside him.

But not anymore.

Jim did not know how long he had been riding. He wasn't even sure what season it was. He had a vague recollection of killing those two back at the general store, but he felt no remorse. They had been in his way and they deserved to die, so he had shot them much in the same way he'd shoot a rattler that was stretched out across the path. They had touched the gown that belonged to Star. For that alone they should have been gutshot and left in the sun to die. Jim had been merciful.

He didn't remember packing the gown, either. But every night he'd take it out and hold it and remember what she had looked like wearing it. Blue was a good color on her. She had liked blue.

He had no plan, any more than a wild cougar, creeping through the night in search of prey, had a plan. He would find the men who had killed his wife, and he would kill them. What happened after that didn't matter. What happened before that didn't exist. The only thing that was real to him was the fire in his belly; it was what kept him going.

His father, Byrd, had been captured by the Shawnee in his younger days; he had endured their torture and learned their ways and lived among them. He had learned to respect them. His uncle Boothe had been a friend to all tribes, revered by them for his "magic." The magic had been second sight, an uncanny knack for seeing the future that was usually passed down to the females of Jim's mother's family. Jim had no such gifts, but he, too, had respected and been respected by the Indian tribes he had known in his life. Since settling on the Platte, he had traded with the Crow, the Blackfoot, the Sioux, and the Arapaho. He had never imagined that there would come a day when he would want to exterminate the Indians as a race.

The Indians who had attacked Star had looked to be Crow, judging from their costumes and the way they painted their horses. Their behavior suggested otherwise, but how could he say? What white man could really know what any Indian would do or why? Their worlds were so different, their minds so unfathomable, that anything was possible.

Perhaps they were Crow. Perhaps they were Pawnee or Shoshone or even Blackfoot disguised as Crow. It didn't matter. They were Indians, and what had happened on the trail had only proved how little any white man would ever know of who they were or what they were capable of; how little they could be trusted.

If questioned and forced to answer, Jim would have said his vengeance was only against those who had killed his wife. But inside he knew he would never think the same way about any Indian again.

The killing had been so senseless. That was what haunted him. So without reason or purpose.

It was near noon when he found the first trail marker. He stopped his horse before it and looked down at it for a long time before finally realizing what it was. And while he looked, the instinctive animal within him gradually receded and the man of reason slowly came forth. By the time he dismounted and knelt beside the marker, he was fully aware for the first time since the murder.

Jim had learned to read trail markers on his trips back and forth to California, for they often made the difference between life and death for the unwary traveler approaching danger on an unfamiliar road. Though a device of the Indians, trail markers were soon in common use among white and red men alike as they traveled across the desert and through the mountains.

An animal skull on a stick or two crossed bones placed before a drinking source warned of poisoned water. A skeletal figure hung on a branch outside an encampment announced the starvation of those within. Three pierced rocks hung on a branch beside a stream indicated an abundance of fish.

Some signs were simple: one stone set upon another indicated a direction; a number of sticks stuck into the ground represented the passage of time; a broken arrow across the path was a clear warning to proceed at one's own peril. Other signs were far more complex, and could tell stories of battles, adventures, and discoveries in as exacting detail as a pictograph.

The trail sign Jim discovered was neither simple nor complex; its message was easy to read for anyone who knew how. A round stone was set in a forked stick pointing west. Upon the stone was etched a crude representation of a doglike creature with the charred wood of a fire. Surrounding it were several sticks, two more piles of stones, and a small tied bundle of grass several days old.

The message was: *The wolf/dog devoured his prey twelve days ago and has gone west from this point. Danger!*

Jim picked up the bundle of grass and hefted its weight in his palm. It was dry; at least a week old. The tracks around the marker were Crow moccasins; the horse's hooves were shod.

There was no reason to believe the marker had anything at all to do with him. Hundreds of people passed this way every month; the message could have been left for any one of them, or for no one in particular.

But there was something about that image, of a wolf devouring its prey. The marker referred to an event that had happened close to three weeks ago. As nearly as Jim could remember, that was about the time Star had been killed.

And the tracks left in the mud at the edge of Donner Lake had been in the distinctive bow shape of a Crow moccasin.

The wolf/dog could be used by an Indian to refer to any creature that was clever and thieving and consistently outwitted its enemies. It could mean a Pawnee. It could mean a literal dog, or even a wolf of the small red kind that was common to these hills. Or it could mean something else entirely.

Jim replaced the bundle of grass. Its aging would mark the passage of time to the next traveler who came by—perhaps the person for whom the marker was really meant.

He remounted his horse and turned it west. He found the path in the woods that was indicated by the marker and followed it.

Chapter Eleven

S arah hoped that travel would be easier when they arrived at the village of Cruces at the head of the Chagres River. There the mud and slime of the river gave way to rocky slopes at the base of the mountains, the Cordillera Central. Sanchez was in a hurry, trying to make up for the time he'd lost in going back for the fever survivors, so there was no time to rest; he immediately ordered them to mount the mules he'd hired and move out as quickly as possible.

Sarah hadn't complained or argued when she realized there was only one pack mule for her, Marie, and Lisanne to share as transport for their belongings. Mules were in short supply, Sanchez advised, the best of them having been hired by the earlier portion of his party. They'd have to pay top dollar for the few scrawny ones that were left.

Because of the scarcity of pack animals, most of their clothes and other possessions would be left behind. Sarah shrugged at the news and began going through her luggage, which had been unloaded from the bongo.

She distributed her dresses and petticoats among the village women, who crowded around expectantly, chattering and laughing at the dispersal of silks and laces, taffetas and satins. It was a scene they'd seen played out again and again.

Sarah's heart gave a little lurch as her new green evening gown, the one that Emilie had given her, disappeared into a hut, draped across the shoulders of a young Indian girl. Then immediately she chastised herself. She was grateful she was alive; losing her belongings was a small price to pay for the privilege. Molly and Madame would never have that luxury.

Sarah and Marie stuffed as much as they could into the pack across the back of a skinny mule, and then they tied a still weak Lisanne onto the back of another and climbed on their own animals. With Sanchez in the lead, the small party of survivors set out. After only a few miles, Sarah realized that the last leg of the journey would be no easier than the first. The path was so treacherous and the grade so steep that they'd have to walk and lead the mules; she only felt safe walking on her own two feet, bent almost double, using her free hand to help pull herself up the mountain.

The Spaniards, who'd crossed the Isthmus three hundred years earlier, hauling treasure from the Pacific coasts of Mexico and Peru to the Gulf of Mexico, had cut steps into the rocky cliffs—mule stairs, they were called. Sarah was grateful for that, but even with the aid of the foot and hand holds, the climb was grueling. Her right hand was scratched and bleeding from the knife-sharp rocks she grasped to pull herself along, and she felt a grabbing pain in her left shoulder from the constant pressure of jerking on the leads of her mule and Lisanne's. Muscles that she'd never used before throbbed painfully in her legs and back. Her dress was stained and tattered, and she reeked of sweat and un-washed clothes, just as the men in the party did. They seemed to have no easier a time than the women and could offer little assistance.

During the brief rest that Sanchez allowed at the crest of the mountain, Sarah pushed a limp strand of hair out of her face and took a look at Panama City in the distance. She wasn't sure she could make it. She wasn't sure of anything anymore except heat and dirt and never-ending exhaustion. Twenty miles from Cruces to Panama City might as well be a million.

"Señoras, let me warn you," Sanchez said, coming to stand beside them and gazing toward the distant town. "It is more dangerous going down than coming up. You might want to walk—"

"We walked all the way up, Sanchez, or didn't you see us?" Marie asked. "Now, I wonder why the hell you made us hire these mules. Except I know the answer, of course. To line your own pockets with more of our money."

He was unperturbed by her criticism. "You will be glad you have the mules for the ride from the foot of the mountain to the city. As I was telling you, señoras, going down can be dangerous." He pointed to the nar-row trail that twisted snakelike down the mountainside. "There are stories of men falling off their mules and hurtling over a cliff to their deaths. *Es verdad*, señoras, and it has happened more than once."

"Well, it ain't going to happen to us, Sanchez," Marie countered, " 'cause we're too close to Panama City to get ourselves killed now!"

Panama City was a walled Spanish town, hundreds of years old, with narrow streets, overhanging balconies, and tiny gardens glimpsed behind wrought-iron gates.

There were several Catholic churches and the ruins of an old fort with rusting cannon by the seashore, where in the seventeenth century Spanish settlers had attempted to hold off the attacks of English pirates led by the fearful Henry Morgan. Once a great and glorious colonial city, it had fallen into near total oblivion, to be revived by the onrush of the forty-niners on their way to the goldfields.

The most amazing aspect of Panama City to Sarah was the large number of Americans. They were everywhere—their voices, their accents, their calls and shouts filling the streets with a rough, raw energy. For a moment, she caught that energy, and her spirits lifted.

Sanchez led them to a small adobe brick hotel on a side street. With a mocking little bow, he left them, after extracting the remainder of his fee. "I wish you well in your travels, señoras, and if you are ever in Panama again—Benito Sanchez is at your service."

"Money-grubbing little bastard," Marie hissed as she watched him lead the mules down the narrow street.

"It doesn't matter," Sarah said. "At least we're here. Now what?"

Marie straightened her shoulders and pushed her tangled hair off her face. "You watch out for Lisanne. She looks like a strong wind could blow her down. I'm going into this place and get us a room—and a hot bath and a decent meal, or there's going to be hell to pay."

The bathwater was lukewarm, but the towels were clean, and the narrow beds with their much-laundered sheets and colorful woven coverlets looked incredibly luxurious to Sarah. Lisanne fell asleep immediately, but Sarah and Marie bathed, threw away their traveling clothes, and put on the one fresh change they'd brought with them. Then Marie set out in search of food.

While she was waiting, Sarah stepped out onto the small balcony that overlooked the hotel garden. The aroma of blooming flowers lay heavy on the evening air. Pigeons picked busily among the beds. Fish in the lily-covered pond made short work of mosquitoes hovering near the surface of the water. There was a feeling of tranquility she hadn't felt in a very long time. She took a deep breath and tried to soak up the serenity. She couldn't see the Pacific, but she was sure she could smell the sea, fresh and salty, on the westward breeze. The sun was setting behind her in a blaze of red and orange across a lavender sky.

"Thank you, God," she said softly. "Thank you for letting me live." She saw the bell tower of a Catholic church over the rooftops, and she vowed that tomorrow she would light a candle in Molly's memory. She dreaded seeing Molly's husband in San Francisco, dreaded telling him what had happened . . .

As she stood in the soft twilight, she was struck with a bittersweet longing for home, not only for the house she'd shared with her parents and brothers and sisters in Cairo, but for the log cabin where she'd lived with Ben and Kitty in Kansas and for the gracious rooms of Deveraux House. But it wasn't the homes that she missed; it was the people—her mother, Kitty, Emilie . . . She thought of all the unkind words she'd spoken, the times she'd wished to be anywhere else but with her family, and she regretted her sharp retorts and whining complaints. She'd never been so far away from her family, and she'd never before realized what they meant to her.

She heard Marie calling from the hall and hurried to open the door. "Let's eat on the balcony," Marie said, "and let Lisanne sleep a while. There'll be plenty of leftovers." The tray she carried was laden with food—

baked yams, rice and tomatoes, slivers of pork in a spicy sauce, and a big loaf of hot bread. There was also a steaming pot of coffee.

"How did you manage?" Sarah asked between bites of bread when they were seated at the little table.

"Americans own this hotel, a man and a woman who know what it's like to cross Panama. Umm—" Marie licked her fingers. "Real butter."

"What are they doing here, besides running a hotel?"

"They started out for California in '50. Seems like there were more boats going into Chagres than leaving Panama City, so lots of travelers got stranded here. Since they couldn't get on a boat going to Frisco, they decided to make their fortune right here. Started this hotel. Other Americans have done the same thing— hotels, saloons, even a newspaper, I hear."

"What if that happens to us?" Sarah said in a panicked voice. "We've missed the *Laura Lee*. What if we get stranded here . . . for months?"

"Don't look on the gloomy side, Sarah. We'll get out. I'll look for a ship schedule tomorrow. Coffee, honey?"

"Please." Sarah sat back in her chair, clean for the first time in days, sated with food, and—most importantly—safe. "Thank you," she said as Marie handed her the cup.

"You're welcome."

"For everything, Marie. For helping with Molly and sticking with me and giving me courage—"

"You're thanking *me?* Good God! Lisanne would be dead if it weren't for you, and I'd have fallen off that damn mountain that's fit for nothing but goats—"

Sarah laughed. "Then you're welcome. Oh, Marie, it feels good to laugh, and at the same time I feel guilty for being happy, because of Molly—"

"Bless her poor little heart."

"She thought I was the strong one, the brave one, but the way she faced death in that awful hellhole of a place—" Sarah shuddered.

"We're all strong when we need to be, I guess."

"Life seems very precious now," Sarah said thoughtfully. "All my life I've been so . . . so greedy for things. A big house and pretty clothes and fancy manners and speaking French and going to balls and parties . . . None of it means as much as this—" She gestured with her hand. "A place to sleep, food, and a friend."

"I guess we've all changed since Chagres."

"I'm glad," Sarah said fiercely. "I know what I want now—my husband, my family, a home—even if it's a shack in a gold camp. Nothing else counts. I don't care about Deveraux House or my ball gowns or being a lady—I just don't care!" As she said the words, Sarah felt a freeing inside; it felt good to let go of those old desires and longings.

"I envy you, honey, being with your family. Lisanne's about the only family I got now."

"Then I want you to be part of mine," Sarah said impulsively.

Marie shook her head. "Oh, no, honey, that would never work. Maybe here in Panama, but not in San Francisco."

"My family's not all that fine," Sarah replied. "I could tell you something about my sister Meg— Anyhow, neither one of us knows much about San Francisco, so let's don't go jumping to any conclusions. Let's just figure out how we're going to get there."

Lisanne was sitting in the sun on the balcony the next morning when Sarah returned to the hotel from the Pacific Steamer office. There was color in Lisanne's cheeks, and her eyes looked more alert than they had in days. She'd washed her long blond hair, and it gleamed softly in the morning sunlight. She looked young and pretty and soft, Sarah thought, without all the paint and powder and curled-up hair. She felt a wave of affection for the girl, who was probably no more than twenty.

"At least there's some good news," Sarah said, joining her. "You look better."

"I feel better, too. Any chance of us getting out of this place?"

"There are two ships this week. One today and one tomorrow morning, and no room on either."

"Shit! We'll never get out of this town!" Lisanne's wide mouth turned down in a grimace.

"Don't let Marie hear you say that. She's determined to look on the bright side—if there is one."

The door opened, and Marie appeared on the balcony. "Did I hear you talking about me, ladies? Well, if I did, I hope you were saying good things—" She was beginning to look like the woman Sarah had first seen on the *Panama Queen*. Her hair was pulled back into an ornate knot at the back of her head; she was wearing rouge and powder on her cheeks, and on her head was a narrow-brimmed straw hat decorated with bright bird feathers.

"*Buenos días*, as we say in Panama. Like my hat?" She took it off and tossed it on the table. "Bought it in the market this morning, along with this fine Spanish shawl." She twirled around, letting the long fringe of the white shawl swirl about her.

"You're mighty chirpy; you must have good news," Lisanne commented.

"That I do!"

"We have passage, thank God," Sarah breathed.

"Not exactly. I have a job, though."

"A job? Where? Why?" Lisanne asked. "I thought we were going to Frisco."

"We are, eventually, but we're running low on money, and when I ran into this fella I know from New Orleans—"

"If you need money," Sarah said, "I can get it. I have a gold piece I haven't spent. It's worth enough to get all of us to San Francisco."

"It ain't just the money, Sarah. It's getting space on the damn steamers. That's going to take time for me and Lisanne, but I think I have a way for you—"

"I checked with the steamship office. The ships are booked; I even tried a bribe. It's just not possible, Marie."

Marie put her hands on her hips and tilted her head to the side. "You're trying to tell me that something isn't possible? Hell, honey, getting you on that boat ain't nothing after what we've been through. You'll be leaving in the morning."

"I really don't understand," Sarah said. "You're making me nervous, Marie. I think you're up to something."

"Damned right. Now, when I was talking to my friend, Harve, down at the Crescent City—that's what he calls his little saloon—I ran into a young gentleman who just happens to have passage tomorrow on the *Pacific Princess*."

"What does that have to do with me?" Sarah asked.

"The less you know, my friend, the better it will be," Marie said mysteriously. "Just leave everything to me and my little helper, Lisanne." She winked at her friend. "We're the experts, after all."

Michael O'Donal was celebrating his upcoming departure from Panama City. As a matter of fact, he'd been celebrating most of the day, going from one saloon to the next, buying drinks for himself and any friendly stranger he might run into. For the past few hours he'd been sitting in the Crescent City, waiting and hoping that his last night in town would be his best.

He was twenty-two years old, short and stocky, with blond hair that, much to his chagrin, was already thinning and a fair, Irish complexion that burned quickly in the tropical sun. After crossing the Isthmus and surviving, he thought of himself as man of the world, an adventurer; however, to most who crossed his path, he seemed a young man who had a lot to learn.

He'd grown up in Philadelphia, where his parents ran a small butcher shop. The senior O'Donals, when hearing of their son's ambitious plans to sail to California and make his fortune in the goldfields, had been vehemently opposed. Their answer to his request for a loan for his passage was a resounding no, which deterred Michael for only a moment. He'd simply "borrowed" a grubstake from the tin box his parents kept under a floorboard in their closet, left a note saying he'd repay them with the proceeds of his gold strike, and taken off for New York and the harbor where ships were loading to sail to Panama.

For three weeks he'd been cooling his heels in Panama City, awaiting the arrival of the *Pacific Princess,* delayed by bad weather off the southern tip of South America. Now the *Princess* was in port, scheduled to sail before dawn, and Mike, more than a little drunk, was in a mood of high anticipation.

He ordered a shot of rum and looked toward the door of the saloon. The veneer of confidence he'd struggled to maintain was cracking a little with each minute that passed. She'd said she'd meet him. Had she just been funning? he wondered. Maybe she wasn't going to show. It wasn't often that a good-looking, older woman like that took an interest in someone like Mike O'Donal.

And then he saw her, sashaying toward him, her head high, her cheeks bright with color, and her eyes flashing. Mike felt a rush of desire just looking at her. God, she was a fine-looking woman. The best-looking woman he'd seen in months, and she seemed interested in him.

She walked right up to the bar and sat down beside him. Her presence, the scent of her perfume, the warmth of her body, almost took his breath away and made him tongue-tied and stuttering. "I—I—thought you might n-not come."

"Not celebrate your last night in Panama? Why, shame on you, Mikey. I gave my word, didn't I?" Marie leaned close so that her full breasts pressed against his arm. "I'm looking forward to this evening as much as you, honey. Now, why don't you buy me a drink? I've got a mighty big thirst on—and get another for yourself."

Mike, already light-headed and anticipating the delights that lay ahead for him this evening, tried to protest. "No, Miss Marie, I don't think so. I've had a lot to drink—"

Marie waved the bartender over. "Don't be silly, Mike. Why, a big, strong man like you ought to be able to hold his liquor. Harve, bring this fella a double, and for me—the regular."

Harve nodded and winked at Marie.

Marie finished her drink in two swallows. "You're not drinking up, honey. Too much for you?"

Mike quickly downed his drink. His giddiness intensified, and he had to blink his eyes several times in rapid succession to focus on her.

Leaning closer, Marie put her face near his. "How you feeling, honey?"

"I feel like raising some hell," he lied. "How about you?"

Her laugh was low and seductive. "Oh, I'd like to raise something else, if you're up to it." Her hand slid between his legs. Mike's reaction, despite the amount of alcohol he'd consumed, was urgent and intense. He groaned as Marie's hand rubbed against his erection.

Her breath was warm against his ear. "Let's leave here, honey. I've got a room—"

Mike was already on his feet, staggering slightly as he tossed bills on the counter to pay for the drinks. "Jus' show me the way," he said, the words slurring together. He slung his arm over her shoulder, and together they wove their way down the narrow street.

Outside the door to the hotel room, Marie paused. "Honey, I've got a real surprise for you inside . . . if you're man enough for it."

"I'm man enough for anythin'," he boasted. He put one hand against the doorjamb to steady himself. "Jus' tell me what you want, Marie."

"I want you to be nice to me . . . and my friend, but let me show you." She opened the door and pushed Mike inside. He gave a little gasp of surprise and disbelief.

"Hello, darlin'. We didn't know if you liked blondes or brunettes, so we decided to give you one of each." Lisanne lay on one of the beds, wearing only her pantaloons and chemise, her hair flowing softly around her shoulders. In the lamplight she looked young and innocent and very beautiful.

Mike tried to speak, but he could hardly get his breath. His heart was pounding like an anvil and the room was whirling wildly around him. He reached for Marie. She was there to steady him and lead him to the bed. "Come on, honey, show us what you can do."

He tottered drunkenly back and forth on the balls of his feet, swaying like a tree in a strong gale. Marie gave him a little push, and he crashed heavily across the bed, facedown. After struggling vainly to sit up, he looked around, a dazed expression on his face, and, as if he'd been struck by a brick, collapsed again.

"Out like a light," Marie said. "Okay, Sarah, you can come out now. Let's get to work."

Sarah appeared from the balcony, her forehead creased with lines of worry. "I'm sure this isn't legal—" she began.

"Of course it's not legal," Marie agreed. "We all know that. Get that rope I bought, girl, and, Lisanne, help me get his clothes off. We'll undress him first and then tie him up."

"You could get into so much trouble for this," Sarah said anxiously. "You could be arrested—"

Marie, who'd been unbuttoning Mike's shirt, put her hands on her hips and glowered at Sarah. "Arrested? Have you seen any sign of law in this place? Anyway, he came here of his own free will, didn't he?"

"But you're going to steal his steamship ticket!"

"For all we know, he could have lost it on the stairs and you happened to come along and pick it up." Marie pulled off his shirt and started on the buttons to his trousers. "Get his boots, Lisanne, and check his pockets for the ticket. Good, there it is. Looks like we're in business."

She tossed Mike's clothes to Sarah. "He outweighs you, but he's not much taller. Put these clothes on, and then we'll do something about your hair."

Sarah stood with the clothes clutched to her breast.

"I can't do this, Marie. This is wrong. When he wakes up, won't he wonder where his clothes are? What are you going to tell him?"

"His valise is behind the bar at the Crescent City, so he won't be running around Panama City in his underdrawers. As for his state of mind—well, after Lisanne and I tell him about what a tiger he was in bed and what we did—honey, he'll be wanting to move in here with us. Believe me, I can handle men, especially men like Mr. Mike O'Donal. Now move, girl. I didn't go to all this trouble just to have you whine like a scared dog. Do you want to find that good-looking man of yours?"

"Well, yes, of course."

"He sure as hell ain't in Panama City, is he? So get moving. Now."

Lisanne tied up a vigorously snoring Mike, and together she and Marie settled him as comfortably as possible on the bed. Sarah, dressed in Mike's clothes, presented herself for inspection.

Lisanne broke into giggles. "You're the silliest-looking man I've ever seen, Sarah. Why, those clothes just hang on you."

Marie was more businesslike. "We'll add another hole in his belt and pad the toes of his boots so they'll fit better. Now for the hair . . ." She picked up a bread knife from the table where the dinner dishes were still sitting.

"That knife is so dull it won't cut hot butter, and you're planning to cut my hair with it?" Sarah was aghast. "The more I know about this plan of yours, the less I like it."

"We ain't got no choice, honey, so sit down."

With a sigh, Sarah sat and Marie went to work. "We'll stick a hat on your head, and if you board while it's still dark, I don't think anyone will pay attention. I'll go down to the port with you, kind of a girlfriend seeing you off. You know, blow kisses and wave." Marie chuckled as she whacked at Sarah's hair.

"You want to be sure I get on the ship, don't you?"

"I didn't go to all this trouble to be double-crossed at the last minute."

"Can I look in a mirror?"

Lisanne shook her head. "If I were you, I'd avoid mirrors for about two months." She giggled again.

"They're going to realize I'm not Mike O'Donal," Sarah argued. "I can't fool anyone for very long."

"And then you pull out your gold coin and bribe the captain, the purser, the first mate—whoever can help you get to California. They ain't going to turn the ship around once you're at sea."

"It sounds so easy when you say it." Sarah wasn't convinced.

"You can do it. I have faith in you."

"I wish you and Lisanne were coming . . . it's not fair. When will you be in San Francisco?"

"Give us some time to make a little money and figure out how to get tickets. Then we'll be there. Your needs are more pressing than ours are right now."

"If I'm not around when you get to San Francisco, remember to look up Meg. Meg Kincaid. She's in business with a man named Sheldon Gerrard. They own a store."

"She's not married to him? I thought you said she had a child." Marie studied Sarah's hair, which stood out from her head in unattractive spikes. She shrugged; it was the best she could do.

"It's not Gerrard's child. Meg was married once; we're not sure what happened . . . Meg is—well, you'll see when you meet her. She's a woman with a mind of her own."

"Then maybe we'll get along," Marie said.

Sarah was thoughtful. "In some ways you're very much alike. That could be good—"

"Or we could fight like two she-cats. Whatever, it's not your concern, honey. Your concern is to get on that ship and find your man." Marie's eyes sparkled with mischief. "And, Sarah, be sure to give him a great big kiss from me."

Sarah stood up and flung her arms around Marie. "How can I thank you? You've been such a friend—"

"You just thank me by finding your husband and starting a new life. That's all any of us wants, and, by God, we're going to get it."

Chapter Twelve

Sarah looked up warily at the scaffolding above her. Workmen scurried around on rafters like busy ants, hauling lumber, sawing, nailing, calling back and forth. In the middle of the chaos in a corner of the half-completed building, she saw her sister Meg Kincaid sitting at a makeshift table, calmly checking figures in a ledger book. Her red hair was upswept under a small bonnet made of ribbons and feathers; her dress of wine-and-green plaid poplin was stylishly cut with an impeccably clean white collar and cuffs. As she made her way through the sawdust, Sarah was painfully aware of her disheveled appearance.

"Meg," she said softly. "I'm here."

For a moment nothing registered on Meg's face but confusion. She looked at Sarah for a long, hard minute, and then she sprang up from her chair, holding out her arms. "As I live and breathe, it's my little sister! Darling, what happened to you? My Lord, we've been so worried. When the *Laura Lee* arrived and you weren't on it . . . Oh, let me look at you!"

"Don't look too hard," Sarah said. She knew her dress hung limply on her too-thin frame, and her hair was frizzing wildly in the damp San Francisco air. "It's been a very difficult trip."

Meg took Sarah's chin in her hand. "It's good to see you, Sarah, and you're as pretty as you can be . . . even with hair that looks as though it was chewed off by dogs."

Sarah put her hand to her hair; she knew that her sister's sharp eyes took in everything—her skin coarsened by the sun, her badly fitting dress, the lines of weariness on her face.

Meg's expression softened. "It's all right, little sister. You're safe now. I can take care of everything. Do you have trunks at the wharf? I can send one of the men."

Pointing to the small valise at her feet, Sarah answered, "That's all the luggage I have. All my worldly possessions. It's a long story, Meg—"

"And I want to hear it, every word. But, Sarah . . ." Meg gripped her sister's fingers tightly, her eyes flooding unexpectedly with tears. "Oh, honey, there's no easy way to tell you this. There's been a terrible tragedy."

The last of the color faded from Sarah's cheeks and her knees went weak. "Jim . . ."

"He's alive," Meg assured her quickly. "At least the last we heard . . ." Her voice trailed off and she swallowed hard to strengthen it. "It's Star. There was an Indian attack at Donner Lake, and Star was—she was killed. Apparently Jim took it badly. He rode off to track down the killers, and last we heard, he had shot two men in Hangtown. He—they say he's lost his mind, Sarah."

Sarah's lips hardly seemed to move as she said, "My God. The dream." She seemed to focus on Meg with difficulty. "Oh, Meg, I had an awful dream about him.

Someone was out to harm him. The wolf! Marcus Lyndsay."

"Captain Lyndsay is dead," Meg replied flatly. "He died in that avalanche back in '43. After what you've been through, I wouldn't put much stock in nightmares. Sounds as though you've been living through one. It's bound to affect you."

Sarah, who usually didn't speak of her dreams to anyone, nodded. The fact that in the past her dreams had come true only made the nightmare more frightening. "What can we do about Jim?"

"Wait for news, I guess. You know your brother better than anyone. He'll do what he has to, and no one can stop him."

"I'm not going to wait," Sarah said decisively. "I'm going to look for Cade and Jim. I'm going to the gold camps."

"I knew you'd say that, and the answer is no. Mr. Gerrard and I won't help you with such foolishness. Just forget it, Sarah. Absolutely not."

Meg's mouth was set in a hard line, but at the look of weary intractability on Sarah's face, her expression softened. "Darling, you're exhausted, and you look as though you haven't eaten in weeks. You need a good meal right away. Why, you're nothing but skin and bones."

"I'm hungry," Sarah admitted. "We didn't have time to eat when the ship docked this morning—"

Meg picked up her shawl. "We'll go to the Colonnade. It's not far from here, and they have a ladies' section and good, filling food." She called out to one of the workers. "Mr. Romero, I'm going out for a while. The brickmasons are due at two. Please don't let them start until I get back." She turned to Sarah. "Mr. Gerrard is so worried about fire that he's insisting we build fire walls. The expense is extraordinary, but he's very stubborn."

"I thought you owned a store," Sarah said. "News travels so slowly—"

"We did, but it burned down. This town seems to burn down every few months," Meg said matter-of-factly. "So now I'm building an opera house—very, very elegant. I'll show you the plans later. It'll fit right in this location on Portsmouth Square. Can you believe this was once the spot where the Spaniards grazed cattle? Then it became a plaza, and now . . . well, it's *the* place to set up a business." She took Sarah's arm and led her into the street.

"See, over there's the St. Francis Hotel, quite a nice place, and then there's the El Dorado, a gambling casino, and the Bella Union and the Verandah—"

"The Verandah?" Sarah looked at the three-story frame building. "Like the gambling house in New Orleans?"

"Well, yes! Now, how did a sister of mine learn about gambling at the Verandah?"

Sarah's mouth curved into a little smile. "From a woman who worked there. She and I became friends on our trip. Marie LaFleur. Remind me to tell you all about her; she's coming to San Francisco soon."

Meg raised an eyebrow. "You've taken up with a fancy lady from a gambling house? Why, what would Mama think?"

"If she knew the whole story, she wouldn't care," Sarah said.

Meg looked surprised. "I guess you've changed a lot from the prissy little girl I knew in Cairo."

"That was over ten years ago, Meg. Lots has happened, and, oh, yes, I have changed. Thank God."

"And I want to hear every word, starting with how you became Mrs. Cade Deveraux."

An hour later, Sarah pushed away her plate and sighed. "I had no idea that food like this existed."

Meg nodded proudly. "We San Franciscans love to eat, and eat well."

Sarah was amused that her sister considered herself a true San Franciscan after only a few years of residence, but she agreed about the meal they'd just completed. They'd started off with oysters from Washington Territory, and then for a main course Meg had chosen quail on toast; and Sarah, mutton pie, ignoring the more exotic listings of veal tartare, wild goose, fricassee oxtail, and hog's head with cranberry dressing.

"Thank you," she said to Meg. "I'm beginning to feel almost human again."

"You've been through it, haven't you?" Meg had listened attentively to Sarah's tales of crossing the Isthmus. "Losing that little friend of yours ... We know some folks in the Presbyterian church out here. I'm sure we can track Mr. Morgan down. He must be frantic about his wife."

"I'd appreciate that. I've dreaded talking to him."

"Mr. Gerrard will take care of it," Meg decided. "He's very good at ... well, taking care of things."

Sarah looked inquisitively at her sister. "What about you and Sheldon Gerrard? You're not interested in marrying him?"

"I have no use for marriage, and as far as I know, I'm still married to Caleb, unless he's dead ... which I hope. I never want him to know about Fiona. Oh, Sarah, she's so wonderful. I can't wait for you to meet her. She's very anxious to see her aunt Sarah."

"I want to see her, too."

The waiter, a slender man with curly brown hair, was hovering near. Meg beckoned to him. "Hank, please take this away and bring my sister a dessert menu. I think she's in the mood, and coffee for both of us." Then she turned back to Sarah. "I still don't understand how you carried off your masquerade on the ship, once they discovered that you weren't Mr. Michael O'Donal."

"Oh, that happened the first night, when I went to my cabin and found it occupied by three other gentlemen. I had to tell the purser, who threw a fit . . . but when I gave him the gold coin—"

"Not the one Mama gave us? Not Grandma Fiona's?"

"Well, of course. What other coin would it be?" She saw the look of dismay in her sister's eyes. "I'm sorry, but I had to. Once I bribed the purser, he decided he could make room for me with another female passenger. The captain never found out who I was—he was too busy trying to make up time. So it all worked out—"

"Except for the poor fella in Panama City."

"I feel terrible about him, but, Meg, I had to get to California. I have to find Cade. Have you heard anything?"

"Nothing at all."

The waiter appeared with coffee and the menu, and stood waiting.

"I'll have cake," Sarah said. "Something rich and creamy with lots of nuts."

Meg laughed. "Bring her the house special with whipped cream on top. You're so skinny you can afford to be decadent."

"Nothing for you?" Sarah poured a huge dollop of cream into her coffee. It tasted wonderful, she thought, but then, everything she'd eaten today had tasted like ambrosia.

"No, I have to get back and talk to the brickmasons." She fiddled nervously with her coffee cup, picking it up and putting it down again. "Sarah, we have to talk about this absurd plan of yours to go to the gold camps. We've lost our precious Star, I'm worried to death about Jim, and I can't bear to lose you." Meg's eyes glittered with tears.

The waiter appeared with Sarah's cake. She pushed it aside and took her sister's hand. "My heart aches for Jim, you know that. But now that Star's dead, it's even more important for me to go. You can't stop me, Meg. I'm a grown, married woman. *You've* always done what you wanted—"

Meg sighed. "As have all the Kincaids."

"Then I'm going."

"We'll discuss it later. Maybe there's another way . . . Mr. Gerrard will have some ideas." Meg looked at the little pocket watch pinned to her bodice. "You stay here and eat your dessert; I'm late for my appointment. Now, my place is only two blocks down California Street—"

"I got across Panama, Meg. I think I can find Portsmouth Square!" Sarah said, indignant that Meg had so easily fallen back into the role of all-knowing big sister.

Meg kept on talking. "If you get turned around, just ask Hank, the waiter, for directions." She lowered her voice. "He's a nice young man; rumor is he was a doctor back east, but some kind of tragedy brought him to California."

Imperiously, she waved the waiter over to their table. "Hank, please put the meal on my bill and see that my sister, Mrs. Deveraux, gets safely back to Portsmouth Square." He nodded and pulled out Meg's chair. She smiled and slipped a bill into his hand. "And as for you, Sarah, no more talk about taking off for the goldfields. I simply won't allow that to happen." She kissed Sarah's cheek and swept grandly from the restaurant.

Sarah picked up a fork and took a bite of cake. Her anger and frustration at Meg weren't going to stop her from enjoying her dessert. It was rich and creamy and packed with raisins and nuts, covered with a layer of whipped cream. She ate quickly, trying to think of ways around her sister. She'd planned to go to the goldfields, and she was going.

Out of the corner of her eye she noticed the waiter standing nearby, watching her. She sneaked another look. He was still staring at her. He was a nondescript kind of young man who would pass unnoticed in a crowd, tall but not too tall, slender, with brown hair and eyes hidden behind gold-rimmed spectacles. He wasn't handsome at all—certainly not like Cade with his sophisticated good looks, or even like her uncle Booth or brother Jim, both of whom had a rugged manliness about them.

She finished the cake, and the waiter was there at her shoulder, pouring another cup of coffee for her. She looked up and smiled. "Thank you."

He seemed ill at ease and hesitant, yet he didn't move away. He continued to stand at her table, looking at her. Sarah met his eyes. Since her journey, she'd learned to deal with men in a straightforward manner.

"Do you want to say something?" She noticed that his eyes were a bluish gray, and that he looked pale and citified, like a man not used to the outdoors.

"I heard you and Miss Kincaid talking about the gold camps . . . about you wanting to go."

"Well, I'm not partial to eavesdroppers, but I guess

you couldn't help overhearing. Yes, I'm going to look for my husband and my brother."

"Would you be in need of a guide?"

"Perhaps," Sarah answered warily.

"Most of the men in this town are pretty rough-and-ready. I don't think your sister would approve of you taking off with them."

"What my sister thinks isn't important. I'm making the decisions," she said shortly.

Of course, he was right, she thought. She'd need to choose a guide carefully, but even then Meg wouldn't agree to the trip . . . if Meg knew. Sarah decided at that moment not to tell her sister anything about her plans. She'd make them, take off for the goldfields, and leave Meg a note. A cowardly thing to do, but with the formidable Meg Kincaid on the other side, it was the simplest solution.

"Can you recommend anyone? Someone reliable and dependable?" She realized she didn't know how far it was to the goldfields or how long it might take. Just as before, she was thinking about taking off on a journey when she hardly knew where she was going.

He looked around the dining room. All the guests except Sarah had left. "May I sit down?" he asked.

"Certainly," she said, surprised at his request.

He settled himself and looked at her, his hands folded in front of him on the table. His fingers were long and slender, his nails clean. Sarah thought of her own broken nails and hands roughened by the hardships of her journey, and hid them in her lap.

"I've been planning on going to the goldfields myself," he said. "Maybe I could escort you out. That's why I came to San Francisco, but then . . . well, I was robbed." The young man looked down at his hands, embarrassed. "All my belongings were stolen, so I've been working here, trying to earn money to get out to the camps."

Sarah frowned. "I don't understand. My sister said you were a doctor and some kind of tragedy brought you out here."

"I was a physician, that's true, but it wasn't any kind of tragedy that led me to California. It doesn't pay to listen to rumors."

"It seems to me you could make a lot of money taking care of sick folks here in San Francisco. Didn't you like being a doctor?"

He raised his head and took off his glasses, massaging his temples. "No, I didn't. I needed a change ... I needed to start over. Isn't that why most men come to California?"

"I guess." He was right, of course. Cade had come to start a new life, and so had Meg and Sheldon Gerrard, and that's what Marie and Lisanne were looking for. Even the unfortunate Michael O'Donal. This man's story wasn't so unusual. "What's your name?" she asked.

"Henry. Henry Corneale. Folks here call me Hank. I guess it sounds more Western." His generous mouth curved in a wry smile.

"But you're from the East, aren't you? Maybe the South?" Sarah wasn't particularly good with accents, but she recognized the traces of a drawl.

"Virginia. I was born near Richmond. I went to school at the university to study medicine and then worked as a physician in Baltimore."

"Oh," Sarah said. Vainly she tried to think of more questions. She'd never hired anyone for anything. She concentrated on what she thought Marie or Meg would ask. "Do you know the route? I mean, if you've never been there yourself, how do I know you can lead me?"

"The way's well known, Mrs. Deveraux. You could do it on your own, except, of course, it's not safe for a woman to travel alone. A few days or so, and we'd be there. I could ask around about your husband and brother. Help you get information. Miners are more likely to trust another man."

"Hmm . . ." Sarah said. Now she was beginning to have cold feet about her journey. She was overwhelmed by the same indecision that she'd experienced on the *Panama Queen.* Maybe going to the gold camps wasn't such a fine idea, but if she didn't, she'd have no way of locating Cade or Jim. Aunt Emilie would be horrified that she was even contemplating such a thing; ladies didn't hire strange men and ride off into the hills with them. But she'd done things these past months that Emilie Gallier couldn't even imagine. Could the trip be any more dangerous than crossing the Isthmus of Panama or any less ladylike than conspiring with two whores to rob a man?

She thought of another question. "How much would you charge? I assume you'd want a fee."

"Money to buy the horses and supplies, and then two hundred dollars for myself to start a stake." His answer was quick, as if he'd been thinking of it for a long while.

Sarah chewed her lip, indecisive. The money wasn't a problem. She was sure that the funds Papa Deveraux had sent had long since arrived in San Francisco and were secure at the Bank of California. She just wasn't sure about Henry Corneale's qualifications.

She pushed back her chair. "I'll think about it, Mr. . . . Dr. Corneale. My plans are . . . well, rather unsure. I'd appreciate it if you wouldn't discuss this conversation with my sister."

"Of course I won't. It will be between us, but I promise you, ma'am, you won't find a more reliable guide."

* * *

Sarah walked slowly back toward her sister's half-finished opera house, deep in thought. Henry Corneale seemed nice enough, polite, well spoken, educated, but could she trust him? Was he the kind of man she needed to get her to Buzzard Creek, where Cade's claim lay? She looked covertly around. The street was filled with men, tough-looking men in denim pants and leather jackets, men with a week's growth of beard and tobacco juice staining their whiskers. They smelled like unwashed animals and their talk was rough. As she passed, she caught portions of their conversations, filled with swear words and remarks about women.

"Goddamn mule gave out on me, so I shot her in the head and then ate—"

"She had legs like a chicken, pardner, but shit, those breasts of hers . . . Why, a man could get lost—"

"You goin' over to the Countess's place tonight? Heard she's got some new girls from Paris, France—"

Sarah walked faster. She couldn't bear to hire a man like those she saw on the street. Sanchez with his snide remarks and posturing and condescending ways to women had been hard enough to take, but at least he'd gotten them safely across Panama. Henry Corneale, though he didn't look like much of a frontiersman, appeared to be a gentleman who wouldn't offend her with rough language or unseemly behavior. A doctor, with his fine education, should be a cut above some of the miners she saw in the street, although it seemed strange to her that he'd willingly give up such a noble profession. Maybe she could talk confidentially to his employer; maybe she could find out about him . . . all secretly, so Meg wouldn't know what she was doing.

Whatever she decided, she'd have to act quickly.

She'd lost too many days in Panama to waste any more time in San Francisco.

When Lobo left the Fort, as he liked to call it, he took two men with him: Charlie because he was loyal, and Cade because he was amusing. He enjoyed Cade as much as he enjoyed anything, though he understood that eventually he would have to kill him. Cade knew far too much ever to be trusted out of sight now, though Lobo had to credit him for not going soft on his first—and only—job. That one would have been a test of character for the most seasoned professional, and Cade had passed.

Cade had a fatal weakness, of course. Lobo had realized from the beginning that he lacked the inner fortitude to endure for the long term. In the meantime, however, Cade Deveraux was the first man he had met since crossing the Divide who knew who William Shakespeare was, and that was an interesting diversion. In many ways he reminded Lobo of the lost indulgences of his youth.

Cade had another refreshing characteristic: he asked questions no one else in Lobo's employ was brave enough, or stupid enough, to ask. Every time he did so, Charlie gave him a look that would have silenced a wiser man, but Lobo indulged him as he would a precocious child.

Lobo stepped away from the trail marker he had left near the stream and led his horse back into the shadow of the woods, where the pine-needle-strewn ground would hide his tracks. There he had instructed the other two to wait.

Leaning back in the saddle, Cade said, "Pardon my ignorance, but it looks like nothing but a bunch of rocks and sticks to me. You say it's supposed to mean something?"

He received another one of those killing looks from Charlie, but Lobo just smiled. "To a trail-wise man, those rocks and sticks read just like writing on a page."

Cade watched as he exchanged the soft, distinctively stitched moccasins for a pair of boots.

"And those moccasins are the signature?"

"That's right."

"Why do you want him to think you're an Indian? For that matter, why are you leaving him a map to find us with? Why don't we just ride back up the trail and find *him?*"

Charlie growled, "You ask too many damn questions, son."

"But valid ones, Charles," Lobo responded easily. He tucked his moccasins into his saddlebag and removed his rifle from the scabbard. Cade watched him warily. "A little curiosity is good for the soul."

He glanced up at Cade. "I don't suppose you do much hunting around New Orleans, now do you?"

"Some," Cade admitted. "Water birds, deer—that kind of thing. For sport."

Lobo smiled. "Sport. That's exactly what I'm talking about. Making the game more interesting. You see, I've been hunting this particular man for almost a decade now. I thought it was only fair that he be allowed to hunt me for a short while in return. Before I kill him, of course," he added matter-of-factly.

"Of course," murmured Cade.

"It's all about control, you see. I will pick the time, I will pick the place, and I will be in control. Disguising myself as an Indian only confuses him, you see, and buys me an extra measure of control. Confusing the enemy is a time-honored strategy in many great battle plans."

Cade was silent for a time, digesting this. He jerked his head toward the marker. "What does it say?"

"It warns of poison water, and points the way toward fresh."

"But the water's not poisoned," Cade pointed out. "We just watered our horses there. If he's smart enough to read the trail marker, isn't he smart enough to figure out the water's clean?"

Lobo just smiled. "By the time he arrives, the water will be quite undrinkable, I'm afraid. So, sadly, will be the stream after that, and the one after that. Now, gentlemen, if it won't trouble you too much to come with me, we have work to do."

An hour later, Lobo watched as Cade and Charlie dumped the carcass of a freshly killed deer into the stream, and understanding finally dawned in Cade's eyes. It really was a pity about Cade, reflected Lobo. He wasn't smart enough to be of any real use to the operation, but he was far too smart to live. Lobo would be sorry to see him go.

Chapter Thirteen

"Why are you dressed like that, Aunt Sarah?"
Guiltily Sarah spun around to meet the inquisitive eyes of her niece. "Don't sneak up on people!" She hadn't meant to snap, but Fiona had taken her by surprise.

"I didn't sneak. I was just walking down the hall and your door was partly open." Instead of being apologetic, Fiona stood in the doorway looking at her with a slightly accusatory expression on her face. "I didn't know you liked to wear trousers."

"I don't—well, I do when I'm going horseback riding. Like this morning." Sarah was irritated for having to make excuses to an eight-year-old. "I thought you left with your mama and papa to go to school."

Fiona walked into the room and sat down on a low walnut rocker. She didn't take her clear blue eyes off Sarah. "Today is a saint's day. The nuns are praying, and we can't have school. Mama and Papa left without me."

Sarah attempted to distract her. "So you go to Catholic school. That must be . . . nice," she finished lamely.

"Umm, it's all right. Papa says they're the best teachers in San Francisco. Why aren't you wearing a riding habit? He's going to buy me one when I get my pony. That's what Papa says ladies wear." Fiona wasn't easily deterred.

"I don't have one, so I thought I'd ride in these clothes today. Maybe I'll buy a habit," Sarah said. She felt guilty lying to a child, but she had no choice. She knew that Fiona would repeat their conversation to Sheldon or Meg at the first opportunity.

"Where did you get a horse? We only have two, and they're hitched to the carriage today."

Sarah gritted her teeth. "I'm renting one. I like to ride early in the morning when it's still cool. It's the best time of day."

"Oh," said Fiona, leaning back in the chair, her legs stuck out in front of her, her position indicating she wasn't about to leave the room.

Sarah made one more attempt to win over the child. She knelt down beside the chair. "Let's play a game, Fiona."

"Maybe . . ." The blue eyes were wary and watchful.

"Let's pretend you didn't see me this morning. If you didn't see me, you can't say anything to Monserrat or Tonio about my going riding."

Fiona's face didn't change expression. "Tonio's not here."

"Then Monserrat, and when Mama and Papa come home and ask about me this evening, then you can tell them that I've gone riding and I left a note for them."

"Why are you going on such a long ride? Won't you be back for supper?"

Sarah cursed the fact that her sister had reared such

a tenacious child. She got to her feet and slipped on the deerskin jacket she'd bought the day before. "It's a very long ride, Fiona."

The little girl was very serious. "I don't think you're telling me the truth, Aunt Sarah. The nuns say that lying is a sin. You might go to Hell."

Sarah propped the note she'd written against the mirror and picked up the broad-brimmed hat she'd purchased along with the other clothes. "You're probably right, Fiona, but there's nothing I can do about it now." She leaned down and gave the little girl a hug. "Wish me luck on my ride and tell your mama that I love her."

Dr. Henry Corneale realized he was in deep trouble. He knew very little about the route to the goldfields in general and Buzzard Creek in particular, and he knew nothing about life on the trail, since he'd spent his entire life in cities. The bad news was that his employer, Mrs. Sarah Kincaid Deveraux, was fast becoming aware of his incompetence.

He kicked dirt over the fire that he'd struggled to make when they stopped for lunch in a grove of willows, and looked surreptitiously at her under the brim of his new hat. During the morning ride, he'd learned that she'd grown up on a farm on the Illinois frontier and then spent years in Kansas Territory, where her sister and brother-in-law ran a horse ranch. She'd told him that she'd ridden into Cheyenne Indian camps to trade horses, information which made him even less secure about his own wilderness survival skills. The damn woman probably knew a hundredfold more than he did about horses, camping, and finding a trail, and she was the kind, he judged, who wouldn't mind letting him know how smart she was.

Sarah got up from the fallen log on which she'd been sitting, brushing away the dry leaves and twigs from her trousers. She'd thought carefully about attire and decided, since the trail wasn't safe for women, that traveling as a man was the wisest thing to do. Her hair was still short and could be tucked beneath her hat, and she'd always ridden astride as a young girl. It wasn't until she became a Deveraux that she'd worn her first riding habit and used a sidesaddle, but her preference still was to ride straddle. She tried not to imagine what Emilie Deveraux Gallier would think; practicality sometimes had to triumph over gentility.

She didn't particularly like horses—or any other animals. She had grown up with an excess of them on her mother's farm in Cairo and at her sister's ranch. Sarah always resented the time and attention animals took, and of all animals, she thought horses were the stupidest. Still, out of necessity she'd become a good rider, and she sat her horse well.

She was a much better rider than Henry Corneale, something she'd noticed a few miles outside the city. Their business arrangement had started out auspiciously that morning, when they'd met at a livery stable where he'd purchased the horses and filled their saddlebags with supplies needed for the journey. To Sarah's inquiries at the Colonnade, Corneale's employer had responded that the man was dependable, didn't use liquor to excess, and kept mostly to himself. That recommendation had spurred her to take on Corneale as her guide, and he'd done well in the initial planning of their secret escape.

However, as the sun rose higher in the sky and their trek continued, Sarah's doubts about him began to grow. He might be a gentleman, but did he know where he was going? The gold hills weren't that far from the

city, but because of the bay and various intervening
creeks and rivers, the trail was convoluted and twisting,
and the trip could take three to five days. A long time,
Sarah thought, to be with a man who wasn't sure on
the trail. Even her sister Kitty had more trail sense than
Corneale. She wiped off her tin plate and fork and
walked toward the horses. Now, she decided, was the
time to confront Henry Corneale.

"Time to mount up, Mrs. Deveraux. We have a few
more hours of daylight left."

Sarah put her utensils in the saddlebag and checked
the strap carefully, but she didn't get on her horse. "Do
you have any idea where we are, Doctor? We should be
riding away from the sun, toward the east. Even I know
the direction of the gold camps."

"The trail turns back on itself, as you know, Mrs.
Deveraux. I have a map, and I can read it."

She gave a sarcastic sniff and glanced around. "It
doesn't look to me like anyone has been on this supposed trail of yours. I think we're lost. As a matter of
fact, I don't think you have an idea in blazes where we
are."

Henry bit back the sharp answer he wanted to give.
"It's time to mount up," he repeated quietly.

"Mount up? For what? To ride in circles? I'm not
getting on that horse until I know where I'm going. I
didn't pay good money to get lost."

It came to him suddenly how much he disliked the
woman. He admired her sister for being a successful
businesswoman; even with her grand airs and slightly
patronizing manner, Meg Kincaid seemed to adhere to
the philosophy of live and let live. But this one . . . She
was controlling, argumentative, and determined to be
right. And, unfortunately, she was exactly right about
him. He wasn't sure where they were. The map was

hard to read, with its squiggling, twisting lines and funny little marks—not like a city map at all, where streets were laid out in a logical grid pattern.

He took the horse's bridle and began walking, not looking back to see if she was following. Sarah called out after him, but he paid no attention. He saw a path, a continuation of the one he'd been following. There was nothing to do but keep on going. He didn't have another plan. He climbed onto his horse, which he'd chosen for its docile manner, and kicked at its fat belly with his heels, but the horse was much more interested in grazing in a patch of tender grass than obeying its rider. Henry kicked again, harder, and this time the animal moved.

Henry refused to look back to see if Sarah was behind him. He decided he didn't care and kept on riding.

Sarah was in a better mood when they made camp that evening. They'd come across two miners heading to San Francisco from the hills, and Henry had confirmed that he and Sarah were riding in the right direction. If they kept on toward the Sacramento River, eventually they'd run into Buzzard Creek, which branched off to the northeast.

Sarah volunteered to cook, and as she dished up the beans and cut slices from the loaf of bread he'd bought, she made an attempt at conversation. The atmosphere between them had grown colder and more distant as the day progressed.

"When I was younger, I used to eat on the trail fairly often. I hated it!" She laughed.

Henry looked up at her. She had a nice laugh, full of joy and youth. She'd taken off her hat, and her hair curled around her face. He'd been surprised when she'd turned up in men's clothing, but after he got used to the garb, he realized how sensible it was for her. She seemed totally unselfconscious about her attire and had been amused when one of the miners on the trail had called her "son." She'd laughed then, too, as if she'd put a joke over on everyone. She was very young, he realized, no more than twenty-two or -three. At thirty-three, he felt old.

She waited for his response. When there was none, she kept on talking. "I wish I could recapture those days. They were so innocent and carefree, and I never appreciated them. Do you ever feel like that, Doctor? That you'd like to recapture the past?" She took her plate of food and sat down, leaning against a tree.

"Henry, just call me Henry. I'm not a doctor anymore. Please don't call me that!" He couldn't control the anger in his voice.

Sarah gazed at him levelly across the fire. Her voice was quiet and determined. "Would you like to explain to me why not? It was my impression that a physician took the oath for life."

His jaw tightened and a multitude of emotions warred in his eyes. He put his plate and cup down. "I gave up the right to be called a physician when I lost my first patient."

"Every doctor loses patients," Sarah said gently. "There's no reason to—"

"This patient was my wife. She had a tumor. I waited too long to operate. I should have saved her, but I couldn't. She was only twenty."

The anguish on his face was awful to behold. Sarah didn't know what to say, so she said nothing.

"I lied about being robbed," he went on in a cool, flat tone. "I barely had enough money to get to California, and I was lucky to find a job at that restaurant. I just wanted to get away—from the memories, from the people who knew me, from being a doctor. I made a mistake and let it slip, what I'd been back east. It got around the restaurant, and I knew I'd have to leave there, too. The gold camps seemed like an easy place for a man to get lost."

"And you really knew nothing about the trails to the camps."

He didn't look at her. "I think we've established that."

Sarah took a deep breath and released it slowly. "Well," she said at last, "I daresay you're not the first man to come west to escape his past. Yet I can't help but wish you'd told me sooner."

He looked at her for a long time in silence. His expression was impossible to read, but it left Sarah feeling as though she had said the wrong thing, or should say something further. It was a very uncomfortable feeling.

Then he said, "Good night, Mrs. Deveraux."

He turned and stretched out on his bedroll, pulling the blanket over his shoulder and facing away from her. The conversation was unmistakably at an end, and Sarah was left to watch the flames alone.

Chapter Fourteen

Times were hard in Cairo, Illinois. The grandiose promises of the 1830s and 1840s lay fallow and unfulfilled. The Cairo City and Canal Company, which had floated a scheme to dig a canal between the Ohio and Mississippi rivers, went bankrupt in 1846; the Illinois Central Railroad never established its projected line from Cairo to Chicago; and the town's one bank, the National Credit Office, closed its doors and fell into disrepair. Under the blazing glare of the sun, the town seemed to be enveloped in a torporific slumber.

But to Katherine Carlyle Kincaid, the low-lying delta land was home, and she had no desire to leave the farm that she and her husband had carved out of the wilderness. Her homestead was self-sufficient, and on the rare occasions when she needed to trade for store goods, the small lean-to shops near the river served her adequately. The great rush of settlers who had once traveled down the Ohio and reprovisioned in Cairo for the trip west had slowed to a trickle. Other routes were now more popular. But traffic on the Mississippi was growing, and

195

steamboats snorting black smoke against the sky stopped regularly to take on supplies and restoke their furnaces from the abundant forests that surrounded Cairo.

One enterprising citizen, who refused to be daunted by the downturn in Cairo's economic affairs, built a large three-story frame building overlooking the Mississippi. It served as the town's inn, saloon, post office, and meeting hall, and its third-floor balcony was the best spot from which to watch for steamboats approaching the town.

"You can't wish that boat to move any faster, Ma." Katherine's daughter Amity came to stand beside her. "They'll be here. Don't worry."

"I'm not worried, I'm just excited and anxious. It's been fourteen years since I've seen my little Kitty, and now she's coming home with her own children."

"I hardly remember her," Amity said. "I was five when she left to go west with Uncle Boothe. I remember her hair, though—all yellow and curly. The only one in the family who didn't have red hair."

Katherine's own red hair was streaked with gray; a year away from her fiftieth birthday, she was still a handsome woman, strong and straight, proud of carriage, able to work from sunup to sundown. She'd been a widow since 1837, and alone she had reared her family and run the farm. She'd had suitors over the years, like Oliver Sherrod, who operated a dry goods store across the Mississippi in Missouri and had wanted desperately to marry her, but there had been only one man in Katherine's life, her husband, Byrd Kincaid.

Like her intrepid grandmother Fiona Carlyle before her, Katherine had chosen to remain a widow and to live her life on her own terms. When she looked back over the years, despite the losses and the pain, despite the fact that four of her beloved children had left home, she was content with her life.

There were two children remaining in Cairo—Amity, her last daughter; and Luke, the youngest, although at seventeen, he hated to be called the baby of the family. "Where is Luke?" Katherine asked. "I want him here when Kitty and the children arrive."

"He saw some friends down on the levee," Amity answered. "He'll keep his eyes open for the steamboat. Don't worry, Ma!"

"All right, all right." Katherine shaded her eyes with her hand against the sun and watched as a big stern-wheeler turned slowly toward Cairo. The *Liberty Bell*. That was Kitty's boat. She felt a lump in her throat and the sting of tears in her eyes. Soon, soon, she'd hold her Kitty again and for the first time nestle Hilda and Carrie and little Ben in her arms.

Kitty was not Katherine's birth child, but she was very much the child of her heart. Kitty had been born in 1820 on a wilderness trail when Katherine had been leading a group of women and children to safety after the wrecking of their river barge. Hilda Werner, Kitty's mother, had died in childbirth, and Katherine had sworn to take the baby and raise her as her own. True to her promise, she and Byrd had made Kitty part of their family. Then in 1837, Kitty had left home, gone west with Katherine's brother, Boothe Carlyle, and Ben Adamson, the man who would become her husband.

Katherine often thought that Kitty was more like her than any of her birth children. After her early years of wandering, Kitty had chosen to stay in one place, at her horse ranch in the Flint Hills of Kansas Territory; there she was rearing her children and making a home in the wilderness, just as Katherine had done in Cairo. Unlike the other Kincaid offspring, Kitty seemed to have found her niche in the world.

Katherine's other children—all except Amity—had the Kincaid wanderlust, and there was nothing Katherine could do about it. Luke was already talking about going to Kansas with Kitty and helping out on the horse ranch. He'd never been west of the Mississippi, and he admitted to his mother that he didn't think he could stay still for much longer. There was too much of the world he wanted to see, and Katherine knew she couldn't hold him.

Her older son, Jim, had been like that. At seventeen, he'd taken off to make his way in the world, and he'd never come back. Katherine sighed. She worried about Jim. Even though he'd married, he still seemed unsettled to her, without roots. Like Boothe, she thought. She hoped that Jim would settle down in California with his sisters. Katherine liked that idea—three of her children being together.

Amity called out to her. "I'm going to walk down to the wharf, Mama. Are you coming?"

"Just a minute, honey. I want to watch the boat come in."

Katherine looked after Amity's retreating back. All her natural-born daughters were different from one another—and none of them were like her. Still home at nineteen, Amity was the quietest and most thoughtful. She seemed content to stay with Katherine and make a life in Cairo. She wanted to be a teacher, but she'd refused to go to Teachers' Training School in Memphis because she hadn't wanted to leave home. Now she helped out with the younger children in the schoolhouse and seemed happy with her life. Selfishly, Katherine was pleased to have Amity with her. She couldn't bear to think how lonely she'd be if all her children left her.

There had been no doubt, of course, that Meg would leave Cairo at the first opportunity. She'd run away with a totally unsuitable man to St. Louis, left him, taken off up the Missouri River, and ended up with Sheldon Gerrard.

At first Katherine had been shocked and horrified. Sheldon Gerrard had been the mortal enemy of her brother, Boothe; their enmity had begun in 1835, when Boothe had led Gerrard's ill-fated wagon train toward Oregon Territory. Gerrard always blamed Boothe for its failure and for the loss of his leg on the trek. Gerrard had spent years trying to get even with Boothe but had only ended up a failure himself. Somehow his meeting with Meg had changed both their fortunes, and they'd built a partnership and provided a family for Meg's child, Fiona.

Fiona was a beautiful child; Katherine knew that from the photograph that had recently arrived. Despite what Meg wrote about her relationship with Sheldon Gerrard, Katherine thought the three looked very much like a family—a proudly beaming Sheldon; Fiona, happy and bright-faced; and Meg, confident and commanding.

Meg had always been ambitious, restless, and opinionated; Katherine had no doubt that her daughter would build a successful life in San Francisco. Sarah, though also restless, was different. She, too, had disliked Cairo and wanted to leave; she'd always longed for what her brother Jim jokingly called "the finer things of life." Luke had teased her, too, and called her "Princess" and "Your Highness," sending Sarah into temper fits, which only made Luke tease her more fiercely. Imaginative, fiery, and emotional, Sarah had never been one to hide her feelings.

She had daydreamed about living in a fine house

with a wealthy, handsome husband, being waited on hand and foot by servants, and having only to ask to make her wishes come true. By her maneuvering and manipulation of the Gallier family, she'd made it happen. For a while Sarah had all that she'd dreamed of, but now Katherine wondered what would happen to her spoiled, though loving, daughter in the rough-and-tumble world of California. She could only hope that the innate values that had been instilled in all her children would triumph, and help Sarah survive.

The *Liberty Bell* gave three more blasts, and Katherine hurried down the steps toward the boat that was bringing her daughter Kitty home.

"There she is!" Kitty shouted over the noise of the whistle's blast. "Look, girls, there's Grandma Katherine and . . . Luke? Could that be Luke? He's so tall, and little Amity— Oh, Lord."

"Don't cry, Mother. Your face will be all puffy," Carrie admonished. "You should be happy."

Kitty tried to control her son, Ben, struggling in her arms. "I am happy. Oh, I haven't been this happy in a long, long time. Look at Grandma! Isn't she beautiful?"

Kitty did not hesitate to push herself and her children to the head of the line; they were the first down the gangplank, Kitty running ahead and flinging herself into her mother's arms, almost crushing a startled Ben between them.

"Oh, Mama, Mama—"

"Kitty, my baby—"

They hugged tightly, tears mingling, laughing and crying at the same time. Ben was transferred to his aunt Amity's arms, where he squealed noisily. For the moment, Katherine paid no attention; all she could think of was holding her beloved Kitty in her arms again.

"Look at you," she crooned, cupping her daughter's face in her hands.

She felt a tug on her arm and then another, and looked down into the serious face of her granddaughter Hilda. "Aren't you going to hug me, Grandma? I've waited a long time." Hilda was tall for her age and thin, and her long blond hair was plaited into two shiny braids.

Katherine swept both girls into her arms. "I'm going to hug both of you. In fact, I'm not going to stop hugging you all day." She looked at Kitty. "They are beautiful children, Kitty. Thank you for bringing them home." She held out her arms to Ben, who went immediately to his grandmother; he'd stopped crying, but his fat cheeks glistened with tears. Katherine fluffed his brown curls with her fingers. "He looks just like his papa. Ben was the cutest little boy—"

Kitty stood with one arm around Amity and another around Luke. "Look at these two. Luke is so tall—I bet you're taller than Jim."

Luke nodded proudly.

"And Amity—all grown up and so pretty." Kitty gave her sister a squeeze. "I've told the girls you were a teacher and could help them with their lessons. We don't have a teacher in the whole territory," she explained, "and you know I was never much of a scholar."

"Papa does most of the teaching," Carrie added.

"And I bet he does real fine," Katherine said. "His mama was a teacher, right here in Cairo."

"Grandma Caroline," Carrie said. "I'm named for her. She got shot."

Katherine frowned at Kitty, who shrugged and said, "I always tell the children the truth. They know about Pa and Miz Caroline getting shot. After all, it's family history. Let me have Ben, Mama. I'm used to carrying him, but he's too heavy for you."

"Don't you dare, Kitty Adamson," Katherine answered in mock irritation. "I've carried babies fatter than this. Now let's get your luggage loaded in that wagon and get on home."

"Home," Kitty said. "What a wonderful word. Isn't it funny that the place you grew up in is somehow always home?"

"I thought you liked our house, Ma," Hilda accused. "It's very nice—all made of rocks," she explained to her grandmother.

"I love our house, you know that," Kitty said, "but Mama's house is . . . special."

Katherine gave her daughter's hand a squeeze. "I hope that never changes—for any of my children."

Luke drove the wagon and the girls sat beside him. Kitty, the baby, Amity, and Katherine scrambled in the back amid the luggage. "I thought you might want to see what Cairo's looking like these days. The streets still aren't paved, but we've got some planked sidewalks now."

"And there's talk of the railroad running a spur in here," Luke called out over his shoulder.

"Oh, there's been talk of a railroad spur coming to Cairo for years," Amity said dismissively.

Luke ignored her. "It's going to happen this time. Wouldn't that be something, a railroad train coming right into Cairo? Why, you could buy a ticket to anywhere, I bet."

"Anywhere that has a railroad," Amity corrected. "You can't ride a train across the Mississippi River!"

"Not yet, but someday. Isn't that right, Kitty?" Luke asked pleadingly.

She looked at Katherine and smiled. "I wouldn't be surprised, Luke. The West's changing mighty fast."

They'd left the town's meager main street and were driving toward the Ohio River, along the curving tree-shaded road that led toward Katherine's farm.

"New levees, Kitty," Luke called out. "The Ohio broke through the old ones last year. Lor-dee, did we have a flood."

Katherine waved away the alarmed look on Kitty's face. "No worse than usual. The bottom pastureland was flooded out, but nothing else. The house is fine, Kitty."

She sighed with relief. "You don't know how much I want to see it, Mama. Is the apple orchard still there? And the garden?"

"Still there, strong and healthy. I have magnolia trees now, too. Sarah sent me seedlings from Deveraux House, and they're doing right well. The blossoms smell so sweet—well, you'll see."

Kitty looked at the familiar scene that was passing by—the rutted dirt road shaded by willows and oaks, elms and cottonwood; the split-rail fence that indicated the beginning of Kincaid land; the lazy hum of bees; the swarming gnats caught in a brilliant shaft of sunlight. She felt content and excited at the same time, and hundreds of memories flooded over her.

"Remember when Ben and Boothe and I set out fourteen years ago, you made us pies to take—"

"Of course I remember." Little Ben had fallen into an exhausted sleep in his grandmother's arms, and Katherine rocked him gently. "I've already cooked up a batch of pies. They're in the pie safe, just waiting."

"Did you hear that, girls? Apple pies tonight!" Kitty bounced up and down with excitement, much to the dismay of her daughters.

"Mo-thur, you're acting like a little girl!" Carrie chastised.

Kitty and Katherine caught each other's eyes and burst into laughter. "She *is* a little girl—at least to me," Katherine said. "My little girl who's come home at last."

Chapter Fifteen

Marie LaFleur knew immediately that San Francisco was her kind of town. New Orleans had always seemed like a great lady, jaded and sadly past her prime, covering her age with paints and powders, pretending that she was forever young. In San Francisco, there was no need for pretense. The city was youthful and vigorous and made fresh each day by the hundreds of settlers who arrived filled with hope and looking for the Promised Land.

Frisco was a place where Marie could re-create herself; what did the past matter when everything around her seemed so new? She'd worked hard in Panama City and done some things she wasn't proud of, but she figured she'd gotten her money as honestly as anyone else. Luck had been with her. One of the patrons of the Crescent City had decided to stay in Panama and open his own saloon, and after a night of persuasion he'd sold his steamer ticket to Marie.

When she arrived in San Francisco, she rented a room in a rambling frame hotel which she considered a firetrap, but the price was right and meals were included. That first afternoon, she walked around Portsmouth Square and observed what was going on. She saw no sign of Sarah Deveraux, but she was certain the red-haired woman who was busy giving orders to workmen at a newly constructed saloon was Meg Kincaid. She wasn't sure why she put off going to see the Kincaid woman that very day; Marie usually wasn't hesitant or indecisive. Maybe it was because Meg Kincaid seemed to have everything, and right now Marie had little but the clothes on her back and a few dollars sewed into her camisole top.

She approached Meg Kincaid the next morning. The day was bright and breezy, and gulls swooped and screamed over the streets that led toward Portsmouth Square. Wind whipped up the water in the bay and brought with it the sharp scent of the sea. Marie needed both hands to anchor her new bonnet of red satin ribbons and her Spanish shawl, which she'd thrown across her shoulders. The breeze was fresh and invigorating, and as different from the humid heat of New Orleans and Panama as night from day.

Windblown and out of breath, Marie arrived at Meg's establishment. The saloon—or opera house— looked huge to her. It was three stories high, with a grand staircase sweeping up from the ground floor to balconied rooms above. Fancy columns of carved wood held up the balconies, and a team of painters was applying the final touches of blue-and-gold paint to the scrolls along the tops of the columns. The place was by no means complete, but Marie could get the feel of it, even with sawhorses and stacks of boards cluttering the floor. It was elegant and grand—just like the woman who owned it.

Meg, wearing a dress of gray taffeta and a smart

black hat, was busy giving orders to the men who were installing a long mahogany bar. She saw Marie but didn't acknowledge her presence. Marie wasn't bothered by that. She didn't expect Meg to drop everything and rush over to a stranger.

When Meg finished her detailed instructions, she approached Marie with a cool "Yes?"

There was definitely a family resemblance, Marie thought. The same red hair and blue eyes, but the shape of her face was different. Meg's chin was squarer and more determined, and her eyes were harder than Sarah's, and not as playful.

Marie held out her hand. "I'm Marie LaFleur. I was with your sister in Panama. I guess she's gone on to the goldfields."

Meg ignored the proffered hand. "She certainly has gone! Sneaked off, more like it. I'm really quite angry with her."

"Oh." This wasn't at all the response Marie had expected. She tried again. "Well, I guess she was in a hurry to find that handsome husband of hers."

Meg's eyes grew even colder. "Oh, yes, the handsome and good-for-nothing Mr. Deveraux. I assume you knew him in New Orleans. Sarah mentioned the Verandah."

"I used to work there," Marie said. She wasn't going to deny to anyone who she was or what she'd been.

"I also assume that Cade used to gamble there, which is what he's probably doing in every gold town in California. I really could wring my little sister's neck," Meg said angrily. "Running off and leaving me a note—dressed like a man, my daughter tells me!"

Marie couldn't stifle her laughter. Sarah, dressed like a man again! What a sight that must have been.

Meg's look was censorious. "I remember that you

and your friend were the ones who concocted that whole male-impersonation scheme to get her here."

"It worked, didn't it? Your little sister showed up in Frisco. In fact, I think it was a pretty damned good idea."

Meg ignored that. "Where's the other one? Leeanne, or something? I know both of you were with her in Panama. Sarah said both of you would be coming on to California."

"Lisanne." Marie grinned broadly. "She didn't come with me." Her grin blossomed into a chuckle. "Lisanne's done gone and got herself married!"

"Married? Who to?" Meg seemed more stunned than curious.

"Why, to Mr. Michael O'Donal, that's who."

"You're not serious, surely. The man you robbed and tied up—Sarah told me the whole story."

"Well, since you know most of it anyway, I might as well tell you the rest." Marie shrugged. "After Mike got over being so damned mad he'd have spit nails if he could, he calmed down and took a liking to Lisanne. He moved in with us at the hotel for a while, got himself a job so he could buy a new ticket—"

"And fell in love with a . . . a . . ."

"*Whore's* the word you're looking for, Miz Kincaid. He ain't the first man and he won't be the last, and who among us, I wonder, is so fine as to cast stones? Who can judge what somebody has to do to survive in this world?" Marie saw Meg flush and knew she'd hit a nerve with the other woman. It gave her a grim satisfaction to know she'd finally found a sore spot in Meg's tough hide.

"So they got married and decided to head back to Philadelphia," Marie went on. "Seems as though Mike owed his folks some money that he needed to pay back.

Lisanne's a good girl. She just needed a good man and some loving. I think they'll do fine. Just like I think Sarah and Cade will do all right, too, once she finds him."

"I don't share your optimism, I'm afraid, Miss LaFleur." Meg glanced down at the watch pinned to her lapel. "Now, if you could tell me what you want." It wasn't a question; her words were a royal command.

Marie took a deep breath. After her frigid reception, she knew what Meg's response would be, but she'd be damned if she'd let the cold bitch stop her from even asking. "Sarah said you might be willing to help me out. With a job. I'm looking for a new line of work and you've got this fine saloon—"

"Opera house," Meg snapped.

"And there's a lot I could do to help."

"I'm not planning to conduct a house of prostitution, Miss LaFleur. My opera house will be high-toned, high-class, and above reproach. I'm afraid—"

Marie's cheeks flamed with anger. "I wasn't applying for a job as a whore, Miz Kincaid. Just like you and a lot of other people, I want to start over out here in California. I want a new life, too. Sarah and I were as close as sisters, and she was the one who said to look you up and see if you'd help me out, but I might as well be asking a rattlesnake for help. You are nothing like your sister! She's got a heart as big as all outdoors."

"Thank God I'm not like her!" Meg shot back. "Making friends with all kinds and falling in love—"

"And you've never been in love?" Marie gave a disparaging snort. "What about that man you've lived with all these years? Don't think Sarah didn't tell me about her fine sister and Mr. Sheldon Gerrard."

"Love has nothing to do with our relationship, if it's any of your business, and it's not." Meg took a shaky breath and struggled for control. "Our conversation is over, Miss LaFleur. If you're looking for a place to work, go find Yancey Connor or Tim Drayton or some of that kind. They run saloons and gambling casinos. Your kind of place."

Without a word, Marie picked up the hem of her skirt and stomped out of the opera house without looking back. Meg sagged against a column. What had come over her? she wondered. There'd been no need to attack Sarah's friend because she wanted a job. A workman approached, a questioning look on his face, and Meg waved him away. She needed time to pull herself together, to become once more the cool and competent and thoroughly in control Meg Kincaid, owner and operator of San Francisco's finest opera house.

Marie brought back all kinds of memories to Meg, unpleasant, painful memories which she'd stuffed into the corner of her mind and tried to forget. She'd once been like Marie, desperate, without friends or family in a strange town, looking for a way to support herself, struggling to start a new life, totally dependent on strangers. Being a woman alone in the West was not only frightening but also dangerous. She could very well have ended up a prostitute working in a saloon—except for a twist of fate that had brought her into the path of Sheldon Gerrard.

Meg walked to the door and drew in long draughts of fresh air. She didn't want Marie around to remind her of her past, of what might have been. It wasn't fair that Sarah had gotten herself tangled up with a woman of the streets and then sent her to Meg to redeem. Well, she wasn't going to do it! Marie would have to make it on her own just as Meg had.

Of course, Meg reminded herself as she turned back

toward the workmen, she hadn't been alone for a long, long time. She'd had Sheldon.

Meg had been right. Yancey Connor hired Marie on the spot. She thought about turning the job down; Connor was a slimy bastard, she knew that from the first meeting, but she needed the work. She'd be waiting tables in his saloon, talking to the men, and making them feel at home. "Loosening them up to gamble a little," Connor had said. "And if you want to make a little money after work—"

Marie didn't, but she didn't say that to Connor. She didn't want him to know anything about her private life, and she tried to stay out of his. But she couldn't help overhearing bits and snippets of Connor's conversations with his henchmen, talk about how he planned to take over the whole of Portsmouth Square someday. He was full of hot air, Marie thought, a bragging windbag, his head filled with schemes that would never come to pass.

The money was good at the Golden Horseshoe; miners loved to outdo one another in tips, and that was fine with her. She'd save up a nest egg and then she'd do what Meg Kincaid was doing. She'd open her own place, maybe a nice restaurant or a little shop. She'd bide her time and save her money.

She was sorry it had ended so badly with Meg, but the woman was a coldhearted bitch and there was no way to excuse her. Oh, sure, Sarah had been stuck-up and spoiled when Marie had first met her, too, but her heart was good. Anyone could tell that. But Meg—ice water surely must run in her veins. Sadly, she was the only contact Marie had with Sarah, and she wanted to know how her friend was faring in the goldfields.

Maybe that man of Meg's, Sheldon Gerrard, was a little more human. Marie thought she might look him up sometime, just for the hell of it. She'd like to meet the man who could put up with years of Meg Kincaid.

Chapter Sixteen

Annabelle Williams awoke to the quiet and terrible certainty that she was alone. She lay on the thin corn-shuck mattress and stared at the inside of the canvas wagon top, straining for some sound from the outside that might prove her premonition false. There was none.

Grafton had insisted that they leave the wagon train as soon as he learned the wagon master intended to take them through the Sierras by way of the Carson route rather than by the shorter, though somewhat riskier, Donner route. He had been warned of the dangers, not only of the route but also of trying to brave them alone. The hazards of the trail could prove deadly for someone who did not know how to negotiate or avoid them. Grafton, of course, had not listened.

When they had left their home in Pennsylvania for the promise of the Golden Shores, it had been in search of a better life for both of them, and for their unborn child. Grafton had never been much of a farmer, but he was sure he would strike it rich in the goldfields. They had planned to reach California in time to stake a claim and get a little house up before the baby came. Then Grafton would go off to work the claim while Annabelle stayed home with the child. Every cent they had and all they could borrow had gone into financing this expedition.

The rigors of the journey wore heavily on Grafton. In many ways it was harder on him than on Annabelle, for though she suffered physically, he had to bear both the physical and the mental burdens. Their meager savings went quickly. They used up supplies faster than anticipated and had to replace a wagon wheel at Ash Hollow. They lost two oxen in the desert, and Grafton had pulled a gun on one of their fellow travelers to force him to sell them his spare ox. It was at that point, Annabelle supposed, that she realized her husband was no longer the man with whom she had begun this journey.

The closer to California they got, the more stories they heard of the fabulous riches that were waiting for them. Annabelle could scarcely credit most of them—nuggets as big as a hen's eggs, for example, that were strewn along the ground just outside Sutter's Fort. She begged Grafton not to believe the stories either. But she could see him change day by day, and what had begun as a hopeful plan for a new chance in the West soon became an obsession, and then a mania.

The wagon train moved much too slowly for Grafton. He had heard that the best claims were being snatched up daily; what would be left for them by the time they finally arrived? With each mile they traveled he seemed to slip deeper into the clutches of gold fever. He had never been a perfect husband or even a particularly good provider, but until this point he had at least been reasonable.

During the nightmare of the Forty-Mile Desert, Annabelle had seen him stand guard all night over a barrel of water when children in the next wagon were crying of thirst. She had seen him drive their oxen until they died in their traces, and once, when she swooned from the heat and her advancing pregnancy, he might have left her there in the sand had not the man in the wagon behind them rushed to her aid. For the man's charity, Grafton had threatened him violently with an iron awl for daring to lay hands on his wife.

They called it gold fever, but it was not a fever at all. It was madness.

Grafton was convinced that as soon as they reached California, gold would practically pour from the sky into his open hands. He was equally convinced that every day they delayed, someone else was collecting the gold that should be his.

He insisted he couldn't afford the delay of the Carson Route, even though people warned him that trying to get the wagon through the steepest parts of the trail alone would be a much slower process than staying with the train on the longer route. Even though there were rumors of Indian troubles, and the story of that horrible massacre at Donner Lake had haunted them all since Fort Bridger. Even though Annabelle, in her eighth month, was less and less able to aid him with the physical chores which might have made the crossing possible, if not easy.

Grafton ignored the advice of his betters and gloated over his victory, for the first part of the trail was smooth and beautiful, marked by bountiful shade and rushing streams. After the desert, it was paradise, and even Annabelle began to believe he was right. They laughed together for the first time since Ash Hollow. They made plans, as they once had done, and dreamed dreams. For

a short while, Grafton was once again the man she had
married.

Then they met up with their first obstacle. The trail
began to climb and reached a point so steep that, even
with the oxen straining until their shoulder muscles
trembled, the wagon wheels began to slide backward.

They'd already left many of their possessions along
the trail, to lighten the load of those last few miles while
they limped along on a damaged wheel to Ash Hollow,
and to further ease the load through the desert after
they lost the oxen. Annabelle's trunk and most of her
clothes, her grandmother Hubble's dishes, the hip bath,
several buckets and cooking pots, a copper washtub,
even a small box of knitted blankets and baby clothes
her sister had given her before she left Pennsylvania.
"You can make more," Grafton had told her when she
had argued that the clothing couldn't possibly weigh
much and took up hardly any room at all.

Now, in the high Sierras, Grafton unloaded almost
all of what remained of their possessions: the cookstove,
iron skillets, his own tools, the extra water barrel. These
they left in scattered disarray at the bottom of the trail,
for they had no thought of coming back for them. The
trail was long and steep and they didn't know what they
were going to find on the other side.

It took a total of two days to unload the wagon and
coax the oxen to pull it—an inch at a time, it
seemed—up the hill. A half day's travel later, they came
upon an even worse disaster. The trail descended so
sharply that there was no way to drive a wagon down
it without crashing and splintering it on the rocks below.

They had encountered much the same problem at
other places along the trail, most notably at Ash Hollow. It had occasionally been necessary to snub the

wagons off by ropes to trees and lower them down by means of a crude pulley system. That was what Grafton would have done then had he not been alone, but Annabelle wasn't strong enough to hold the ropes and he couldn't do it by himself.

It was plain to see that other wagons had made the slope, though scars in the bases of the trees along the way testified to the ropes they had used for the descent. Others, Grafton insisted, had simply found an easier way, and he backtracked until he found what appeared to be an alternate trail cutting through the mountains.

That had been three days ago. Grafton had expected the alternate trail, which was much narrower and rougher, to join up with the main route within a mile or two, five miles at the most. When it hadn't, he had been noticeably anxious. After two days he was furious.

There were many minor cutoffs through the mountains, most of them leading toward one or more of the gold camps that had sprung up over the past two years. Some of those trails could support a wagon; most could not. Grafton and Annabelle might travel another day or another week before the trail narrowed so as to become impassable; it was even possible that they might come to the end of the trail, only to find it had taken them miles out of their way and ended nowhere. There was no choice but to retrace their steps back to the main trail and once again face the problem of getting the wagon down the slope.

Annabelle should have known that no matter what, he wouldn't turn back. Perhaps in her secret heart she had known.

She got up, cumbersome in her heaviness, and parted the wagon flap. A soft mist lay over a blue-gray dawn, drifting through the rises and hollows, obscuring the shadows of the surrounding timber. The clearing looked as if it were filled with ghosts, and she repressed a shiver.

She climbed out of the wagon stiffly, still holding onto a forlorn hope that she might be wrong, that Grafton might suddenly appear in the mist or walk around the corner of the wagon or turn from the stream. The oxen munched on grass. The riding horse was gone. Grafton did not appear.

Annabelle stood there looking, waiting while the mist evaporated and the first rays of the sun rounded the mountain peaks and picked out silver on the tops of select trees. Incongruously, she thought how beautiful it all was.

She felt the baby move, and pressed both hands over her abdomen as though the gesture could protect the infant inside. Her eyes flooded unexpectedly with tears and she whispered, "It's all right, little Michael or Pearl." She had narrowed down the list to two names: Pearl, in honor of her mother; Michael, simply because she liked the sound. It was a game that had helped pass the monotonous days of the journey, a game in which Grafton had never shown any interest. Pearl or Michael, yes. That was all that mattered now.

She took a breath and said in a slightly stronger voice, "Mama will take care of you. It will be all right. It will."

She squeezed her eyes shut briefly as she fought one last wave of helplessness, terror, and despair. She knew she had no energy to spare on emotions that would only make her weaker. Not if she was going to get herself and little Michael or Pearl back to civilization alive.

She took another breath, squared her shoulders, and went to check the provisions. He hadn't taken much. He had probably been too anxious to get away, to make up for lost time. The water barrel was almost full. She topped it off from the stream, then forced herself to eat a breakfast of cold gruel. Her plan was simple. She would somehow get the wagon turned around, and she would head back to the main trail. There she would turn east, not west.

She didn't care if she had to give birth on the side of the road and carry her baby in her arms across the desert; she was going home. There was nothing for her here. She was going home.

The first step lay in figuring out how to harness the oxen.

"This can't be right," Sarah said. "You made a mistake. You took the wrong turn. This isn't it."

Henry made no reply. He didn't have to. The sign, hand-painted on a broken board and now swinging loosely by one nail, clearly read "Buzzard Creek."

They had passed through several mining camps before reaching this one, and each was more disappointing than the last. Sarah did not know what she had expected, but these shantytowns of rough-and-ready men and overwhelming filth were hardly the environment in which she could picture the elegant Cade Deveraux. She could not, in fact, picture her husband even making the journey she had endured to get here.

The previous camps had been ugly and frightening, with their mud-pitted paths and their lewdly grinning men and the stench of latrines fouling the countryside for what seemed like miles. But at least they had been *alive*. There had been movement, activity—sometimes too much of both for Sarah's liking—raucous voices, cursing and shouting triumph; men running or walking or digging or hammering; men standing over a rocker or carefully sorting through the debris in a pan. This place was a ghost camp in comparison.

It had rained last night, and Sarah had spent a miserable and furious time trying to keep dry under a blanket and a broad-leafed tree because Henry had forgotten to bring a tent. The skies were still leaden and drizzling, which did nothing to improve her temperament or her first view of Buzzard Creek.

Tents, many of them leaning and tattered, were scattered up and down the network of muddy paths that led to the stream. Toward the center of the little village, if it could even be called that, a kettle was hung over a low smoky fire, and the odor of what simmered inside was nauseating. Though claims dotted the stream and climbed the hill, only two or three miners were present. Those were skeletal-thin and hollow-eyed, and moved as if the mere act of walking were a monumental task that was hardly worth the effort. One man stood in the middle of the stream, leaning on his shovel, staring glassy-eyed at nothing. Another was stooped over with a hacking cough that sounded as though it was shredding his lungs; he continued to swirl water in a pan, over and over again.

Cade couldn't be here. He just *couldn't.*

Henry nudged his horse forward reluctantly, a look of horrible understanding slowly deepening on his face as he moved his gaze from tent to tent. The reins were slack in his hand and his horse kept plodding onward. Henry didn't stop him, as if he were drawn forward on a compulsion.

Sarah followed him closely, wrinkling her nose in distaste. "Excuse me!" she called to a miner who was crossing the path a few yards in front of them, his shovel thrown over his shoulder. "You there!"

The miner didn't even glance in her direction.

Henry drew his horse to such an abrupt halt that Sarah had to rein her own mount sharply to avoid a collision. She scowled fiercely at him. "Will you be more careful? Watch what you're doing!"

"Mrs. Deveraux," he said hoarsely, "we have to turn back. We can't go any further."

"Don't be absurd." She raised herself in the stirrups and called, "You! Yes, you!"

The miner turned a rheumy gaze on her. He looked old, with a scraggly pale beard and thin yellow hair and sunken eyes and bowed shoulders; Sarah was startled to realize, on second glance, that he was not much older than she was.

She dismounted and, leading her horse, walked up to him. "Can you help me?" she inquired. "I'm looking for someone."

The man spat a stream of filthy brown liquid on the ground. "Depends. Who isn't?"

"Cade Deveraux. He has a claim here."

But even as she spoke, she knew, with a peculiar combination of disappointment and relief, that she would not find her husband here. This place was played out. Cade had left long ago, was probably back in San Francisco now, or even in Louisiana, waiting for her. She had made the long, horrible trip for nothing.

The man was silent for a long and thoughtful time. Then he spoke slowly. "Good-looking man, blond, fancy-talking? From N'O'leans or thereabouts?"

Sarah's heart leapt. "Yes, that's him."

The man scratched his head. "Hell, ma'am, somebody's been pulling on your leg, you'll pardon me a-saying so. That fella ain't never had no claim here or nowheres elst. Used to work the camps, card-sharpin' and what-all, till he got drove out. Last I heard, he was roamin' the trail, stealing what he couldn't earn at gunpoint from honest folk."

Sarah felt the blood drain from her cheeks, then rush

back into them, flaming scarlet. "That's quite impossible," she said coldly.

The man ran his fingers through his fine hair. "Ma'am," he said tiredly, "I'm just a poor boy from Missouri, come west to get a little put by for my wife and two little girls. A little is just what I got, and now it don't look like I'm ever gonna get out of this place alive. I got no reason to lie to you, ma'am."

He swung his shovel onto his shoulder again and resumed his weary trek downstream.

Sarah stood where she was, staring after him yet not really seeing him at all. She could feel Henry's gaze boring into her. The miner's words kept echoing in her head. The worst part was, they all rang true.

She let the reins drop into the mud and walked toward the stream, standing with her back to Henry. She supposed there was a part of her that had always known that the weakness inside Cade was just one step from criminal. She had excused his indolence as elegance, his laziness as refinement, but she had been raised by such men as Byrd Kincaid, Boothe Carlyle, Jim Kincaid, and Ben Adamson. She knew the difference between an honest man, a good man, a strong man—and a man like Cade Deveraux. In her heart she had always known. She had simply made Cade into the kind of man she wanted him to be, and she had fallen in love with that illusion.

Why hadn't she listened more carefully to Marie, asked more questions about her husband and New Orleans? She knew the answer . . . because she hadn't wanted to know the truth. She'd needed to keep on living the lie of Cade waiting for her, making a home for her, needing her, wanting her. Lies. All of it, lies.

A thief. A common thief, skulking through the mountains like a snake, striking at the unwary and then crawling away to hide. Sarah's heart broke at the final admission, but not for herself so much as for Emilie and Père Lucien. How could she break this news to them?

Or perhaps they, like she, had always known.

She felt Henry beside her. "I'm sorry, Mrs. Deveraux," he said quietly.

She didn't look around. "I at least expected to find a claim. He said there was a claim."

A note of urgency crept into Henry's voice. "We have to go now. We shouldn't have come this far."

She watched the pale-haired man as he stuck his shovel into the dirt, leaned his foot on it, and turned over a spadeful. The effort seemed to exhaust him.

"I have no place to go."

"Of course you do. Back to San Francisco, to your sister. Back to wherever's home for you. Just come on, let's go. *Now.*"

Sarah muffled a cry of alarm as she saw the miner crumple and fall to the ground. Ignoring Henry's grasp on her arm, she ran toward him.

The man was sparrow-thin, and when she turned him over, she could feel the bones of his shoulders beneath her fingers—bones and searing heat. His face was chalk-white, and he was burning with fever.

Henry bent over her, pulling at her shoulders. "Mrs. Deveraux—Sarah—get away from him. Leave him alone. Come away from there, now!"

She turned on him in horror and indignation. "What kind of doctor are you?" she cried. "This man is sick. Can't you see that?"

Henry's face was tight. "I know he's sick. Everyone in this camp is sick! It's the fever and we're already at risk. This whole place should be under quarantine. The longer we stay, the greater the danger. Now, will you *come away?*"

The fever. Abruptly, Sarah was plunged back into the nightmare on the Isthmus of Panama. Molly, Madame, Lisanne . . . the stench, the suffering, the cries of pain in the night. Molly . . .

Numbly, she allowed Henry to pull her to her feet, but when he started to turn her away, she balked.

"No," she said. "I'm not leaving."

Impatience mixed with pain crossed his face. "There's no point in staying—"

"People are dying! Isn't that reason enough?"

"There's nothing we can do for them!"

"You're a doctor," she accused. "You took an oath to save lives. I'm tired of watching people die and I should think you would be, too!"

He blanched. Though she had not intended to wound him, she could see her attack had struck home. "There's nothing I can do," he repeated stiffly. "I don't have any medicine or equipment—"

"You packed medicine in your saddlebags, I saw you!"

"That was just for us! In case one of us got sick or hurt. There's not nearly enough for this whole camp."

But she could see his hesitation, his mind reviewing the possibilities, negative and positive, with horrified fascination. Sarah said, "It's more than they have now."

He looked away, and she could see the tension gripping his shoulders, working in his jaw. When he looked back at her, there was more agony in his eyes than Sarah had ever known a man could endure. His voice was low and strained. "What if I *fail?* They're dying and . . . what if I can't save them?"

"Then at least you will have tried. Can you keep running for the rest of your life?"

There was a long moment in which she thought he still might walk away. Then his shoulders relaxed with the decision, and the hint of a resigned smile touched his lips. "No," he said. "I guess not."

He walked back to his horse and started unpacking the saddlebags. But before he had turned away, Sarah saw in his eyes the one thing she had never seen in Cade's: courage.

Nobility was an attribute that Cade Deveraux had always considered more of a vice than a virtue; morality was a matter of convenience more than conscience. It was not that he approved of what had happened back at Donner Lake, nor would any civilized man. But he had not been required to participate, only to watch while the others killed the Indian woman, and he'd known he was being tested. Had he balked or in any way shown his distaste, he had little doubt he would not have lived to see another morning. For the sake of his own survival he could endure much worse, and so he had concealed his horror and kept his silence.

He knew, however, that his time was limited. He had been chosen to accompany Lobo on this insane mission while a dozen more qualified, and trustworthy, men were left behind. He had seen Lobo unmasked. He had seen the way out of the canyon fort. He knew he would not be returning alive. Even if he had wanted to remain with the band of outlaws, who were all virtual prisoners to their own greed and unspoken fear of their leader, Lobo was too clever to trust him. Too clever, and too concerned with his own survival.

Cade knew his only chance was to escape before Lobo completed his mission, whatever that might be, and turned his attention to cleaning up the excess baggage. The problem was that until now Cade had no place to escape to. He knew exactly the extent of Lobo's tracking and trapping skills. He knew precisely the nature of his ruthlessness and determination. If Cade somehow managed to escape the camp, he would be tracked down and killed before sunrise. Of that there was no doubt.

Nonetheless, he continued to watch for an opportunity, to ask questions, to play his role ... and to be ready when the chance came. It came when they had been on the trail for so long that he had almost given up hope. It came in a manner he least expected.

The trail wound down to a path so narrow and steep a goat would hesitate to use it, but Lobo led them onward. That night they camped above a blind wash that was protected on three sides by sheer rock cliffs, and on the fourth by deep timber. Exercising more intuition than trail sense, Cade said, "Is this it, then? Is this where we trap him?"

"You sound eager."

Cade shrugged. "No more than you." He looked back down the wash, shadowed and eerie in the deepening twilight. "What makes you think he'll follow this far? What makes you think he's still following at all?"

Lobo just smiled. "The hunter always knows his quarry. Jim Kincaid is a highly motivated, very determined man. He's still back there. And he won't give up. He'll walk right into my trap and be glad to do it, because he's the kind of man who doesn't believe he *can* be trapped. It won't be long now. You'll see for yourself."

But Cade was staring at him. "Kincaid? Did you say Jim Kincaid?"

Lobo gave him an odd look. "You know the man?"

Cade's head was still ringing with astonishment and he almost didn't think of the lie quickly enough. "By name," he admitted casually. "Headed up a wagon train or two, didn't he?"

"Did he?" Lobo turned back to unsaddle his horse. "I wasn't aware."

Kincaid. Jim Kincaid. Cade couldn't believe this was the first time he'd heard the name of the man they were stalking ... the man he himself had targeted to rob. The man whose squaw Charlie and the others had murdered at Donner Lake.

Jim Kincaid. His brother-in-law.

And why not? Those damn Kincaids were all over the West, to hear his bride tell it. And Jim ... how many times had he heard *that* particular name since he'd been married?

He wasn't alone anymore. Now he knew how he could escape. Jim Kincaid.

It seemed like destiny somehow.

Chapter Seventeen

At the deepest part of the night, after the moon had set and the campfire embers had burned away, Cade Deveraux slipped silently from the camp. Carrying his saddle until it was safe to stop and saddle his horse unheard, he led his mount down the trail.

Charlie slipped his pistol from its holster and cocked it, rising on the balls of his feet to follow. A firm hand on his arm stopped him.

Lobo's face was deeply shadowed, but his eyes glittered with an odd and dangerous fire. "Let him go," he said quietly. "He's doing exactly what I wanted him to do. At first light, we follow."

By the time Jim reached the second poisoned stream, he knew he was being led into a trap. Yet with a single-mindedness that bordered on the kind of madness that leads the moth to be consumed by the flame, he continued to follow. Once, he detoured from the trail markers to fill his nearly empty canteen from the spring that was the source of the polluted stream. Though the task took him only half a day out of his way, it was two days before he picked up the trail again, and by that time he was close to panic, fearing he had lost the only connection he would ever have to the men who had killed his wife.

He knew several things now. There were three men, all riding shod horses. The one who consistently dismounted to leave the trail markers wore the distinctive half-crescent-shaped Crow moccasin. The men who had attacked Star had ridden shod horses and left moccasin prints, too smudged and trampled to be identifiable as to tribe, in the mud beside her body.

They were poisoning the water after their horses had drunk and they had filled their own canteens; that Jim could tell by the nature of the tracks left beside the stream. The path on which they were leading him was winding and circuitous, taking him deeper into the mountains and away from familiar trails. They were now less than three days ahead of him.

And for days now, there had been no water at all.

He was in the part of the Sierras where timber was scarce and scraggly, cliffs were rugged, and trails were narrow. An ambush could come from any direction at any moment. Turning back was pointless; even if he could force himself to abandon the chase, his horse would never make it back to fresh water.

It was clear, even to a mind muddled by the thirst for revenge, that he was riding into his death. But at this point his only chance of survival was to keep riding forward.

And then he saw the wagon.

It was a little after noon when Annabelle's water broke. She had resigned herself to giving birth alone in the wilderness. On the day after Grafton had deserted her, after struggling half a day to get the oxen in their traces and turn the cumbersome wagon around on the narrow trail, after having traveled a total of no more than five miles back toward the main trail, the wagon hit a rut and the front axle snapped in two. There was nothing she could do but cry. And she refused to do that.

She had made her camp where the broken axle stranded her, and waited. She tried not to think about marauding animals or wild Indians or the massacre at Donner Lake. She tried not to think what would happen when her supplies ran low or how isolated this place was or how long it might be before anyone came this way. Most of all, she had tried not to think about the moment she went into labor.

And yet, now that it was upon her, she was surprisingly calm. Today, or perhaps tomorrow, her baby would be born. The waiting would be over.

She changed into a clean dress and covered the mattress in the wagon with an extra blanket. Then she went to gather firewood.

When she returned with her arms full of dried branches and broken sticks, a man stepped out from behind the cover of the wagon, his rifle pointed at her.

He had dark red hair, visible below the brim of his hat, and a bushy, ginger-colored beard. His eyes were dark and flat and as cold as death, yet they seemed to soften into something resembling surprise or even confusion as they moved over her swollen figure. He said, "Where's your husband?"

Annabelle was too shocked even to feel fear, and perhaps that was best. How far could she run before he caught her? If she screamed, who would hear?

She bent her knees and let the firewood slide to the

ground beside the embers of the morning's fire. "I don't know," she answered. "He left almost a week ago."

Wariness was evident in his tone, if not in his eyes. "Where'd he go?"

She straightened up again with difficulty. "To look for gold."

She didn't think he believed her. He didn't lower the rifle, and nothing at all was evident on his face. "I need water and food."

"Take what you need. I can't stop you."

There was a moment when he almost seemed to war within himself, and Annabelle thought he might put the gun down. Instead, he took a step back, gesturing slightly with the rifle toward the wagon.

"You do it."

He held the gun on her while she filled a pail with water for his horse, and then two canteens. When she held the dipper out to him, he hesitated. Then he reached forward and took it from her, letting the barrel of the rifle slide toward the ground. Annabelle took her first deep breath and moved back toward the fire to dish him up what remained of the cornmeal mush she had made for breakfast.

He sat on a log across from the fire and ate with his rifle leaning against the log beside him. She set the coffee on to boil; it disagreed with her at this stage of her pregnancy, so she didn't make it for herself anymore.

Jim alternated between watching her and scanning the hills surrounding them as he ate. He had long since abandoned any faith in God, and therefore accountability in the afterlife, but it occurred to him to wonder, in a vague and detached way, how a man might explain on Judgment Day why he had once held a gun on a pregnant woman while she watered his horse.

He hadn't known what to expect when he approached the wagon, but a woman alone and so hugely pregnant as she was would have been his last guess. And when he first saw her, he didn't expect the cramp of pain and remembered loss that squeezed through his muscles. He saw her, and he thought of Star.

She was nothing like Star, of course. Her face, though pleasant, was rather plain, drawn with the discomfort of her condition and the lines of anxiety he had put there. She had wheat-colored hair that she wore in a fat, not altogether tidy braid down the center of her back, and tired hazel eyes that had endured too much for her to be frightened of him now.

Nothing about her was similar to Star, yet he looked at her and he saw the wife he had lost and the child he would never know. It was foolish.

She handed him a tin cup of coffee, just as if he were a welcome guest at her dining room table, and he took it, though not without another small twinge of guilt. The stirring of emotions seemed particularly vivid to him now because he had felt nothing for so long.

He said, "How come you ended up way out here?"

She pressed a hand to the small of her back. There was a small stool drawn up before the fire, but she did not sit down. "My husband decided it would be faster to go through Donner Pass than follow the Carson River like the rest of the train. When we got to a place too steep for the wagon, he decided to try to go around it. That's how we ended up so far off the trail."

Jim's gaze moved from his slow examination of the shadowed hills to a brief perusal of the campsite.

"Your husband's not coming back?"

"No." Her voice held very little emotion. "I was trying to get the wagon back to the main trail."

He had noticed the broken axle when he first arrived. Even if it could be repaired, she would encounter nothing but poisoned water between here and the main trail. Again he felt a faint stirring of unfamiliar emotion, but there was nothing he could do for her even had he been of a mind to.

He finished his coffee in silence. She stood and watched.

"I'm sorry for your troubles, ma'am," he said. He placed the tin mug on the ground beside the log and stood up. "And I thank you kindly for the grub."

He picked up his rifle and was about to advise her that her best chance for fresh water, as well as civilization in the form of a rude gold camp or mining claim, lay in the opposite direction from which she was headed. But then he stopped, his attention caught by a glimpse of something in the distant hills.

It was the glint of sunlight on metal.

His jaw tightened briefly, and he added, "And I'm sorry to bring more trouble to your door. But it looks like we've got company."

She made a little sound low in her throat, and before he could catch her, she collapsed on the ground.

Thunder Eagle had long ago discovered the futility of trying to know another man's mind. The only truth was what he saw with his own eyes and from that he drew no conclusions. He resisted the urge, therefore, to speculate on who his quarry might be or what he might be after.

He had had no difficulty picking up the trail of the man with the spotted horse. Intent as he was on following the sign left by the others, he made no attempt to hide his own tracks or watch his back. His behavior was that of a trail-wise man who, for reasons of his own, had grown careless.

At the second poisoned stream Thunder Eagle began

to see the pattern. It required no speculation to see that the man on the spotted horse was being led into a trap, and by someone who knew the back trails of the Sierras well enough to call them home.

Thunder Eagle had started out hoping the renegade was part of Lobo's band; with each passing day, that possibility became more remote. But the more Thunder Eagle trailed him, the more he was convinced it was Lobo himself who was leading the way.

Though his home was in the Rockies, Thunder Eagle had traveled the Sierras enough over the past years to have a certain familiarity with the back trails and rabbit paths along which they were now being led. He knew where to find water when the major sources were fouled, and eventually he recognized enough of the country through which he traveled to project where the trail might end.

He circled wide, and left the man on the Appaloosa behind him. That night he came upon Lobo's encampment.

Throughout the night and for the better part of the next day, he lay as still as a lizard on a rock, watching and listening. He learned nothing that would help him.

He was a wily hunter and he could have taken the wolf and his pack that night, one by one, before any of them knew he was there. Then he could have circled back for the red-haired one. But killing them there would not have served his purpose, and would have left too many questions unanswered.

He rode back and picked up the trail of the Appaloosa.

From the beginning, little about this chase had been predictable. Until he saw the man with his own eyes, he hadn't even been sure he was on the right trail at all. He still wasn't entirely certain what role the red-haired man played. Now there was the woman, and he certainly hadn't counted on that.

Neither, he had to believe, had Lobo.

Fortunately, patience was something Thunder Eagle had learned from his mother's people at an early age. He chose a spot in the sun with a view of the wagon below, and he settled back to watch.

Jim thought about how easy it would be to ride away, and how much smarter. He was a sitting duck here on the flat trail surrounded by high rocks and timber—and so was she. If he had tried, he couldn't have set himself up for a better ambush. There had even been a moment when he thought it might be a trap—the broken axle, the beckoning campfire and full water barrel, the helpless woman—but the moment had been fleeting. It was a testament to the state of his reasoning that the thought had occurred at all.

And it was too late now to ride away.

He carried her to the wagon and made her as comfortable inside as he could. Then he went back out and tried to see what he could tell about the man who was hiding in the hills, without being too obvious about it and without making too much of a target out of himself. He figured the best thing to do, for now at least, was to let whoever it was believe he was still unobserved. When Jim moved out of the cover of the wagon and no rifle shot cut him down, he knew he'd made the right decision.

Yet that was at the basis of his quandary: he didn't *know* who was out there or what he wanted. Had he brought a killer to this woman's door, or was his presence now keeping one away? And there was still the matter of her missing husband. Jim knew full well what the rigors of the Overland Trail, combined with raging gold fever, could do to a man, and it was not beyond belief that a husband could simply walk off and leave his pregnant wife behind. Still, perhaps this husband had come back.

Or perhaps whoever was up there wore the moccasins of a Crow and was simply biding his time.

When Jim pushed aside the flap of the wagon canvas, she was lying on her side on the mattress; at his appearance, she pushed herself to a sitting position and moved clumsily toward the back of the wagon.

Jim hesitated. "I just wanted to see how you were feeling, ma'am."

Her gaze came to him from the shadows, steady and unafraid. "Are you going to kill me?"

For a long time he could not even form an answer. He thought of Star. In her last moments, had she seen a man like him and known she was going to die? Had he become the very thing he hunted, to strike fear into the hearts of the helpless? The notion made him feel slightly ill.

He thought of his mother, who had raised her sons to defend the weak and honor all women. He thought of his sister Sarah, to whom he had always been closer than anyone in the world except Star, and how horrified she would be to know that he had considered, even briefly, deserting this woman in her time of travail.

For the first time in what seemed like centuries, he thought about who he was. Jim Kincaid. Son of Byrd Kincaid. Nephew of Boothe Carlyle. The oldest male in a line of men who were destined to leave their mark upon this land.

He knew then what he had to do. Perhaps he had known it from the first moment he had laid eyes on this woman.

He said quietly, "No, ma'am, I'm not."

He stepped into the wagon, and did not blame her for flinching. He set the rifle on the floor near the door.

"But there's somebody up in those hills who might be planning to kill us both," he said. "I was wondering if you had any idea who it might be."

She shook her head, leaning it back against the canvas tiredly. A lock of her hair had come loose from the braid, and Jim could see a fine film of perspiration on her face.

"I haven't seen anyone . . . since we left the trail."

Jim nodded. "I'll wait till sundown, then scout around. Meantime, we'd better fort up for trouble. Where are your weapons?"

She drew in her breath softly, and her face tightened with pain. In a moment she answered, "There—aren't any. Grafton took them all."

Jim's lips compressed briefly against a surge of anger for the kind of man who would leave a woman stranded in the wilderness with a half-empty wagon and no weapons with which to defend herself. Then he forced himself to relax his expression as he turned his attention to more immediate problems.

"Is it very bad with you, ma'am?"

She shook her head hesitantly. "Not yet. There's time. Hours yet."

He nodded and picked up his rifle. "I'll be outside."

He left the wagon to make what preparations he could for sundown.

Thunder Eagle had hidden himself in rocks above the wagon being used by the white woman and her red-bearded companion. Four days down the trail was a gold camp supporting twenty or thirty men; not much to look at, but substantial enough in its own way. The California Trail, with its well-rutted paths and promise of civilization just over the next rise, was more than a week away in the opposite direction. And almost within shooting distance now, headed up the trail toward the wagon, was one of Lobo's men.

Thunder Eagle knew that because just at the palest gray-purple hour of twilight he had seen the flicker of a fire; doubtless the traveler had thought the flame couldn't be seen against an almost light sky, and he had screened the fire well to filter the smoke. Thunder Eagle had crept down the trail on foot to investigate and recognized the blond man from Lobo's camp.

He wondered if the red-bearded man was expecting the rendezvous. Or if the blond man was an assassin sent to dispose of them both.

One thing was certain. Lobo's man had no idea how close he was to the camp; if he had, he wouldn't have stopped for the night and he certainly wouldn't have made a fire—however small and however brief. It therefore followed that he didn't know about Thunder Eagle—who still had the advantage of surprise.

Thunder Eagle pondered his situation as he made his way back to his own rude camp above the wagon. He felt himself becoming pinned in on two sides by the unknown: on the trail below him was the wagon, the mysterious woman, the red-bearded man he had been tracking since Hangtown. On the trail behind him was a member of Lobo's band who he knew, but could not prove, had been involved in the massacre that would soon push white men and Indians to the brink of war.

He could not afford to wait until sunrise to have his questions answered.

"And there's my sister Sarah. She married some fancy-pants dude down New Orleans way. Never figured her for that, but she always did like to put on airs for herself. Underneath, though, she had more sense than just about anybody in the family. She just didn't like to let on."

"And your sister Meg?" the woman prompted. Her voice was tight and her breathing ragged from the last pain, but she wouldn't let the silence fall. "What happened to her?"

Jim had brought her water in the heat of the afternoon, and started talking to her just to get the frightened look out of her eyes. And because he didn't want to think that that same look might have been in Star's eyes right before she died. It was dark now, inside the wagon as well as out, but his eyes had adjusted well enough to see her damp, tangled hair and the smudged circles around her eyes. This baby was not going to be quick in coming, and she was tired already.

"Well, after the big potato strike, she up and moved to San Francisco, her and her whole family. She opened a store that made money faster than she could spend it. Now she's starting a fancy opera house."

The woman smiled faintly. "So now I can say I did know someone who struck it rich in California."

"Yes, ma'am." But he found it hard to say anything at all, because suddenly he was remembering, poignantly, that last night with Star, when he lay awake thinking about all the money he had and what it was going to buy for his child and how it had never meant anything until there was someone whose future it could build. Now it meant nothing again.

Another pain seized her and she arched on the mattress, clamping her lips tightly together. All this time and she hadn't made a sound. Jim turned and wrung a cloth out in the bowl of water at his side. When the pain was over, he placed the cloth on her forehead.

"If you don't mind my asking, ma'am, what made

you up and take off for California, being in your condition and all? It's hard enough on the average man."

She let her eyes drift closed for a moment. "A woman goes . . . where her husband takes her." Then she looked at him. "Where is your wife?"

Jim didn't remember saying he was married, but he must have. He answered briefly, without looking at her, "She's dead."

That was the first time he had ever said those words. They were not easy, but not impossible either. And they were words, he knew, that needed saying.

He moved his eyes back to her. "She was killed. Murdered on the trail."

Her gaze didn't waver. "That man out there—is he the one who did it?"

Jim didn't reply right away. Then he said, "I think so."

"Then you have to go after him."

Her tone was matter-of-fact, but her eyes held dread and forced courage. She hadn't asked for any of this. She had been stranded in the wilderness to give birth alone, and now the only thing that stood between her and the same kind of massacre that had taken place at Donner Lake was a stranger who had held her at gunpoint only hours ago. She couldn't have run if she had wanted to. Yet perhaps the thing Jim admired most about her was that he didn't think she would have run in any case.

He answered gently, "Yes, ma'am. I do."

And he had to do it now. He knew it, and so did she. He saw it in her eyes.

He picked up his rifle and got up, staying low to avoid brushing his head on the canvas.

She said, a little quickly, "When you get back— maybe you can tell me the potato story again."

She caught her breath sharply with another pain. Jim watched as her face contorted and her body writhed, her fingers tearing holes in the mattress ticking. When it was over, her muscles sagged and her breath came in exhausted, erratic gasps.

"If you want to yell, ma'am, it's all right."

"No." She took a couple of deep breaths and met his eyes. "If he's out there, I don't want him to hear."

Jim knew then the definition of bravery.

He inclined his head toward her in silent understanding and respect, then turned to push open the flap.

"Wait."

He looked back.

"What—what is your name?"

"It's Kincaid," he told her. "Jim Kincaid."

"I'm—Annabelle."

He smiled a little and touched his hat. "Pleasure, Miss Annabelle."

"Mr. Kincaid . . ." Again he saw the dread, the uncertainty, in her eyes. The courage. "You will come back, won't you?"

He thought about Star and all the things she would never know, the things they would never share. He thought about his own child, who would never draw a breath or see a sunrise. He looked at the woman across from him, her face drawn with pain and her eyes filled with pleading, and he said quietly, "Yes, ma'am. I'll be back."

Until Jim actually saw the moccasin print in the soft earth alongside the trail, he held out hope that he was wrong, that he had imagined the glint of sunlight on a rifle barrel, that the third person on the trail was an innocent passerby who chose not to make himself known for reasons that had nothing to do with Jim Kincaid. It

might be the woman's husband, after all, or a refugee
from the gold camps, or even a common trail thief. But
the starlight illumined the ground too well, and Jim's
eyes, which had grown too accustomed to scouting for
signs over the past weeks to miss anything so obvious,
easily picked out the curved half-bow of a moccasin
print.

A surge of rage went through him, so swift and so
strong that for a moment it left him paralyzed. He was
here. The filthy, murdering Indian who had slaughtered
his wife was here, within firing range. He was *here*, and
Jim could almost taste the blood, his instincts for killing
were that strong. He was here, vengeance was within an
arm's grasp, and for a moment that was the only thing
that registered on his brain, the only thing that mattered.

And then he saw the direction in which the footprints
pointed. Toward the wagon and a woman called
Annabelle, who was helpless and alone.

Jim whirled and started back down the path as silently as he had come, but much more swiftly. The only
sound in the night was the pounding of his heart in his
ears. Sometimes it almost seemed the night was gone
and bright morning sun beamed down as he ran, stumbling and plunging down the mountain toward the lake.

He was less than two hundred yards from the shadowed hulk that was the wagon, darting from tree to
shrub and ever mindful that even now he might be in
the killer's sites, when there was a flash of movement to
his left. Instinctively he swung toward it, raising his rifle
and firing in one smooth motion.

The thunder of his gunfire echoed through the
mountains like a roar of triumph: *this* time he wasn't too
late. *This* time there was justice. Then, before he could
take a step toward his target, before the echo had died

away, something tangled in his hair, jerking him backward, and he felt the sharp bite of steel across his throat.

"Drop the rifle, Red Beard," a voice said low in his ear. "Tonight you will die."

Chapter Eighteen

Two things were very clear to Jim as he weighed his options. The voice that spoke to him was not that of an Indian, and if he moved so much as an exhaled breath, he would be dead. There was a pistol in his belt and a knife in his boot; he saw no clear way to reach either one of them. The best he could do was to toss his rifle away, a few feet in front of him, so that his captor could not reach it. The movement caused a trickle of blood to seep down his throat into his shirt.

The fingers that were wrapped around his hair maintained a steady pressure, and the knife edge did not ease away from his throat. The voice demanded, "Who are you? Tell the truth, because you don't want to meet your Maker with a lie on your lips."

"I've got no reason to lie to you, mister. I don't even know who you are or what you want with me."

The fingers tightened on his hair, hard enough to make him see stars for a moment. "What I want from you is the truth. And just so you know, this knife will kill you just as dead quick or slow, and right now you're bleeding to death by drops. Are you working with Lobo?"

"No. I don't know who you're talking about."

Jim's head was tilted back and to the side; the blade was so sharp he couldn't feel the sting, only the damp mist of blood on his skin. He could see nothing but the shadowed shape of the wagon straight ahead and, by shifting his eyes downward, his own booted foot.

And, next to it, the foot of the man who held him captive. It was clad in a buckskin moccasin, with the distinctive shaping of the Crow tribe.

"Who are you?" the man demanded again roughly. "Were you at Donner Lake?"

Jim's heart was beating slow and strong. His muscles felt like iron. "My name is Jim Kincaid," he answered low. "I was at Donner Lake. The woman you killed was my wife, you bastard."

Thunder Eagle loosened his hold and Jim took advantage of it, stabbing back with his elbows, kicking backward with his hard-heeled boot. In another instant Thunder Eagle was on the ground and Jim was above him, the barrel of his pistol pressed into the hollow of the other man's throat. Thunder Eagle had not relinquished his hold on the knife. A single downward thrust would bring it squarely between the ridges of Jim's spine.

"Think about it," Jim said, breathing hard. He cocked the pistol. "Who's going to die first?"

For a long moment neither man moved. Looking into the broad, flat features and dark eyes of the Indian countenance that had become the stuff of his nightmares, Jim did not know why he hesitated. He should have pulled the trigger. He wanted to feel the body jerk with the impact, feel the splash of hot blood on his face, know the dark satisfaction of death come at last, an end to the nightmares.

Thunder Eagle opened his hand and Jim heard the knife clatter to the ground. Slowly he lowered his arm. "I'm not going to kill you," he said.

"That's right, you're not." Jim's finger tightened on the trigger. "I've waited a long time for this."

Thunder Eagle's voice was calm, and his eyes showed no fear. "Then you're going to be disappointed. I'm not the man you want. One of them's backtracking you and camped less than an hour away. The rest can't be too far behind. They'll be here before sunrise. Your gunfire made sure of that."

The white-cold fire inside Jim dampened a little; confusion licked at the corners of his mind. The man was unarmed, but why should such a thing matter to him now? Unarmed and unafraid.

"Do you think I'm a fool?" he said harshly. "I've been tracking you all over these mountains. Those are Crow moccasins you're wearing. It was Crow Indians who murdered my wife!"

"Will you kill a man for the boots he wears, Jim Kincaid?"

"If that's all I've got to go on."

But doubt was pounding at him now, eating at his rage, his certainty. There had been three of them. Maybe this man was one of them, but the questions he had asked Jim when he had a knife to his throat didn't sound like the kind that would be asked by a man who had been leading him through the mountains with false trail signs and poisoned streams. Maybe he was one of the killers . . . but maybe he wasn't.

He was an Indian, and Jim had seen Indians—Crow Indians—fleeing the scene of the massacre. That was proof enough.

But what if this man was telling the truth? What if he had not been among the killers?

He was an Indian. Did it matter?

In frustration, Jim pushed the barrel of the pistol deeper into his victim's throat, but he didn't squeeze the trigger. "Where have you been leading me?"

"I've been tracking you—or rather, I was tracking Lobo. It's my guess he was leading you into an ambush."

Perspiration dripped into Jim's eye and clouded his vision. "Who the hell is this Lobo you keep talking about?"

"He's the man who killed your wife. Why, I don't know. But he disguised his men as Indians and made a lot of white men real nervous—nervous enough to start a war, given half a chance. As for the Indians—the Sioux, the Pawnee, the Shoshone—some of them have been wishing for war longer than I've been trying to stop them. Shoot me now, Kincaid, and they're going to get their wish."

Confusion was pecking at Jim now from all sides like a hundred hungry birds, tearing at his resolve, shredding apart what he believed to be the truth. And then something else distracted him. There was a sound from the wagon, low and muffled, a cry smothered in agony.

She had said she wouldn't cry out.

It lasted for only a moment, but his concentration was broken. He glanced toward the wagon; for an instant his grip on the pistol slackened. It was only for a moment, but it could have cost him his life. He knew the strength and the reflexes of the man beneath him; in that one moment the Indian could have taken advantage of Jim's distraction and reversed their positions. He could have disarmed him, snatched up his knife, slit his throat.

But he didn't.

"It can start here," Thunder Eagle said quietly. "This war that both our people are waiting for. Or it can end here. Whichever it's to be, do it now. The woman in the wagon needs your help, and the men who killed your wife will be here before the night is over."

For a long time Jim did nothing. Then he heard a muffled cry again.

He slowly lowered the hammer of the gun and stood up, taking a step backward. "Get out of here," he said.

Thunder Eagle stood up and retrieved his knife. He replaced it in its scabbard, and met Jim's eyes one last time. Then he turned and disappeared into the trees.

Chapter Nineteen

"I'm sorry," Annabelle gasped. The viselike grip of her fingers around Jim's relaxed slightly as another spasm passed. "I tried . . . I promised . . . I gave away our position!"

"You didn't give away anything," Jim assured her quietly. "It's all right. The only thing you have to worry about now is getting this baby born."

But the words felt hollow, and Jim wondered just how big a mistake he had made. Had he set them both up to die? Would yet another woman and child be murdered because he had failed to protect them? Why hadn't he blown a hole in the Indian's throat when he had had the chance? Then at least he would be sure.

But he hadn't. He had believed the man against all evidence, and he might well live to regret it. But even if the one he had allowed to escape was telling the truth, the worst was not over yet. The Indian had said it was a man named Lobo who had been setting the traps. If that was true, so was something else—the shot

Jim had fired would lead the enemy straight to their camp.

Annabelle's fingers dug into his hand and she smothered a cry as she rode out another long spasm. Her face and hair were drenched and her breathing was labored. It wouldn't be much longer.

She whispered, half moaning, "My poor baby. I never meant to do this to you. You deserve better than this. My poor baby . . ."

Jim tried to distract her. "What will you name it?"

She looked at him, her eyes tormented. "I don't even have anything to wrap it in. To be born here in the middle of the wilderness without even a blanket to call your own . . . Why did I do this?" she sobbed. "Why did I ever leave home?"

Jim got up quietly and left the wagon.

The night was thick and black in the hour just before dawn. If there was an attack, it would be now.

Somewhere in the rocks beyond, at least one pair of eyes watched him; he could feel the gaze as if it were a physical thing. He was a fool to leave the camp unguarded while he was inside the wagon, but he couldn't let her go through labor alone. Star wouldn't have wanted him to do that.

But Star wouldn't have wanted him to let Annabelle die, either.

He stood still for a long time, scenting the air, his eyes scanning the shadows of the surrounding ridge until he had memorized every dip and contour. Then, silently, he moved around the wagon to the front wheel, the most defensible position, where he had left his saddlebag. He knelt and filled his pockets with ammunition, stuffing extra cartridges into his belt. Hesitating for only a moment, he reached into the second bag and took out the blue dress. He held it in his hands for a time, feeling its texture and smelling its scent. Then he rose and took it inside the wagon.

"I found something to wrap the baby in," he told Annabelle.

Meg wrapped the shawl more tightly around her shoulders and leaned against the mantel, gazing down into the fire. She hated foggy days when the dampness seeped in through cracks in windows and doors and permeated the house with its gloom. San Francisco was known for wintry summers and for autumns that seemed like summer, but this coolness seemed unseasonable even for the city by the bay. The heavy gray mist that swirled outside the windows was both depressing and foreboding.

When Tonio appeared in the parlor doorway, she turned from the fireplace, unable to hide the worry on her face. "Is he awake yet?"

"He just woke, señora." Tonio's expression was grave.

"I'll take dinner to him," Meg said briskly. "Fiona's in the kitchen with Monserrat, making his favorite soup. I think it will do him good to eat."

Tonio shook his head. "I don't think the señor can eat at all. The pain in his belly is too great."

"No," Meg said sharply. "I won't accept that. Mr. Gerrard must eat. He has to keep up his strength. Isn't that what the doctor said? And where is that doctor? I thought he was going to come by every day."

"He was here this morning, señora, when you were at the opera house. He left some more medicine, but . . ." Tonio shrugged his shoulders in an expressive gesture of despair.

"Well, this is absolutely ridiculous," she said. "I'm going in to see Mr. Gerrard right now, and I guarantee,

Tonio, that he will eat. You go tell Monserrat to prepare his tray."

She strode determinedly down the hall, aware of Tonio's sorrowful gaze on her. Tonio! He and Monserrat were such doomsayers. When Sheldon had suddenly taken to his bed, they'd come to her with their woeful tales of the seriousness of his illness, stories which she absolutely refused to believe. Sheldon was still a young man; he was stronger than most and had endured hardships which would have killed lesser men. Of course he would recover!

She'd see to it that he had another doctor. The physician who'd been treating him was obviously a total charlatan, giving him laudanum for the pain when he simply needed to change his diet, keeping him doped up and in bed when he needed to move around and regain his energy—

She stopped, her hand on the door to his room. Despite her brave show, she hated to go inside. She hated to see him lying pale and thin in the huge bed. She couldn't accept that he was ill. *Oh, God,* she cried silently. *Please don't let this be happening. Please.*

Straightening her shoulders and taking a deep breath, Meg stepped into the room. Tonio had lit a fire there, too, but a chill hung in the air. She stood beside Sheldon's bed, feigning good cheer. "Now, what is this I hear about no dinner? Why, your daughter is making your favorite soup."

Sheldon's skin was pulled tightly across the bones of his face; the dark circles beneath his eyes stood out in sharp contrast to his pallor. His eyes were dull with pain and drugs, and he spoke slowly, as if to form the words was a struggle. "I'm not really hungry, Miss Meg. I just don't think I can . . ."

She pulled up a chair and sat beside him. "Of course

you can. You must try. I'm sure if you try, you can get well. This . . . this little upset is just temporary. I know it." Her lips tightened defiantly. "I know you will get better. You've always had such a strong will—"

Sheldon's hand reached for hers, grasped it, and held on. Meg felt a tenderness envelop her that she only experienced toward her child. Unbidden tears came to her eyes, and she blinked them away. How many times in their years together had she and Sheldon touched? So few . . . so few, and now all she could think of was holding onto him and keeping him with her for as long as she could.

More tears flooded her eyes and trickled down her cheeks. "I'm sorry, Sheldon. I'm so sorry."

His grip tightened. "For what, Miss Meg? Now, why should you be sorry?"

"For the times I was sharp with you and turned away. I'm sorry because . . . because I never let you love me." The words were out, and she looked at him, astounded that she'd said them. *Love* was a word never mentioned between the two of them.

He laughed softly, and for a moment she saw the old Sheldon in his eyes. "But I do love you, Miss Meg, and our little girl. I don't care who her father was; she is mine, heart and soul."

Meg prayed that she could control the emotions that were building in her, feelings that made her want to throw herself across Sheldon's bed and sob until she had no more breath left in her. In a strangled voice she said, "I don't see how you could love me. I've been so hard and cold—"

"You acted the way you thought you must to protect yourself, Miss Meg. I guess a man like me admires that in a woman. I know there's goodness inside you. If not, you wouldn't have put up with me all these years. Good

Lord, you saved my life back there in Bellevue. You and Fiona gave me a new life, and it's been wonderful. I'm a lucky man."

Lucky. She felt as though her heart would burst with pain. "It can still be wonderful. I need you with me, Sheldon. I need you to help me with the opera house and to see Fiona grow up. How can I raise her without you? How can I?"

"You'll do just fine, Miss Meg. You always do."

"No, no, I don't! I can't do it without you. You're giving up on me," she accused him angrily. "You're just giving up and I won't have it! No, I won't."

He smiled again, but more weakly. "I wouldn't leave you and Fiona if I had a choice. But our child is very much in my thoughts—you know I have no claim to her legally."

"That doesn't matter."

"Oh, but it does. I've talked to my lawyer about my will. Of course, everything goes to you and the girl."

"I don't want to hear about your will," she said stubbornly.

"You must listen to me, Miss Meg, and listen hard." He was gasping for breath, pushing past his pain with a desperate will. "The lawyer says that Fiona must be protected. I want her to have everything I own. I want her to be the richest woman in San Francisco, and she will be someday. In ten years my property will be worth millions. Not hundreds of thousands, but millions. We've got to get married, Miss Meg."

"Married? But I'm already married. We can't . . ."

"He's dead. Killed in a bar fight years ago. You are a widow. I had my lawyer look into that, too, and I want you to marry me. Tonight. For our child."

Meg withdrew her hand from his and stood up. She wiped her tearstained cheeks with the back of her hand.

She felt disoriented and afraid. Everything was changing, and she didn't want it to. Her safe, secure world was shifting and sliding away from her. "No, Sheldon, I can't marry you. After all this time . . . after—"

"I should have asked you years ago, Miss Meg, but I always thought you'd say no. You can't say no now. I love you, and I love that little girl of ours. For my widow and my child, there can be no questions about my will."

Meg shook her head. "I can't . . . I can't take it all in. I need to think."

"We can't think too long, Miss Meg. We don't have time."

There was a soft knock at the door. "Papa, I have your dinner. Can I come in?"

"Of course, angel. Meg, open the door."

Meg stepped back into the shadows and watched as Fiona led the way into the room, followed by Monserrat carrying a tray. Meg knew that Sheldon was exhausted from their conversation, yet he mustered energy for a smile.

"Give Papa a kiss, Fiona."

She wiggled up on the bed and kissed his sunken cheek. "We made your favorite soup, Papa. It has chicken and potatoes and all kinds of vegetables. Monserrat let me do most of it."

"Thank you, sweetheart. It smells wonderful, but I'm too tired to eat right now."

"But you must eat it, Papa," Fiona ordered. "It will make you strong. I can help you if you're too tired." She motioned to Monserrat with a gesture very much like her mother's. "Put the tray here on this table so I can feed Papa. Would you like that? Would you like me to feed you a tiny bit at a time?" Fiona bent close to Sheldon's pillow.

Meg bolted from the room, her hand pressed over her mouth, stifling her sobs.

Hours later, Meg sat in front of the dying fire, swaddled deep in her shawl, consumed by the past, remembering. The first time she'd seen a drunken Sheldon Gerrard was in a ramshackle saloon in Bellevue, on the Missouri River. She was running away from her abusive husband, and Sheldon was running away from his failures. They'd been quite a pair, she thought. Two people with nowhere to go. She remembered the night six months later when Fiona was born; Sheldon had paced up and down outside her room in the trading post on the Platte River as if he indeed had been the natural father. The first time he'd held Fiona in his arms, his eyes had filled with tears and he'd vowed to give the child the sun and the moon and the stars.

He'd protected them and shared with them, guided them and put up with Meg's temper and bossiness. She'd always thought it was because he loved Fiona so much, but could it have been because he loved her just a little, too?

She looked down at the daguerreotype she was holding in her hands. Sheldon, Meg, Fiona. Father, mother, child. A perfect family, the photographer had said. Meg remembered scoffing at the idea, but it was true. They were a family, bound together by love and pain and hardship and joy. How could she have been so blind not to see what she had? After her brutal marriage to Caleb O'Hare, she'd vowed never to marry again, and never to let herself love another man. What a fool she was.

Years wasted ... happiness thrown away because of her stubbornness and selfishness ...

At the most meaningful times of her life, Sheldon had

been by her side. Why did it have to be something as dreadful as his impending death that made her see that? Meg was terrified by the thought of going on without him. She was so afraid that her fear had made her deny the reality of what was happening. But now time was running out.

A sudden knock on the front door startled her, and she jumped at the sound that echoed loudly through the quiet house. Still clutching the photograph, she went to the door and looked through the glass panel. A woman stood in the shadowy fog. Meg pulled open the door.

"What are you doing here?"

Marie LaFleur stepped past her into the hall. "I know it's late, and I know you don't want me here—"

"You're right, Miss LaFleur. Mr. Gerrard is very ill. We can't ... we can't receive guests."

Marie's sharp eyes sized her up. "You look like death warmed over, Meg Kincaid, and I know you're hurting, but there's worse to come."

"What are you talking about?"

"I've been working for Yancey Connor. Now, he's a real weasel of a man, but I'm used to that in my line of work. What I don't like is working for a criminal. That bastard is plannin' to burn down your opera house tonight."

"Connor! That skunk— Wait a minute." Meg caught herself. "Why would he tell you that?"

"He didn't! I overheard him talkin' to two fellas. If he'd knowed I heard, I wouldn't be here. I'd be floatin' in the bay."

Meg was still suspicious. "I have a night watchman at the opera house, you know."

"They know it, too," Marie said grimly. "He's probably already knocked out and tied up."

Meg retreated into the parlor, and Marie followed. "I don't know why I should believe any of this—it's so preposterous. My opera house has fire walls, first of all—"

"They're plannin' to burn it down from inside. Look here, Miz Kincaid, Connor ain't no fool. If he fired the whole block, the flames might jump the street and burn his own place down. But if he pours turpentine all over your new wood floor and lights a match—" She made an explosive sound with her lips. *"Pouf!* The inside of your opera house will burn just like a fire in a grate. The Sydney Ducks get blamed, and you're out of business for a while."

Meg's mind raced. "Why are you telling me this? You didn't have to . . ."

"Well, it ain't because you've been nice to me; it's that sister of yours. She treated me like I was family. I couldn't let her down."

Meg had made up her mind. "How'd you get here? Do you have a carriage?"

"I walked. Hell, after walkin' across Panama, a hike out here ain't nothing. A little fog compared to a million mosquitoes and snakes and alligators—"

"You're a determined woman, Miss LaFleur. If Connor finds out about what you've done—well, we both know what will happen. I'll take care of you, though—if any of this is true. If not, then you're on your own."

"You're a hard woman, Miz Kincaid."

Meg's face softened. "No, I'm not. I'm just a good actress. Wait here and pour yourself some sherry. It's on the table. I'm going to get Tonio and have him hitch up the horses. We need to alert the volunteer firemen—"

"You know any men with guns? That's what we need."

"The vigilantes." Meg was halfway down the hall. "You can stay here, Miss LaFleur. Marie."

"I ain't a quitter, Meg Kincaid. I'm goin' with you, and I'm seein' this one through."

Chapter Twenty

Charlie had long thought that the root of Lobo's power lay in the fact that he was so damn spooky. He never guessed wrong. He knew people's minds. He could see in the dark better than a cat and a damn sight better than Charlie's horse, and he could track like an Indian in that same pitch blackness.

Of course, if Lobo's theory was correct—and Charlie had no reason to believe it wasn't—there was not a lot of tracking to be done, simply back-trailing. If Cade Deveraux, who was no frontiersman by anyone's measure, could do it in the dark, they certainly could.

They had the handicap of staying far enough behind Cade to avoid detection, however, and more than once Charlie thought they'd lost him. Then they spotted the wagon, and the Appaloosa horse tied behind it. He felt a surge of triumph.

There was, however, no sign of Cade Deveraux.

They left their horses deep in the woods and walked back down the trail, taking up a position above the wagon in the cover of the rocks. Charlie wondered why they didn't storm the wagon and shoot Kincaid where he slept, but he knew better than to ask.

He had to ask one question, though. "What about Deveraux, Captain?" He whispered it so quietly that his lips barely moved. "Do you want me to scout for him?"

"No need," Lobo answered calmly. "I've got him in my sights."

As hard as he searched the darkness, Charlie found nothing that remotely resembled the figure of a man.

Lobo slid a glance toward him. The glitter in his eyes was the only light Charlie had seen since moonset. "Be patient, my friend," he murmured. "You're about to see the beauty of life's unpredictability as our two quarries lure each other into battle. They will not, however, finish each other off." And the glint in his eyes hardened to ice. "That pleasure I reserve for myself."

"Miss Annabelle," Jim said, blotting her forehead one last time as she collapsed against the mattress, drained. "It's almost dawn. I need to scout around. I can't promise how long I'll be gone."

Panic flashed in her eyes and he saw her fight to subdue it. Jim's admiration for her surged.

She nodded. "Be—careful."

"Yes, ma'am."

He ducked his head and stepped out into the night.

Immediately every sense flared into alertness. Something was different. Something was out there, something was wrong, something was about to happen; the night was charged with it. Some small, vital part of his brain picked up on the signals and tingled and throbbed with them. Perhaps it was a movement, half caught out of the corner of his eye, or a sound just barely within the range of his hearing. Perhaps it was the way his horse held its ears, alert to a sound that might come again, or nothing more than a change in the quality of the darkness. But something was there.

And then he saw it. A movement off to his left, a shadow flitting between the shadows, moving down the trail toward the wagon fifty yards away. Jim turned toward it silently and drew back the bolt on his rifle. He would not make the same mistake twice and fire blindly into the darkness. But he would be ready.

Cade dropped down behind the boulder as he heard the click of the rifle bolt. His throat was dry, his heart pounding. He hadn't anticipated Kincaid's lying in wait for him. He had counted on reaching the wagon before anyone knew he was there, and he shouldn't have. Now he didn't know what to do. If he moved, Kincaid would blow him again; his skill with a rifle was legendary, according to Sarah.

As quietly as he could, Cade searched his pockets for a scrap of something white but was frustrated. What had happened to the days when he never left his room in the morning without a white handkerchief? Would he ever know those days again? Finally he shrugged out of his jacket and, making as little noise as possible, ripped off the sleeve of his shirt.

"Kincaid!" he called, staying low as he tied the scrap of cloth around a stick. "Jim Kincaid! Hold your fire!"

From the hills opposite, a single look passed between Charlie and Lobo, and without a word they began to move in.

Jim saw the white flag appear above the rocks, but he did not lower his rifle or change his stance. He was standing in the deep shadow of the wagon, and he did not think he could be spotted from that distance unless he did something to call attention to himself, but he had to move. A stray shot, or even an accurate one, would penetrate the wagon and had a good chance of striking the woman inside. He had to get away from the wagon before opening fire—or before allowing them to.

The voice that called to him did not belong to the Indian he had encountered earlier; that much he knew. But he was far too smart, and had far too much to lose, to be lulled by a white flag. So he held his ground, and waited, and considered his options.

"Listen to me!" The flag rose a little higher. "My name is Cade Deveraux! I'm married to your sister Sarah!"

Jim's heart thumped hard against his ribs. Deveraux! That was the right name. And he'd heard that Sarah's husband had gone to the goldfields; Sarah had written him about it herself. His finger did not ease off the trigger and he kept his eyes on his target.

"The men you're tracking, they're leading you into a trap!" There was desperation in the voice. "They're after me, too! We have to team up. I'm coming down!"

Jim wanted to shout at him to hold his position, but knew the sound of his voice would give away his location. He watched as the flag rose higher, and slowly a figure appeared among the rocks.

He stood there for a moment in full view, his arms high above his head, the flag of truce in one hand. "I know you have no reason to believe me," he called, "but I'm telling the truth! I can prove it!"

Jim could hear the tightening of the other man's voice as his dilemma became clear, as he struggled to think of something that would convince Jim of his identity. Then he burst out, "The coin! That's it! Sarah had a gold coin with foreign writing on it—she showed it to me once. She said her great-gran Fiona had given a bunch of them to her mother, and her mother gave one to each of her daughters for luck. How would I know that if Sarah hadn't told me?"

Slowly Jim lowered the rifle. It was true. The coins were deeply embedded in a family tradition as old and as cherished as the talisman he wore around his own neck. Sarah wouldn't share such a thing with a casual stranger.

Jim stepped cautiously out of the shadow of the wagon. "Come in with your hands up!" he called out. "Slowly!"

Two shots rang out. The first exploded in the dirt a yard to his left; the second caught Cade Deveraux and flung him backward. Both shots came from the east, and Jim reacted instinctively, swinging in that direction and firing as he dove for the ground. But two rifle blasts rang out—his own and another, close behind him. From inside the wagon Annabelle cried out and broke into sobs racked with pain and terror. Jim rolled beneath the wagon bed, holding his rifle close to his chest, every sense alert as he tried to guess from which direction the next shot would come—east or west. He was surrounded, and anything he did would only draw fire on the innocent woman inside the wagon.

He lay there breathing hard, trying to reason it out. He had to get away from the wagon, and he had to do it now, while darkness still gave him some protection. If he could get into the rocks and circle around from east to west, picking them off one by one . . .

It was an insane plan, with little chance for success. But it was the only one he had.

Making as little noise as possible, he crawled on his hands and knees farther beneath the wagon bed. Annabelle cried out again, and the sound was agonized and smothered, as though her face were buried in a pillow. Her time was near and his heart wrenched for her.

How could he leave her? But if he didn't, she would surely die.

The sky was lightening, casting the shadows of the boulders into treacherous relief. Staying low and moving fast, Jim made a break for the nearest clump of shadows. He hadn't gone half a dozen running steps when a rifle blast split the ground at his heels. He hit the dirt and tried to swing around to fire back, but before he could, another blast thundered—toward the direction of the first shot, not from it.

Someone was covering him.

Jim ran beneath the crossfire toward the rock-shadows and the flash of gunfire that was clearly illuminated there. He dropped down beside his ally and returned three rounds of fire before looking to see who had come to his aid.

It was the Indian.

"There are two of them," he said, reloading. "One is circling east. He'll have the sun behind him when it rises and we'll be blinded. The other one is behind that clump of rocks that looks like a bear. They are the ones who killed your wife," he said without emotion. "The one who said he was married to your sister was with them. It might have been a trap. They shot him—I didn't."

Jim studied the landscape beyond, confirming as best he could what the other man had said. Then he glanced at his companion. "What's your name?"

"They call me Thunder Eagle."

"Jim Kincaid."

Thunder Eagle returned his glance briefly. "I know."

The gunfire had died down, and they both concentrated on the countryside before them, watching the shadows for signs of movement. Jim said, "What's your stake in this?"

Thunder Eagle hesitated, as though debating whether to answer. Then he said, "Peace."

From the wagon came another muffled cry that diminished at last into a weak, exhausted moan and a series of choking coughs. Thunder Eagle said, "Her time is near."

"Yes."

"They will attack at dawn. The one from the east will try to draw our fire into the sun while the one in the west takes us from behind."

From the wagon was another muffled, choked cry, prolonged and anguished. The sobs sounded like a plea—for help or release.

"Go to her now," Thunder Eagle said, "while it's still dark. I'll cover you."

Jim knew he was right. He couldn't leave the woman in the wagon to give birth alone; he had promised her. He had promised Star. With someone to draw the fire away from the wagon, this might be his only chance to return. But if he went back to the wagon now, he might well be leaving Thunder Eagle to fight the battle to its conclusion by himself.

He had a feeling the other man knew that.

"I'll be back," Jim said.

Thunder Eagle fired his rifle into the hills as Jim ran a zigzag pattern back to the wagon.

They arrived too late. Orange-and-red flames shot into the night sky, illuminating Portsmouth Square in an eerie, satanic glow. Meg clutched Marie's arm and watched her dreams turn to ashes.

Consumed were the ornate columns of the opera house, the balconies, the painted gold scrolls. The oil paintings of the three Graces that she'd hung that morning on the balcony level were fodder for the raging flames. The gilded cupids bought to adorn the four corners of the gentlemen's smoking room melted, their little features blistering and dissolving like hot wax. Meg's wonderful mahogany bar crackled and sizzled in the heat. Flames ate through paint and wood like a hungry animal whose appetite could not be sated. Finally, with a crash, the grand sweeping stairs collapsed, falling into a sea of flames. Gone. All of it gone.

Marie slipped an arm around Meg's shoulder; the women stood mesmerized by the terrible power of the fire. Before its awesome rage, they were helpless; there was nothing to do now but wait.

Volunteer fire-fighting brigades came racing through the foggy streets, alerted by the clanging of the great fire bell. Coded strokes of the clapper pinpointed the location of the blaze, and volunteers were outdoing one another to reach the fire first. Three companies converged on Portsmouth Square almost simultaneously—Knickerbocker Five, Crescent Ten, and Harvard Five—manned by settlers from the New York, New Orleans, and Boston areas.

They set their hand-pulled engines in position and then began to pump streams of water on the blaze that was engulfing the interior of the almost finished opera house. Some of the firemen had taken time to don slickers and boots; others were in street clothes, a few in fancy evening wear. The regionally named companies were fierce rivals, and each wanted the credit of being first on the scene. No one could criticize their zeal or their efforts to do a good job, but at times the fires were too intense for their expertise and equipment; blazes consumed whole blocks, leapt from street to street, and burned large portions of the city.

But a fire like the one at the opera house—contained and fairly small—responded well to their hand-pumped fire hoses spewing out a steady stream of water. The wooden interior of the building went up like kindling, but the fire walls held and the fire did not spread.

When the fire was out, and there was nothing left of the bar and balconies, the columns and arches, but a smoldering pile of ashes, Meg thanked each of the volunteers and promised them a free evening at the rebuilt opera house when it opened. She held her head high and pretended optimism, but inside she felt as if she were burned out, too scarred by the events of the past few hours ever to recover. She was determined not to cry; the opera house was only wood and bricks, not flesh and blood, and if she had the will, she could rebuild. If she had the will . . .

Sam Brannan, San Francisco's most famous entrepreneur and self-proclaimed first citizen, had appeared on the scene just after the volunteer firemen arrived. He was in charge of the city's vigilantes and immediately dispatched his henchmen to look for likely suspects; he'd also taken charge of Meg's night watchman, whom he'd found bound and gagged in an alley. Brannan's questioning of the man revealed little, only that he'd been hit over the head from behind and had seen nothing.

Dressed in his dark frock coat and high silk hat, with his black beard giving him an almost sinister look, Brannan approached Meg and held out a comforting hand.

"Miss Kincaid, my deepest regrets." His quick dark eyes glanced rapidly about. "No structural damage to your fire walls—"

"We were lucky," Meg said grimly. "Thank God I had a warning."

"And thank God for the fire companies, and, I might add, for the vigilantes." Brannan never missed an opportunity to take credit for his accomplishments. There was a commotion on the street, and Brannan called out, "Bring him up here, boys. I want Miss Kincaid to see the culprit face-to-face."

Two men dragged forward a struggling third. "Jack Henley," Brannan intoned. "Second in command of the Sydney Ducks, found loitering in the area. Very suspicious, I'd say."

Henley, a short, burly man, pulled against the grasp of his captors. "You're daft, Brannan. I was over at the Golden Horseshoe for a pint, mindin' me own bloody business. These two ruffians of yours jumped me when I was leavin' the place. I don't know one bleedin' thing about any fire."

Meg looked over at Marie, who was standing behind the men. Marie shook her head.

"I don't believe this man is involved," Meg said. "I have evidence that this fire was set by men Yancey Connor hired."

Brannan seemed truly surprised. "Oh, no, Miss Kincaid! Connor's a member of our vigilantes; he's a fine citizen. Why, he's done a great deal to bring business into Portsmouth Square."

"It's my business he doesn't want here," Meg said. "He's afraid I'll ruin that gambling den of his. He's afraid that men might actually want to patronize a place run by a woman."

Brannan held up a conciliatory hand. "Now, now, if this fire had gotten out of control, Connor's saloon might have burned, too. He wouldn't have taken that kind of a chance."

"He knew I had fire walls," Meg said. "He knew he was safe. All he wanted to do was to scare me and make me back down—"

"Right-oh, miss," Henley called out. "It ain't always

the Ducks, but we always get the blame. Why the bloody hell, if you'll pardon me, miss, would I be burnin' down your place? Why, there ain't nothin' here to steal."

"One more reason to put the blame on Connor," Meg answered.

Brannan ignored Henley's denial. "Your reasoning about Connor seems a little farfetched, Miss Kincaid. I know this whole episode has been upsetting for you—"

Meg caught Marie's eyes again. In them she saw a look of resignation. Who would believe the story of two women?

Brannan continued to talk. "There's plenty of room in San Francisco for all of us—"

"Connor doesn't think so." Slowly Meg's resolve was returning. She was in no mood to be pitied or patronized by Brannan. "Let's go ask Connor. That seems the easiest way to get to the truth."

Brannan looked worried. "I don't know about that. I don't think this is the time, with you being so emotional and all. I think it's best for you to go home and lie down—"

Meg wasn't going to be dismissed by anyone, not even by the most important man in San Francisco. "This is exactly the right time. I have a witness, if she will come forward—"

It was as if Marie had been primed and waiting. She shot forward and grasped Sam Brannan by the sleeve of his very expensive coat. "I heard Connor talkin' to two men about torchin' this place. I heard him say that Meg Kincaid was a stuck-up bitch who needed to be put in her place. I heard him say he has a friend who wants the property she's on."

"And who are you?" Brannan asked.

Meg was quick with her answer. "She's Marie

LaFleur, an old family friend, and her truthfulness is above reproach."

Brannan didn't look convinced. "But this accusation, based on the word of—"

"A woman?" Meg cut in.

"One person," Sam allowed.

"You didn't mind arrestin' me with no bloody witnesses," Henley argued. "I think the ladies have a point. I think we ought to see what Yancey Connor has to say for hisself."

Meg's despair had left her, replaced by a powerful anger. There was much in her life that enraged her— her inability to stay the ravages of Sheldon's illness, Star's brutal and senseless murder, the fire that had burned her out, and now Brannan's attempts to smooth it all over and send her home as if she were a hysterical schoolgirl. She'd been a fighter all her life, and she wasn't going to stop now.

"You're right, Mr. Henley. We should all face down Mr. Connor." She turned to look at Marie.

"I said I ain't a quitter, Miz—Meg. I'll say in front of Connor's face what I heard and what I saw."

Meg picked up the hem of her skirt and strode through the smoky debris of her opera house. She sailed into the night like a grand ship, with the others trailing in her wake. The streets were deserted; the excitement of the fire was over, and curious onlookers had drifted back into the saloons and hotels that rimmed the square. Meg stalked purposefully into the Golden Horseshoe.

Brannan tried one more time. "Miss Kincaid, this is very unlady—"

By then Meg had pushed through the swinging doors and was standing inside the smoke-filled saloon. A few customers looked up from their mugs of beer, but most of the men were intent on their card games of vingt-et-un and monte. A thin girl in a too-short flounced skirt sitting atop an upright piano was singing a nasal rendition of "Sweet Betsy from Pike."

Meg barged past them all and approached the bar. The bartender, a tough-looking man with one crossed eye, ignored her. Meg spoke up over the tinny noise of the piano. "I'd like to see Mr. Connor, please."

There was no response. Meg knew the man recognized her; he'd passed her in the street a dozen times. She'd even wondered if he was spying on her, he'd watched her so intently.

"I said, I'd like to see Mr. Connor. Call him out." This time there was no *please*.

The bartender leaned against a stool and stared off into space. Meg turned to Brannan and asked smoothly, "May I borrow your walking stick, sir?"

"Certainly, but why—" He handed over the gold-headed cane.

To everyone's amazement, including her own, Meg raised the walking stick high above her head and brought it down with all her might across the bar. The head of the cane cut into the wood of the bar and the sound reverberated like thunder. The piano player paused in mid-stroke; the singer slid nervously off her perch; gamblers put down their cards and drinkers their mugs. All eyes were on the red-haired woman at the bar.

"What the hell—" the bartender muttered.

"Now that I have your attention"—Meg's eyes blazed blue fire—"I'd like to see Mr. Connor."

He appeared almost instantaneously from a back room, buttoning up his brocade vest and smoothing back his hair. "What's the racket?" Then he noticed Meg and behind her Sam Brannan, along with Marie and two vigilantes holding a now quiet Jack Henley. Meg was sure she saw a quickening of anxiety in his face. "Sam, maybe you can explain what's happening here," Connor said.

Brannan began to talk. "Just a little misunderstanding, Yancey. This pretty lady here believes that you—"

Meg brought the cane crashing down on the bar again. "I'll explain. This very angry woman here knows, Connor, that you hired some lawless savages to burn down my opera house. Well, it didn't work, and I'm here to warn you—"

Connor's face turned beet red and his eyes darted from Meg to Brannan and then to Marie. "Now just a minute. You have no business making accusations like that. Everybody knows you're a troublemaker. A decent woman would stay home with her family, not go flaunting herself—"

Brannan was growing uncomfortable at the tone of the exchange and jumped in to play peacemaker. "I think if we just go into the back room and discuss this privately, we can work—"

"Nothing in private," Meg said. "Everything I have to say can be said in front of witnesses." She waved her hand at the fascinated customers of the Golden Horseshoe. The room was eerily quiet. Meg felt a growing sense of empowerment. "Come over here, Marie, and tell everyone what you saw and heard."

Marie stepped forward and faced Connor brazenly. "I heard Mr. Yancey Connor hire two men to torch Meg Kincaid's opera house. He wanted it done quiet, and he didn't want the fire to spread. He said he wanted the stuck-up bitch out of business once and for all."

Connor made a move for Marie, but Sam Brannan blocked him. "You're not going to listen to her, are you,

Sam? Why, she's nothing but a two-bit whore from New Orleans. I hired her out of the goodness of my heart so she wouldn't end up sleeping on the street. I had nothing to do with any fire."

"You ain't callin' me a liar!" Marie, fingers outstretched, leapt for Connor's eyes, but Meg was there to grab her arm.

"Miss LaFleur," she announced as she had before, "is an old family friend who saved my sister's life in Panama." Meg knew she was exaggerating, but in many ways Marie had been a lifesaver for Sarah. "I trust her implicitly and I believe her, but I know you for what you are, a liar and a coward, Yancey Connor." Meg stared defiantly at him; her hair flamed golden red in the light from the lamps, and her cheeks were flushed.

"You're out of your mind, woman," he said.

Meg looked at Sam Brannan for support; she knew his slippery mind was working hard, trying to think of a way to turn the scene to his advantage and end the encounter peacefully, but Meg didn't want peace. She wanted victory.

"What do you have to say, Jack Henley?" She turned to the Australian.

"I say that the lady knows what she's talkin' about. I say it's time someone else got the blame for what's been going on around here. It ain't always the Ducks who cause problems, and I think Yancey Connor ought to be dragged off to jail."

Among a certain element, Jack Henley was a popular figure, and there was a small smattering of applause. The two vigilantes dropped Henley's arms and shrank a little into the crowd.

Everyone was looking at Meg.

"Oh, I see no reason for Mr. Connor to go to jail,"

she said. "Not now at least. I think, however, that he should pay a fine—to me, to rebuild my opera house."

"Pay you?" Connor shouted angrily. "Why should I pay you? I had nothing to do with your opera house burning down."

There was a stirring in the crowd. A voice called out, "Jack Henley was drinking with me. I know he didn't do it."

Someone else shouted, "The lady's got a witness. It don't look good, Connor."

"Never," Connor said through gritted teeth. "Never."

Meg looked up at Sam Brannan. She could smell victory in the air. "What do you think, Mr. Brannan? Who's in the right?"

Brannan looked uncomfortable; his answer was thoughtful and deliberate. "I think we made a mistake tonight, arresting Mr. Henley. My apologies, sir."

Henley smirked and made a mocking bow.

"And it seems to me, in the spirit of fairness and for the good of the business community, that we take up a collection to restore the interior of Miss Kincaid's sal—uh, opera house. And I think it only fitting that Mr. Yancey Connor make a substantial contribution. Now. Tonight."

Connor started to protest, then sagged against the bar. No one in San Francisco wanted to be at war with Sam Brannan.

Brannan smiled. "Is that satisfactory to you, Miss Kincaid?"

Meg debated. She hated for Connor to have any out at all, but she knew the realities of life. "Yes," she answered. "But I have one more thing to say. If there's any more trouble at my establishment, I think we'll all know where to look."

Brannan nodded.

Henley had one more thing to add. "And if anyone tries to harm these two fine ladies in any way, they'll have Jack Henley to answer to."

"Thank you, Mr. Henley," Meg replied. "My friend Marie and I appreciate that. She'll be under my protection—and Mr. Henley's."

Connor shot Meg a nasty look, and Meg smiled sweetly. "And now, gentlemen, if you'll excuse me, Marie and I are going home to my husband. Oh, your walking stick, Mr. Brannan. I don't think I'll need it anymore this evening."

Meg took Marie's arm and swept out of the saloon on a sea of cheers.

"Good God, Meg, I didn't know that you and Gerrard was married," Marie whispered.

Meg waved at Tonio, who was waiting with the carriage. "If God is truly good, Marie, we will be before this night is over."

Chapter Twenty-one

A half hour after the gunfire started, Annabelle Williams gave birth to a small, angry baby boy. Compared with the miracle that was taking place inside the wagon, the battle that was going on outside faded in significance. It almost seemed to Jim to have nothing to do with him at all. Outside, the madman who had killed Star was waiting, plotting, moving in to kill again. But inside there was life renewing itself, and that magnificent wonder seemed to bring everything else into balance.

One part of Jim's mind did keep track of the pattern of gunfire, and at first it puzzled him. The shots were sporadic, more like warning shots than a heated gun battle. It was clear they had Thunder Eagle pinned down, but they neither moved closer nor retreated. Thunder Eagle returned fire but did no damage. It was a standoff.

And then Jim realized why. They weren't interested in the Indian; they were only using him to draw Jim out. If Thunder Eagle hadn't prevented it, they would have stormed the wagon, but as it was, they would wait—until they got a clear shot at Thunder Eagle, or until Jim came to defend him.

It was Jim they wanted. It was he they intended to kill.

But when he wrapped the tiny, mewling infant in Star's blue dress and placed him in Annabelle's arms, all of that seemed far away. Already today he had seen life triumph over death, and what happened in the hills outside could neither change nor diminish that.

Annabelle was weak and exhausted, but her smile was radiant as she looked at her son. "Oh, my," she said softly. "Oh . . . my. He's wonderful, isn't he?"

Jim smiled, touching one small, waving fist with his forefinger. "He's a fighter, all right." He met her eyes. "So are you, ma'am."

The moment was shattered by yet another volley of gunfire. Thunder Eagle was positioned close enough to hear the infant's cry, and he knew Jim would be leaving the wagon soon. He was offering him the cover of fire to do so.

Annabelle looked at him anxiously. "Who are they? What do they want from us?"

"You're safe in here, Miss Annabelle," Jim said. He picked up his rifle. "You just keep that little one warm."

Terror tore across her face. "Please! You won't let them—"

But she was unable to finish the sentence. She pressed her newborn son tightly, possessively, against her breast.

Jim gazed at her for a moment, then took the pistol from his belt and placed it beside her on the mattress. "No," he said quietly, "I won't. Not while I'm alive."

She closed her eyes in brief and painful understanding.

Jim paused at the flap covering the wagon opening, gathering his concentration for what he knew would be a life-and-death dash between bullets to cover. She spoke very softly behind him.

"His name is James Michael Williams."

Jim felt the warmth of surprise and gratitude, and then his chance came. Thunder Eagle fired a round and fire was returned. Jim leapt into the storm.

Jim knew they expected him to circle to the east, to join his ally in that easily defensible position behind the lowest clump of rocks. Jim turned west, dividing the enemy's fire and making sure the wagon would never be in the line of fire, whether the bullets were aimed at him or at Thunder Eagle. He had a distance of about seventy yards to cross before he reached cover, and he estimated his chances for success at about twenty percent.

But he had reckoned without the help of Thunder Eagle.

He had gone about twenty yards when, out of the corner of his eye, he saw the Indian leave his cover and start to work his way east. Immediately the gunfire was drawn to him, for he made a much clearer target against the morning sky. Thunder Eagle fired back; then the rifle clattered from his hands as a bullet caught him in the chest and he staggered backward.

Jim dropped to one knee and took aim at the form on the opposite ridge as he turned to regain his cover. Without drawing a breath, he squeezed the trigger and watched the man fall. Now the odds were even: one against one.

But instead of pursuing his course and going after the remaining man, without thinking about it at all, Jim ran back to the spot where Thunder Eagle had fallen. No gunfire followed him, and he knew why. What he was doing was insane. He was running right into his enemy's trap. But Thunder Eagle might still be alive.

He was. "You are a fool!" he gasped as Jim dropped down beside him. He had pulled himself to a sitting position against the back of a stump. His face was gray and his right arm was limp and drenched in blood. Blood continued to blossom from the wound in his chest. "I gave you your chance."

"Thanks," Jim said briefly. He took out his knife and cut away the other man's shirt. "Where's the other one?"

Thunder Eagle shook his head weakly against the stump. "I lost him. He moves like a panther circling. He could be behind this rock right now."

Jim's hand had frozen in mid-motion, and he was staring at Thunder Eagle's chest. The bullet had made a dark, ugly hole just above his breast muscle that oozed blood faster than it could be wiped away, but that was not what held Jim's attention. He closed his fingers around a small, carved wooden ornament that hung from a thong around Thunder Eagle's neck.

"Where did you get this?" he said hoarsely.

A flinch of new pain crossed Thunder Eagle's face. He waited until it had passed. "My father . . . gave it to my mother before he went away."

Jim lifted his eyes to him. "Who was your father?"

"A white man. They called him the Firebird."

The silence was long and sharp. Then Jim reached inside his shirt and brought out the Celtic cross he wore. His was of iron; Thunder Eagle's was of wood. But they were identical.

"His name was Boothe Carlyle," Jim said quietly. "He was my mother's brother."

Thunder Eagle looked at the iron ornament for a

long time, and then at Jim. He closed his eyes, as though the effort exhausted him. "I'm glad I didn't kill you, then," he mumbled.

Jim worked quickly to pack the wound with strips from Thunder Eagle's shirt. His efforts slowed the bleeding but couldn't stop it. The other man's lips were white and his eye sockets hollow; he was holding onto consciousness through will alone. He would be doing no more fighting today.

"I've got to try to get above him," Jim said. "He's been using his front man to cover him while he moved in closer, I'll bet on it. Now he's got to stay put. Our only chance is if I can circle behind him."

He saw Thunder Eagle's pistol beside him on the ground. He checked the load, cocked it, and put it into Thunder Eagle's hand. "I'm going to draw his fire," he said. "When you hear the shot, fire this. That'll throw him off-balance for all the time I need. Just fire it in the air. Can you hold on that long?"

Thunder Eagle swallowed hard but did not waste energy replying. His fingers closed on the pistol butt.

Jim squeezed his shoulder gently and picked up his rifle.

"When I was a boy," Thunder Eagle said weakly, "I used to wonder who the father of the white man was. Now I think . . . there is only one father." He opened his eyes and regarded Jim steadily. "Good luck, Jim Kincaid."

Jim nodded in silent understanding, then moved quickly between the rocks.

He circled up and back, staying to cover as much as he could, expecting the shot that would either end his life or lead him to the enemy to come at any moment. It never did. He was coming up on a bare stretch of about twenty-five feet where no cover would be possible, and he had to decide whether to take to ground now and rethink his strategy, or to take his chances through the open. He plunged onward.

He had taken three low, running strides when suddenly his feet were snatched out from under him and he landed facedown on the rocky ground. His rifle clattered from his hands. He was so stunned, it took him a good two seconds longer than it should have to recover himself.

He sat up, untangling the thin length of wire from about his ankles, and just as he realized what that signified, he heard the click of a rifle bolt. He darted a glance to his own rifle, a good two yards out of reach, but it was too late.

"It was a good plan, Kincaid. A noble effort."

Jim knew that voice. He knew it so well that the sound froze his blood.

"Stand up, if you're able," the man invited easily. Footsteps crossed the rocky ground and stopped half a dozen paces from Jim. "Satisfy your curiosity."

Jim stood slowly, and turned to face his enemy.

A long time ago the man had been handsome. Hardship and deprivation had hardened his eyes and thinned his hair, yet the right side of his face was still recognizable. The left side had been all but burned away; scar tissue had closed his left eye and drawn the left corner of his mouth downward in a perpetual sneer.

Star had scarred him eight years ago when she thrust a burning log into his face to save Jim's life. His name was Marcus Lyndsay, and he had died in an avalanche.

He smiled. It was a grotesque expression. "You look surprised to see me. You shouldn't be. You should have known I'd track you down—even if I had to return from the grave to do it."

In an instant, time was wiped away. Lyndsay kept

talking, but Jim didn't hear. He was on a snow-covered Rocky Mountain peak eight years ago, watching help-lessly as this man held a gun to Star's head, as his uncle Boothe walked slowly and deliberately into the line of fire ... mesmerized, perhaps, as Jim was now, by the evil this man represented. Sunlight winked on the ring he wore on his finger, and Jim's eyes were helplessly drawn to it. It was an onyx and silver ring, with the head of a wolf worked into the crest.

Watch out for wolves, Sarah had said, all those years ago.

His name was Marcus Hunt Lyndsay, and he had killed Jim's wife. He had killed Jim's uncle. Now he would kill Jim.

If he could.

In a surge of rage, Jim grabbed for the pistol that was always in his belt, but it was gone. He had left it with Annabelle in the wagon.

Lyndsay just smiled. "I know it's not very sportsman-like, but I shall enjoy killing you in cold blood. I've hunted you fairly and cornered you shrewdly. Some-what to my surprise after all these years, you've even been a fairly worthy opponent. Now I'll take the plea-sure of the kill. But first, I have something for you."

He reached into his shirt and drew out a bundle of something soft and dark. He tossed it through the air and instinctively Jim caught it. It was long and silky, blue-black in color. It was human hair.

Star's hair.

With an inarticulate roar Jim lunged at him bare-handed. The rifle discharged, but Jim did not feel the bullet. He kept on coming. He saw the look of surprise on Lyndsay's face, and then, just before Jim launched himself at him, Lyndsay fell forward into the dust. The handle of a knife protruded from the back of his neck.

For a long time Jim stood over the dead man, breathing hard, staring down in disbelief. In those first few moments he was not certain whether he felt gratitude or resentment, whether he felt cheated or indebted. And then he realized that the shot had gone wild only because the knife had already found its target. If it had not, Jim would be lying dead now.

"I've stolen your victory," Thunder Eagle said. Though the words were formal, the voice was flat, the breathing labored. "I should apologize."

Jim looked up at him. He was leaning against a boulder a few feet away, his face ashen and filmed with perspiration, his injured arm held stiffly by his side. Jim bent down and removed the knife from the body, wiping the blade on the ground.

He presented the knife to Thunder Eagle. "He murdered your father," he said.

Thunder Eagle looked at the corpse without passion, then took the knife and resheathed it. "All debts are paid," he said simply.

Jim went back to the body and stood over it for another moment. Then he bent down and removed the ring from the dead man's finger and put it in his pocket.

"Yes," he said. "They are."

He went back to Thunder Eagle and, getting an arm around the injured man's waist, helped him back to camp.

Meg felt a sickening lurch in the pit of her stomach. There was a familiar carriage in front of her house. "The preacher," she said to Marie. "Oh, dear God, I'm too late. They've fetched the preacher."

"Don't mean nothing," Marie answered. "Probably just here to give some comfort."

"In the middle of the night? No, something awful has

happened. I know it." Meg scrambled down from the carriage. "Sheldon's dead. Oh, dear Lord."

The two women burst into the house. A robust, red-faced man rose from the sofa in the parlor. "Ah, Miss Kincaid. I've been waiting—"

She was shaking so, she could barely speak. "Reverend DeLong, is he . . . is . . . ?"

"He's resting quietly, but of course he's worried about you."

Meg sagged against the door. "I didn't tell him about the fire, didn't want him to worry." She raked a hand through her hair. "When did he send for you? Tonio was with me."

"He arranged this morning for me to come back tonight. We assumed you'd be here. He said there was to be a wedding—"

"Yes—oh, yes. Thank you. Please tell him I'm back, and get Monserrat and Tonio. Marie, come with me. We'll wake Fiona." Meg felt infused by a great rush of energy. Sheldon was still alive; she wasn't too late.

She pulled Marie up the stairs behind her and into her bedroom. "Find something you'd like to wear. Something bright and cheerful." Before Marie could move, Meg swung open the door of the wardrobe. "I'm wearing this lavender dress. Sheldon always liked it . . . Sheldon likes it," she corrected herself. Her hand touched a yellow sprigged cotton. She pulled it out and handed it to Marie. "You'll look like sunshine in this. It should fit you."

Not waiting for Marie to answer, Meg moved to the door. "Monserrat!" Her maid appeared at the bottom of the stairs. "Please get Fiona up and put her white dress on her, and change yourself. Wear the new dress the señor gave you for Christmas. We're having a wedding."

Marie was standing openmouthed, staring. "You sure do like to give orders," she observed.

"You'll get used to that," Meg said, stripping off her soot-stained dress and tossing it on the floor.

"Pardon?"

"When you go to work for me at the opera house. Now, surely you didn't think I'd take you in and not have you work for your keep. Of course, there'll be a salary, too."

"Well, now," Marie said, smiling. "Well, now, how about that?"

Meg stopped in the middle of repinning her hair. "You will help me, won't you? I need someone . . . for a while. I can't . . ." In her agitation, her hands trembled so much that she dropped her brush. Meg put her head in her hands and fought for control.

Marie touched her tense, taut shoulder. "I told you earlier that I was here to see it through with you, and I ain't never gone back on my word."

Half an hour later, Meg entered Sheldon's room. He lay quietly, eyes closed. In the low light of the oil lamp, she couldn't be sure if he was breathing. Meg fought back her fear and knelt beside him. She took his hand. It was warm in hers, and she grasped it tightly. "I'm here."

His eyes opened and he smiled, a tired, wan half-turning-up of his lips. "I was worried about you, Miss Meg. Where were you?"

"At the opera house. There was a break-in," she lied, "but everything is fine now. It's all taken care of."

"That's my Meg. You can handle anything."

"No," she whispered, "I can't. Not everything . . ."

He squeezed her hand briefly. "Yes, you can. Just believe in yourself the way I believe in you."

Meg rested her cheek against his frail hand.

He went on, struggling for words. "I've been thinking about that fancy place of yours, and I've decided you're doing the right thing. Remember that talk we had years ago on the Platte—about the dreams we had that didn't come true? Well, it's time for your dreams to come true, Miss Meg, and if it's that opera house, then I want you to have it. Use whatever money I leave you to make it the best damn place in San Francisco. Hire someone to run it for you and build that new house on Nob Hill for you and Fiona. I'd like to know you were living in a fine brick house—"

"I will," she said. "I promise." She fought back her tears. "What about *your* dreams? Oh, my dearest Sheldon, your dreams?"

"My dreams have all come true—you and Fiona. Our wedding—" His voice was so weak and faint that she had to lean close to hear him. "You're a beautiful bride, Miss Meg."

She mustered a tremulous smile. "Reverend DeLong is waiting outside. How did you know we'd need him, Sheldon? How did you know I'd say yes?"

"If a man's ever known a woman, I know you, Miss Meg, everything about you—"

Tears she'd held tight inside began to course down her cheeks. "And you still love me?"

"I will love you forever."

She put her head down on the bed and did what she'd longed to do earlier. She sobbed in pain and anguish, in anger and loss. All the tears that she'd stored up over the years seemed to burst forth in a huge torrent of emotion that she couldn't contain, that she didn't want to control. Sheldon stroked her hair as if she were a little girl. "Don't cry, Miss Meg. I want you to be happy. I never meant to make you sad."

Meg sobbed until there were no more tears to be shed, then raised her tearstained face to look at him. "You've never made me sad, Sheldon Gerrard. You've made me angry and frustrated with your stubbornness, but you've never made me sad, and I shall love you all the days of my life."

He closed his eyes and sighed. "Thank you for that, Miss Meg. Just love our child and take care of her."

"With my life," she vowed.

His voice was low, his breathing more labored. "I don't have much time, Miss Meg. I think you'd better get the preacher—"

Meg wiped her eyes; shakily she made her way to the door. Worried faces stared at her from the hall: Marie, tired and brave in her bright yellow dress; Monserrat and Tonio in their Sunday clothes, their eyes shimmering with tears; Fiona, her little face reflecting confusion and fear.

"We're going to have the wedding now," Meg said to Reverend DeLong. She lowered her voice. "And no one is to be sad or cry. No one." She bent down to kiss her daughter. "This is going to be a joyous time for us to remember. Your papa wants it this way. We're all going to be as brave as he is."

She saw Monserrat's shoulders shaking, and she gave the woman a hug. "Do this for the señor. Make our wedding day glorious, filled with those he loves. Promise."

"I promise, señora. I would do anything for the señor."

Meg took a deep, trembling breath. "Marie, you will be my bridesmaid, and Fiona, my flower girl. Tonio, will you give me away?"

"Señora, it is my deepest honor." He held out his arm, and she took it.

"We're ready, Reverend." Meg's head was high, and her eyes were clear. She was filled with love and a peace she'd never known before. She could feel love flowing all around her, giving her strength, and she was no longer afraid of anything that lay ahead.

Slowly the procession moved into the room, and they took their positions. Meg reached for Sheldon's hand and held on tightly as the minister began.

"Dearly beloved, we are gathered together in the sight of God and man . . ."

Outside, the fog had rolled away, and somewhere far over the mountains the sun was shining on a bright new day.

Chapter Twenty-two

Sarah left the tent and sank wearily onto the up-turned crate that served as a stool outside it. The odor of sulfur and death clung to her despite the cool dawn breezes. She did not think that smell would ever go away, no matter how much she washed or how much time passed.

She bore scant resemblance to the pampered young woman who had left New Orleans less than three months ago. Her hair was tied up in a scarf; her clothes were spotted and stained and hadn't been changed in almost a week. There were blisters on her hands and deep circles under her eyes. She sat slumped wearily with her knees apart, and her elbows resting on them to ease the strain in her back, and she did not even think what Tante Emilie would say if she could see her sitting like that.

For the biggest changes were not in Sarah's appearance. They were in the way she looked at things that once had seemed so very important and now hardly seemed worth remembering at all.

Henry came out. His movements were just as leaden as hers as he removed his wire-rimmed glasses and polished the smudges from them with the corner of his shirt. His face was sparsely stubbled with a week's growth of beard, his hair badly in need of combing.

He said, "The man who came in Thursday is dead. Said his name was Williams. Grafton Williams."

Sarah nodded dully. It had been her job to inscribe the names of the dead onto placard slabs to be placed at the head of the graves in lieu of a more fitting memorial. Her fingers were black with the charcoal she used to do the job. That was another thing she did not think would ever wash away.

Henry squatted beside her. "He said he left a wife back there on the trail, but I don't know. He was so delirious he might not have known what he was saying. He asked me to make sure she got this."

He weighed a small cotton bag in his hand. Sarah had seen many such bags since coming to the camps.

She took it from him. "Why, it's almost empty! There can't be more than an ounce here."

He nodded gravely. "Not worth dying for, was it?"

Sarah returned the bag to him without answering.

"The worst is over, Sarah," he said in a moment. "The rest of them are mending, but Williams—he was half starved when he got here, in no shape to start working a claim. There was nothing we could do for him."

Sarah nodded again. "I took down the quarantine signs yesterday. More men were back to work today."

Henry shook his head, rubbing his temples. "They'll kill themselves yet."

"Gold," was Sarah's only comment.

Henry turned the little bag over in his hand. "A few more days," he said, "and things should be stable enough here for me to leave." He glanced at her. "I promised the man I'd make sure his wife got this. The least I can do is try to find her."

As tired as she was, Sarah managed a smile. "The Henry Corneale I knew two weeks ago wouldn't have done that."

"The Henry Corneale you knew two weeks ago would never have found himself here, either."

His gaze traveled across the muddy little camp, the fires that sputtered under boiling cauldrons filled with clothing being disinfected, the shabby tents and lean-to, the scarred and rutted ground. "I don't suppose this will be the last camp I'll come across in need of a doctor, either."

Sarah felt a surge of pride that was completely out of place, she was sure, but she couldn't keep her approval from showing in her eyes. "Do you mean it?"

He nodded. "As soon as I get you back to San Francisco. There's an awful lot of healing left to be done, Sarah, and an awful lot of reasons to do it. You've shown me that."

She dropped her eyes. "I'm not going back to San Francisco."

"What are you talking about? You can't stay here."

She rubbed the back of her neck. "I know. But what I came here for doesn't seem important anymore. And what I left behind in New Orleans . . . well, I see now it never really belonged to me. I've seen so much suffering since I started out—first in Panama and now here. So much dying. And I was thinking . . ." She lifted her head and met his gaze boldly. "You're going to be needing a nurse."

The smile that slowly filled his eyes spread to his lips, gentle and quiet. "You're right," he said, "I will."

He took her hand and closed his fingers around hers in a strong, warm grip. They held each other's eyes, and though nothing more was said, in that moment the promise between them was sealed.

At last Sarah looked away, then frowned a little as something caught her eye on the horizon. She raised a hand to her forehead, shielding her eyes against the sun. "Visitors coming," she said.

They watched until the group got close enough to be distinguished. There were three of them, and they weren't typical miners. One man walked out front, leading two horses. His head was down and his steps were plodding and weary. On one of the horses was a man who was slumped so far over the saddle that he looked as though he might tumble off before they reached camp. On the other horse was a woman, riding sidesaddle, with an infant in her arms.

"They look sick," Henry said, getting to his feet and starting forward. "See if you can stir up something hot for them to eat, and prepare that tent down by the Olson claim. If they're contagious, we don't want it to get started here again. We might have to—"

But he broke off at the look on Sarah's face. She had risen to her feet, her eyes large in a white face, her hand pressed against her throat as though to hold back a cry. She whispered, "Jim?"

Then she cried, "Jim!"

She ran toward the group, her arms open.

Jim looked up and stared at the onrushing figure as though he couldn't believe what his eyes told him. He dropped the reins of the horses and took one uncertain step forward. Then he shouted, "Sarah!" and started to run.

The two met in a fierce embrace. Jim swept her off her feet, whirling her around. His hat fell off, revealing his dark red hair, and he pushed back her scarf, freeing her brilliant copper tresses.

"Dear God, Jim, thank God—"

"Sarah, so much—"

"How did you—"

"What are you—"

And then they broke off, holding each other at arm's length, drinking each other in.

"Oh, Sarah," Jim said softly, "you are like a breath of fresh air after a lifetime in a dungeon."

Sarah touched his bearded cheek gently. "Jim, I'm so sorry about Star."

He lowered his eyes and drew her into his embrace again, holding her tight for a long time.

"Oh, Jim, I have so much to tell you. A lifetime's worth of telling . . ."

She pushed herself away and could not hold back her joy as she looked into his eyes. But her gaze was drawn beyond his shoulder, to where Henry was helping the injured man dismount. He was an Indian, with hair that fell below his waist. The woman on the horse behind him held an infant that couldn't be over a week old. Sarah looked back at Jim. "And you have a lot to tell me," she added.

He stroked her hair, and though the joy in his eyes at seeing her was not feigned, his smile seemed a little strained. "Those people with me are very special, Sarah. I'll tell you about them, and you'll meet them, but first . . . honey, everything I have to tell you isn't good."

She gazed up at him and waited. He did not try to soften the news, for to do so would have shown a lack of respect for his sister.

He said, "It's your husband, Sarah. There was a gun battle back up the trail, and he was killed."

"Did you kill him?" she asked steadily.

"No. It looks like he'd teamed up with a bad lot. But

at the end he was trying to get out, and that's how he was shot. I'm sorry, honey."

The pain was evident in Sarah's eyes, but she bore it bravely and even managed a sad smile. "I've had to face some hard truths about my husband, Jim—and about myself. I can't say I'm surprised, but ... I'm sorry, too."

She lay her head against his shoulder. "Oh, Jim, at least you're alive. Thank God you're alive! I've been having those dreams again, the ones about the wolf. I've been so frightened for you. Do you think the dreams will ever go away?"

Gently, Jim pushed her away. "Yes," he said, "I do."

He reached into his pocket and brought out the ring, silver etched in onyx with the head of a wolf. He placed it in her hand. "He's dead, Sarah. This time, he's really dead."

She looked from the ring in her hand to Jim, and her eyes were dark with puzzlement and wonder.

Jim put an arm around her shoulders. "We've got a lot to talk about," he said, "but plenty of time to do it in."

Sarah slipped her arm around his waist. "A lot of time," she agreed.

Smiling at each other, they turned to follow Henry, who was leading the others toward the shelter of a tent and a hot meal while the rising sun, glinting on the treetops overhead, etched their westward shadows across the land.

The WONDER of WOODIWISS

continues with the publication of
her newest novel in trade paperback—

FOREVER IN YOUR EMBRACE

☐ #89818-7
$12.50 U.S. ($15.00 Canada)

**THE FLAME AND
THE FLOWER**
☐ #00525-5
$5.99 U.S. ($6.99 Canada)

ASHES IN THE WIND
☐ #76984-0
$5.99 U.S. ($6.99 Canada)

**THE WOLF AND
THE DOVE**
☐ #00778-9
$5.99 U.S. ($6.99 Canada)

A ROSE IN WINTER
☐ #84400-1
$5.99 U.S. ($6.99 Canada)

SHANNA
☐ #38588-0
$5.99 U.S. ($6.99 Canada)

**COME LOVE A
STRANGER**
☐ #89936-1
$5.99 U.S. ($6.99 Canada)

SO WORTHY MY LOVE
☐ #76148-3
$5.95 U.S. ($6.95 Canada)